PRAISE FOR
The Art of Racing in

"Couched in the drama of a young middle-class family in Seattle is one of those stories that may earn its place next to Richard Bach's *Jonathan Livingston Seagull*, Paulo Coelho's *The Alchemist*, and Yann Martel's *Life of Pi*. . . . A fable with a heart. Like its bestselling brethren, it casts a sleeping spell on the readers' native cynicism and persuades us to dust off old questions about faith and humankind's better traits."
—*Portland Oregonian*

"Splendid." —*People*, 3½ out of 4 stars

"*The Art of Racing in the Rain* is the perfect book for anyone who knows that some of our best friends walk beside us on four legs, that compassion isn't only for humans, and that the relationship between two souls who are meant for each other never really comes to an end. Every now and then, I'm lucky enough to read a novel I can't stop thinking about: this is one of them." —Jodi Picoult

"Joyful in its language, creative in its narration, and affecting in its story, this is a terrific book that speaks to our fundamental desire to commune and communicate with animals." —*Seattle Times*

"Enzo sees the world with wry humor, a sense of wonder, and otherworldly depth, and in the hands of a gifted writer, the story rings with truth. This is a book for anyone who has ever looked into a dog's face and seen the wisdom of an old soul in his sweet brown eyes. It's a heartfelt story of hope, redemption, and the transformative power of love." —Susan Wiggs

"Irresistible." —*Seattle Post-Intelligencer*

"It's impossible not to love Enzo." —*Minneapolis Star Tribune*

"I savored Garth Stein's *The Art of Racing in the Rain* for many reasons: a dog who speaks, the thrill of competitive racing, a heart-tugging storyline, and—best of all—the fact that it is a meditation on humility and hope in the face of despair. Since finishing this engagingly unique novel, I've found myself staring at my own dog, thinking, *Hmm, I wonder...*"   —Wally Lamb

"Fans of *Marley & Me*, rejoice."   —*Entertainment Weekly*

"*The Art of Racing in the Rain* has everything: love, tragedy, redemption, danger, and—most especially—the canine narrator Enzo. This old soul of a dog has much to teach us about being human. I loved this book."   —Sara Gruen

"These seemingly disparate elements are so masterfully worked and blended that it didn't take long to fully engage me, the very skeptical reader.... A compelling, entertaining, and transporting story."   —*Bark* magazine

"*The Art of Racing in the Rain* by Garth Stein had me riveted to its pages until the book was finished.... Just read it."
—*Road & Track*

"Enzo ultimately teaches Denny and the reader that persistence and joie de vivre will see them through to the checkered flag. Stein (*Raven Stole the Moon*) creates a patient, wise, and doggish narrator that is more than just fluff and collar. This should appeal to fans of both dogs and car racing."
—*Library Journal*

"Moving.... Folds thrilling track scenes and driving lessons into the terse family drama.... Readers will ... delight in Enzo's wild, original voice; his aching insights into the limitations and joys of the canine and human worlds; and his infinite capacity for love. A natural choice for book clubs."   —*Booklist*

"*The Art of Racing in the Rain* takes you on an unforgettable journey through another kind of mind, through the eyes—and nose—of a dog. I found it fascinating." —Temple Grandin

"You won't forget Enzo anytime soon." —*Arizona Republic*

"Truly a masterpiece of our time. It is one of those rare tales that will leave you both fulfilled and allow you to look at society a little differently long after you are through reading the last page." —*Tacoma Weekly*

"Captivating, compelling, and thoroughly entertaining."
—*Orange County Register*

"Enzo is a charming and witty narrator. His tale, while hilarious at times, is quite often heartbreaking, but it is ultimately uplifting and heartwarming." —*Bookreporter*

"An extraordinary book: rich, innovative, and believable."
—*Roanoke Times*

"*The Art of Racing in the Rain* is not an instructional manual. It is a fictional novel that pulls at your emotions. Love, devotion, death, and betrayal—life's highs and lows, all paralleled with the sport of automobile racing and narrated by a dog name Enzo." —*Toronto Star*

"Like a dog's wet nose thrust enthusiastically into your hand, the intent—and the effect—is loving, heartfelt, and true."
—*St. Petersburg Times*

"If you're a dog lover, read—or listen—to *The Art of Racing in the Rain*; it is filled with insight and affection for the dogs who know us, at times better than we know ourselves."
—*New Orleans Times-Picayune*

"Tough to put down. . . . After reading this story, I can guarantee you'll wonder what your own dog is really thinking." —*St. Louis Post-Dispatch*

"Uses a dog as narrator to clever effect. . . . Inspirational."
—*Kirkus Reviews*

© Frank Huster Photo

About the Author

GARTH STEIN is the author of two novels, *How Evan Broke His Head and Other Secrets* and *Raven Stole the Moon*, and a play, *Brother Jones*, and he has also worked as a documentary filmmaker. He lives in Seattle with his family.

the art
of
racing
in
the rain

A NOVEL

GARTH STEIN

HARPER

NEW YORK • LONDON • TORONTO • SYDNEY

HARPER

A hardcover edition of this book was published in 2008 by HarperCollins Publishers.

HarperCollins books may be purchased for educational, business, or sales promotional use. For information, please email the Special Markets Department in the U.S. at SPsales@harpercollins.com or in Canada at HCOrder@harpercollins.com.

FIRST HARPER PAPERBACKS EDITION PUBLISHED 2009. MOVIE TIE-IN REISSUED 2019.

Designed by Sarah Maya Gubkin

The Library of Congress has catalogued the hardcover edition as follows:
Stein, Garth.
    The art of racing in the rain : a novel / Garth Stein.—1st ed.
        321 p. ; 22 cm.
    ISBN 978-0-06-153793-6
    1. Dogs—Fiction. 2. Automobile racing drivers—Fiction. I. Title.
PS3569.T3655 A88 2008
813'.54 22   2007033890

Library and Archives Canada Cataloguing in Publication Information is available upon request.

ISBN 978-0-06-236491-3 (movie tie-in)
ISBN 978-1-4434-5915-0 (Canada)

19 20 21 22 23 LSC 10 9 8 7 6 5 4 3 2 1

For Muggs

"With your mind power,

your determination,

your instinct,

and the experience as well,

you can fly very high."

—AYRTON SENNA

1

Gestures are all that I have; sometimes they must be grand in nature. And while I occasionally step over the line and into the world of the melodramatic, it is what I must do in order to communicate clearly and effectively. In order to make my point understood without question. I have no words I can rely on because, much to my dismay, my tongue was designed long and flat and loose, and therefore, is a horribly ineffective tool for pushing food around my mouth while chewing, and an even less effective tool for making clever and complicated polysyllabic sounds that can be linked together to form sentences. And that's why I'm here now waiting for Denny to come home—he should be here soon—lying on the cool tiles of the kitchen floor in a puddle of my own urine.

I'm old. And while I'm very capable of getting older, that's not the way I want to go out. Shot full of pain medication and steroids to reduce the swelling of my joints. Vision fogged with cataracts. Puffy, plasticky packages of Doggie Depends stocked in the pantry. I'm sure Denny would get me one of those little wagons I've seen on the streets, the ones that cradle the hindquarters so a dog can drag his ass behind him when things start to fail. That's humiliating and degrading. I'm not sure if it's worse than dressing up a dog for Halloween, but it's close. He would do it out of love, of course. I'm sure he would keep me alive as long as he possibly could, my body deteriorating, disintegrating around me, dissolving until there's nothing left but my brain floating in a glass jar filled with clear liquid, my eyeballs drifting at the surface and all sorts of cables and tubes feeding what remains. But I don't want to be kept alive. Because I know what's next. I've seen it on TV. A documentary I saw about Mongolia, of all places. It was the best thing I've ever seen on television, other than the 1993 Grand Prix of Europe, of course, the greatest automobile race of all time in which Ayrton Senna proved himself to be a genius in the rain. After the 1993 Grand Prix, the best thing I've ever seen on TV is a documentary that explained everything to me, made it all clear, told the whole truth: when a dog is finished living his lifetimes as a dog, his next incarnation will be as a man.

I've always felt almost human. I've always known that there's something about me that's different than other dogs.

Sure, I'm stuffed into a dog's body, but that's just the shell. It's what's inside that's important. The soul. And my soul is very human.

I am ready to become a man now, though I realize I will lose all that I have been. All of my memories, all of my experiences. I would like to take them with me into my next life—there is so much I have gone through with the Swift family—but I have little say in the matter. What can I do but force myself to remember? Try to imprint what I know on my soul, a thing that has no surface, no sides, no pages, no form of any kind. Carry it so deeply in the pockets of my existence that when I open my eyes and look down at my new hands with their thumbs that are able to close tightly around their fingers, I will already know. I will already see.

The door opens, and I hear him with his familiar cry, "Yo, Zo!" Usually, I can't help but put aside my pain and hoist myself to my feet, wag my tail, sling my tongue around, and shove my face into his crotch. It takes humanlike willpower to hold back on this particular occasion, but I do. I hold back. I don't get up. I'm acting.

"Enzo?"

I hear his footsteps, the concern in his voice. He finds me and looks down. I lift my head, wag my tail feebly so it taps against the floor. I play the part.

He shakes his head and runs his hand through his hair, sets down the plastic bag from the grocery that has his dinner in it. I can smell roast chicken through the plastic. Tonight he's having roast chicken and an iceberg lettuce salad.

"Oh, Enz," he says.

He reaches down to me, crouches, touches my head like he does, along the crease behind the ear, and I lift my head and lick at his forearm.

"What happened, kid?" he asks.

Gestures can't explain.

"Can you get up?"

I try, and I scramble. My heart takes off, lunges ahead because no, I can't. I panic. I thought I was just acting, but I really can't get up. Shit. Life imitating art.

"Take it easy, kid," he says, pressing down on my chest to calm me. "I've got you."

He lifts me easily, he cradles me, and I can smell the day on him. I can smell everything he's done. His work, the auto shop where he's behind the counter all day, standing, making nice with the customers who yell at him because their BMWs don't work right and it costs too much to fix them and that makes them mad so they have to yell at someone. I can smell his lunch. He went to the Indian buffet he likes. All you can eat. It's cheap, and sometimes he takes a container with him and steals extra portions of the tandoori chicken and yellow rice and has it for dinner, too. I can smell beer. He stopped somewhere. The Mexican restaurant up the hill. I can smell the tortilla chips on his breath. Now it makes sense. Usually, I'm excellent with elapsed time, but I wasn't paying attention because of my emoting.

He places me gently in the tub and turns on the hand-held shower thing and says, "Easy, Enz."

He says, "Sorry I was late. I should have come straight home, but the guys from work insisted. I told Craig I was quitting, and . . ."

He trails off, and I realize that he thinks that my accident was because he was *late*. Oh, no. That's not how it was meant. It's so hard to communicate because there are so many moving parts. There's presentation and there's interpretation and they're so dependent on each other it makes things very difficult. I didn't want him to feel bad about this. I wanted him to see the obvious, that it's okay for him to let me go. He's been going through so much, and he's finally through it. He needs to not have me around to worry about anymore. He needs me to free him to be brilliant.

He is so brilliant. He shines. He's beautiful with his hands that grab things and his tongue that says things and the way he stands and chews his food for so long, mashing it into a paste before he swallows. I will miss him and little Zoë, and I know they will miss me. But I can't let sentimentality cloud my grand plan. After this happens, Denny will be free to live his life, and I will return to earth in a new form, as a man, and I will find him and shake his hand and comment on how talented he is, and then I will wink at him and say, "Enzo says hello," and turn and walk quickly away as he calls after me, "Do I know you?" He will call, "Have we met before?"

After the bath he cleans the kitchen floor while I watch;

he gives me my food, which I eat too quickly again, and sets me up in front of the TV while he prepares his dinner.

"How about a tape," he says.

"Yes, a tape," I reply, but of course, he doesn't hear me.

He puts in a video from one of his races and he turns it on and we watch. It's one of my favorites. The racetrack is dry for the pace lap, and then just after the green flag is waved, indicating the start of the race, there is a wall of rain, a torrential downpour that engulfs the track, and all the cars around him spin out of control into the fields and he drives through them as if the rain didn't fall on him, like he had a magic spell that cleared water from his path. Just like the 1993 Grand Prix of Europe, when Senna passed four cars on the opening lap, four of the best championship drivers in their championship cars—Schumacher, Wendlinger, Hill, Prost—and he passed them all. Like he had a magic spell.

Denny is as good as Ayrton Senna. But no one sees him because he has responsibilities. He has his daughter, Zoë, and he had his wife, Eve, who was sick until she died, and he has me. And he lives in Seattle when he should live somewhere else. And he has a job. But sometimes when he goes away he comes back with a trophy and he shows it to me and tells me all about his races and how he shone on the track and taught those other drivers in Sonoma or Texas or Mid-Ohio what driving in wet weather is really about.

When the tape is over he says, "Let's go out," and I struggle to get up.

He lifts my butt into the air and centers my weight over my legs and then I'm okay. To show him, I rub my muzzle against his thigh.

"There's my Enzo."

We leave our apartment; the night is sharp, cool and breezy and clear. We only go down the block and back because my hips hurt so much, and Denny sees. Denny knows. When we get back, he gives me my bedtime cookies and I curl into my bed on the floor next to his. He picks up the phone and dials.

"Mike," he says. Mike is Denny's friend from the shop where they both work behind the counter. Customer relations, they call it. Mike's a little guy with friendly hands that are pink and always washed clean of smell. "Mike, can you cover for me tomorrow? I have to take Enzo to the vet again."

We've been going to the vet a lot recently to get different medicines that are supposed to help make me more comfortable, but they don't, really. And since they don't, and considering all that went on yesterday, I've set the Master Plan in motion.

Denny stops talking for a minute, and when he starts again, his voice doesn't sound like his voice. It's rough, like when he has a cold or allergies.

"I don't know," he says. "I'm not sure it's a round trip visit."

I may not be able to form words, but I understand them.

And I'm surprised by what he said, even though I set it up. For a moment, I'm surprised my plan is working. It *is* the best thing for all involved, I know. It's the right thing for Denny to do. He's done so much for me, my whole life. I owe him the gift of setting him free. Letting him ascend. We had a good run, and now it's over; what's wrong with that?

I close my eyes and listen vaguely in a half sleep as he does the things he does before he sleeps each night. Brushing and squirting and splashing. So many things. People and their rituals. They cling to things so hard sometimes.

2

He picked me out of a pile of puppies, a tangled, rolling mass of paws and ears and tails, behind a barn in a smelly field near a town in eastern Washington called Spangle. I don't remember much about where I came from, but I remember my mother, a heavy bitch of a lab with pendulous teats that swung to and fro as my littermates and I chased them down from across the yard. Honestly, our mother didn't seem to like us much, and she was fairly indifferent to whether we ate or starved. She seemed relieved whenever one of us left. One fewer yipping mammal tracking her down to bleed her of her milk.

I never knew my father. The people on the farm told Denny that he was a shepherd-poodle mix, but I don't believe it. I never saw a dog that looked like that on the farm,

and while the lady was nice, the alpha man was a mean bastard who would look you in the eyes and lie even if telling
the truth would serve him better. He expounded at length
on the relative intelligence of dog breeds, and he firmly believed that shepherds and poodles were the smart ones, and
therefore would be more desirable—and more valuable—
when "bred back to a lab for temperament." All a bunch of
junk. Everyone knows that shepherds and poodles aren't
especially smart. They're responders and reactors, not inde-
pendent thinkers. Especially the blue-eyed sheep dogs from
Down Under that people make such a fuss over when they
catch a Frisbee. Sure, they're clever and quick, but they don't
think outside the box; they're all about convention.

I'm sure my father was a terrier. Because terriers are
problem solvers. They'll do what you tell them, but only if it
happens to be in line with what they wanted to do anyway.
There was a terrier like that on the farm. An Airedale. Big
and brown-black and tough. No one messed with him. He
didn't stay with us in the gated field behind the house. He
stayed in the barn down the hill by the creek where the men
went to fix their tractors. But sometimes he would come up
the hill, and when he did, everyone steered clear. Word in
the field was he was a fighting dog the alpha man kept separate because he'd kill a dog for sniffing in his direction. He'd
rip the fur from a nape because of a lazy glance. And when
a bitch was in heat, he'd mount her good and go about his
business without a thought about who was watching or who

cared. I've often wondered if he sired me. I have his brown-black coloring and my coat is slightly wiry, and people frequently comment that I must be part terrier. I like to think I came from a determined gene pool.

I remember the heat on the day I left the farm. Every day was hot in Spangle, and I thought the world was just a hot place because I never knew what cold was about. I had never seen rain, didn't know much about water. Water was the stuff in the buckets that the older dogs drank, and it was the stuff the alpha man sprayed out of the hose and into the faces of dogs who might want to pick a fight. But the day Denny arrived was exceptionally hot. My littermates and I were tussling around like we always did, and a hand reached into the pile and found my scruff and suddenly I was dangling high in the air.

"This one," a man said.

It was my first glimpse of the rest of my life. He was slender, with long and lean muscles. Not a large man, but assertive. He had keen, icy blue eyes. His choppy hair and short, scruffy beard were dark and wiry, like an Irish terrier.

"The pick of the litter," the lady said. She was nice; I always liked it when she cuddled us in her soft lap. "The sweetest. The best."

"We were thinkin' a keepin' 'im," the alpha man said, stepping up with his big boots caked with mud from the creek where he was patching a fence. That was the line he always used. Hell, I was a pup only a dozen weeks old, and

I'd already heard that line a bunch of times. He used it to get more money.

"Will you let him go?"

"Fur a price," the alpha man said, squinting at the sky, bleached a pale blue by the sun. "Fur a price."

3

"Very gently. Like there are eggshells on your pedals," Denny always says, "and you don't want to break them. *That's* how you drive in the rain."

When we watch videos together—which we've done ever since the very first day I met him—he explains these things to me. (To me!) Balance, anticipation, patience. These are all vital. Peripheral vision, seeing things you've never seen before. Kinesthetic sensation, driving by the seat of the pants. But what I've always liked best is when he talks about having no memory. No memory of things he'd done just a second before. Good or bad. Because memory is time folding back on itself. To remember is to disengage from the present. In order to reach any kind of success in automobile racing, a driver must never remember.

Which is why drivers compulsively record their every move, their every race, with cockpit cameras, in-car video, data mapping; a driver cannot be a witness to his own greatness. This is what Denny says. He says racing is doing. It is being a part of a moment and being aware of nothing else but that moment. Reflection must come at a later time. The great champion Julian SabellaRosa has said, "When I am racing, my mind and my body are working so quickly and so well together, I must be sure not to think, or else I will definitely make a mistake."

4

Denny moved me far from the farm in Spangle, to a Seattle neighborhood called Leschi where he lived in a little apartment he rented on Lake Washington. I didn't enjoy apartment living much, as I was used to wide-open spaces and I was very much a puppy; still, we had a balcony that overlooked the lake, which gave me pleasure since I am part water dog, on my mother's side.

I grew quickly, and during that first year, Denny and I forged a deep fondness for each other as well as a feeling of trust. Which is why I was surprised when he fell in love with Eve so quickly.

He brought her home and she was sweet smelling, like him. Full of fermented drinks that made them both act funny, they were hanging on each other like they had too many clothes between them, and they were pulling at each other, tugging, biting lips and jabbing fingers and yanking at hair, all elbows and toes and saliva. They fell onto the bed and he mounted her and she said, "The field is fertile—beware!" And he said, "I embrace the fertility." And he plowed the field until it grasped the sheets in its fists, arched its back, and cried out with joy.

When he got up to splash in the bathroom, she patted my head, which hovered low to the floor, me still being immature at just over a year old, and a little bit intimidated by all the screaming. She said, "You don't mind if I love him, too, do you? I won't come between you."

I respected her for asking, but I knew that she *would* come between us, and I found her preemptive denial to be disingenuous.

I tried not to act off-putting because I knew how infatuated Denny was with her. But I admit I was less than embracing of her presence. And because of that, she was less than embracing of me. We were both satellites orbiting Denny's sun, struggling for gravitational supremacy. Of course, she had the advantage of her tongue and her thumbs, and when I watched her kiss and fondle him sometimes she would glance at me and wink as if to gloat: *Look at my thumbs! See what they can do!*

5

Monkeys have thumbs.

Practically the dumbest species on the planet, next to the duck-billed platypus, who make their dens underwater even though they breathe the air. The platypus is horribly stupid, but is only slightly dumber than a monkey. Yet monkeys have thumbs. Those monkey-thumbs were meant for dogs. *Give me my thumbs, you fucking monkeys!* (I love the Al Pacino remake of *Scarface*, very much, though it doesn't compare to the *Godfather* movies, which are excellent.)

I watch too much TV. When Denny goes away in the mornings, he turns it on for me, and it's become a habit. He warned me not to watch all day, but I do. Fortunately, he knows I love cars, so he lets me watch a lot of Speed Channel. The classic races are the best, and I especially like Formula

One. I like NASCAR, too, but I prefer it when they race on the road circuits. While racing is my favorite, Denny told me it was good for me to have variety in my life, so he often puts on other channels, which I enjoy very much as well.

Sometimes if I'm watching the History Channel or the Discovery Channel or PBS or even one of the kids' channels—when Zoë was little I'd end up spending half the day trying to pry goofy jingles out of my brain—I learn about other cultures and other ways of life, and then I start thinking about my own place in the world and what makes sense and what doesn't.

They talk a lot about Darwin; pretty much every educational channel has some kind of show about evolution at some point, and it's usually really well thought out and researched. However, I don't understand why people insist on pitting the concepts of evolution and creation against each other. Why can't they see that spiritualism and science are one? That bodies evolve and souls evolve and the universe is a fluid place that marries them both in a wonderful package called a human being. What's wrong with that idea?

The scientific theorists go on and on about how monkeys are the closest evolutionary relative of people. But that's speculation. Based on what? Based on the fact that certain ancient craniums have been found to be similar to modern man's? What does that prove? Based on the fact that some primates walk on two feet? Being bipedal isn't even an advantage. Look at the human foot, full of bent toes and calcium deposits and pus draining from ingrown claws that aren't even hard enough to scratch at the earth. (And yet, how I yearn for the moment my soul inhabits one of these poorly designed bipedal bodies and I, too, assume the health concerns of a man!) So what if man's body evolved from the monkeys? Whether he came from monkeys or fish is unimportant. The important idea is that when the body became "human" enough, the first human soul slipped into it.

I'll give you a theory: Man's closest relative is not the chimpanzee, as the TV people believe, but is, in fact, the dog.

Witness my logic:

Case-in-Point #1: The Dew Claw

It is my opinion that the so-called dew claw, which is often snipped off a dog's foreleg at an early age, is actually evidence of a preemergent thumb. Further, I believe that men have systematically bred the thumb out of certain lines of dog through an elaborate process called "selective breeding," *simply in order to prevent dogs from evolving into dexterous, and therefore "dangerous," mammals.*

I also believe that man's continued domestication (if you care to use that silly euphemism) of dogs is motivated by fear: fear that dogs, left to evolve on their own, would, in fact, develop thumbs and smaller tongues, and therefore would be superior to men, who are slow and cumbersome, standing erect as they do. This is why dogs must live under the constant supervision of people, and are immediately put to death when found living on their own.

From what Denny has told me about the government and its inner workings, it is my belief that this despicable plan was hatched in a back room of none other than the White House, probably by an evil adviser to a president of questionable moral and intellectual fortitude, and probably with the correct assessment—unfortunately, made from a position of paranoia rather than of spiritual insight—that *all dogs are progressively inclined regarding social issues.*

Case-in-Point #2: The Werewolf

The full moon rises. The fog clings to the lowest branches of the spruce trees. The man steps out of the darkest corner of the forest and finds himself transformed into . . .

A *monkey*?

I think not.

6

Her name was Eve, and at first I resented how she changed our lives. I resented the attention Denny paid to her small hands, her plump, round buttocks, her modest hips. The way he gazed into her soft green eyes, which peered out from under stylish strands of straight blond hair. Did I envy her engaging smile that eclipsed anything about her that might have been considered less than special? Perhaps I did. For she was a person, unlike me. She was well groomed. Unlike me. She was everything I wasn't. I went for extended periods without a haircut or a bath, for instance; she bathed every day and had a special person do nothing else but color her hair to Denny's liking. My nails grew too long and scratched the wood floor; she frequently attended to her nails with sticks and clippers and polishes to make sure they were the proper shape and size.

Her attention to every detail of her appearance was reflected in her personality as well: she was an incredible organizer, fastidious in nature, constantly making lists and jotting down notes of things to be done or gotten or assembled, frequently creating what she called "Honey-Do" lists for Denny and me, so that our weekends were filled with trips to the Home Depot or waiting in line at the Disposal and Recycling Transfer Station in Georgetown. I didn't like painting rooms and fixing doorknobs and washing screens. But Denny liked it, apparently, because the more she gave him to do, the more quickly he completed his tasks so he could collect his reward, which usually included a lot of nuzzling and stroking.

Soon after she moved into our apartment, they were married in a small wedding ceremony, which I attended along with a group of their closest friends and Eve's immediate family. Denny didn't have any brothers or sisters to invite, and he explained his parents' absence simply by saying that they didn't travel well.

Eve's parents made it clear to all involved that the house in which the wedding took place, a charming little beach cottage on Whidbey Island, was owned by close friends of theirs who were not in attendance. I was allowed to participate only under strict rules: I was not to roam freely on the beach or swim in the bay, as I might track sand onto the expensive mahogany floors. And I was forced to urinate and defecate in a very specific location next to the recycling containers.

Upon our return from Whidbey, I noticed that Eve

moved through our apartment with a greater sense of authorship, and was much bolder in her actions to move or replace things: towels, linens, and even furniture. She had entered our lives and changed everything around. And yet, while I was unhappy with her intrusion, there was something about her that prevented me from mustering any real anger. I believe that thing was her swollen belly.

There was something about the effort it took for her to lie down on her side to rest, having removed her shirt and undergarments, the way her breasts fell just so across her chest as she lay on the bed. It reminded me of my own mother at mealtime when she sighed and shrugged herself to the ground, lifting her leg to expose her nipples to us. *These are the devices I use to feed you. Now eat!* And while I greatly resented the attention Eve lavished on her unborn baby, in retrospect, I realize I had never given her a reason to lavish that same attention on me. Perhaps that is my regret: I loved how she was when she was pregnant, and yet I knew I could never be the source of her affection in that way because I could never be her child.

She devoted herself to the baby before it was even born. She touched it regularly through her tightly stretched skin. She sang to it and danced with it to music she played on the stereo. She learned to make it move around by drinking orange juice, which she did frequently, explaining to me that the health magazines demanded she drink the juice for the folic acid, but she and I both knew she was doing it for the kick. She once asked if I wanted to know what it felt like, and I did, so she held my face against her belly after she had drunk the acid, and I felt it move. An elbow, I think, pushing out perversely, like something reaching out from the grave. It was hard for me to imagine exactly what was going on behind the curtain, inside Eve's magic sack where the little rabbit was being assembled. But I knew that what was inside of her was separate from her, and had a will of its own and moved when it wanted to—or when prodded by the acid— and was beyond her control.

.I admire the female sex. The life makers. It must be amazing to have a body that can carry an entire creature inside. (I mean, other than a tapeworm, which I've had. That doesn't count as another life, really. That's a parasite and should never have been there in the first place.) The life that Eve had inside her was something she had made. She and Denny had made it together. I wished, at the time, that the baby would look like me.

I remember the day the baby arrived. I had just reached adulthood—two years by calendar count. Denny was in Daytona, Florida, for the drive of his career. He had spent the entire year soliciting sponsors, begging, pleading, hustling, until he got lucky and found the right person in the right hotel lobby to say, "You've got balls, son. Call me tomorrow." Thus, he found his long-sought sponsor dollars and was able to buy a seat in a Porsche 993 Cup Car for the Rolex 24 Hours of Daytona.

Endurance racing is not for the meek. Four drivers each spending six hours behind the wheel of a loud, powerful, challenging, and expensive race car is an exercise in coordination and determination. The 24 Hours of Daytona, which is broadcast on television, is as unpredictable as it is exciting. That Denny was presented with a chance to drive it in the same year that his daughter would be born was one of those coincidences that turn on interpretation: Eve was dismayed by the unfortunate timing of the events; Denny celebrated the bounty of opportunity and the feeling that he had everything he could possibly ask for.

Still, the timing was off. On the day of the race, even though it was more than a week before schedule, Eve felt the contractions and called the midwives, who invaded our home and quickly took charge. Later that evening, as Denny was, no doubt, driving the circuit in Daytona and winning the race, Eve stood bent over the bed with two round ladies who helped her by holding her arms, and with a monstrous bellow that seemed to last an hour, squirted out a little bloody blob of human tissue that wriggled spastically and then cried out. The ladies helped Eve into her bed and rested the tiny purple thing on her torso until the baby's searching mouth found Eve's nipple and began to suck.

"Could I have a minute alone—?" Eve started.

"Of course," one of the ladies said, moving to the door.

"Come with us, puppy," the other lady said to me on her way out.

"No—" Eve stopped them. "He can stay."

I could stay? Despite myself, I felt proud to be included in Eve's inner circle. The two ladies bustled off to take care of whatever they needed to take care of, and I watched in fascination as Eve suckled her new babe. After a few minutes, my attention drifted from the baby's first meal to Eve's face, and I saw that she was crying and I wondered why.

She let her free hand dangle to the bedside, her fingers near my muzzle. I hesitated. I didn't want to presume she was beckoning me. But then her fingers wiggled and her eyes caught mine, and I knew she was calling me. I bumped her hand with my nose. She lifted her fingers to the crown of my head and scratched, still crying, her baby still nursing.

"I know I told him to go," she said to me. "I know that I insisted he go, I know." Tears ran down her cheeks. "But I *so* wish he were here!"

I had no idea what to do, but I knew not to move. She needed me there.

"Will you promise to always protect her?" she asked.

She wasn't asking me. She was asking Denny, and I was merely Denny's surrogate. Still, I felt the obligation. I understood that, as a dog, I could never be as interactive with humanity as I truly desired. Yet, I realized at that moment, I could be something else. I could provide something of need to the people around me. I could comfort Eve when Denny was away. I could protect Eve's baby. And while I would always crave more, in a sense, I had found a place to begin.

The next day, Denny came home from Daytona, Florida, unhappy. His mood immediately changed when he held his little girl, whom they named Zoë, not after me, but after Eve's grandmother.

"Do you see my little angel, Enz?" he asked me.

Did I *see* her? I practically *birthed* her!

Denny skated carefully through the kitchen after he returned, sensing that the ice was very thin. Eve's parents, Maxwell and Trish, had been in the house since Zoë was born, taking care of their daughter and their new baby granddaughter. I began calling them the Twins because they looked very much alike with the same shade of artificially colored hair, and because they always wore matching outfits: khaki pants or polyester slacks partnered with sweaters or polo shirts. When one of them wore sunglasses, the other did, too. The same with Bermuda shorts and tall socks pulled up to their knees. And because they both smelled of chemicals: plastics and petroleum-based hair products.

From the moment they arrived, the Twins had been admonishing Eve for having her baby at home. They told her she was endangering her baby's welfare and that in these modern times, it was irresponsible to give birth anywhere but in the most prestigious of all hospitals with the most expensive of all doctors. Eve tried to explain to them that statistics showed exactly the opposite was true for a healthy mother, and that any signs of distress would have been recognized early by her experienced team of licensed midwives,

GARTH STEIN

but they refused to yield. Fortunately for Eve, Denny's arrival home meant the Twins could turn their attention away
from her shortcomings and focus on his.

"That's a lot of bad luck," Maxwell said to Denny as they
stood in the kitchen. Maxwell was gloating; I could hear it
in his voice.

"Do you get any of your money back?" Trish asked.

Denny was distraught, and I wasn't sure why until Mike
came over later that night and he and Denny opened their
beers together. It turned out that Denny was going to take
the third stint in the car. The car had been running well, everything going great. They were second in class and Denny
would easily assume the lead as the sunlight faded and the
night driving began. Until the driver who had the second
stint stuffed the car into the wall on turn 6.

He stuffed it when a Daytona Prototype—a much faster
car—was overtaking. First rule of racing: Never move aside
to let someone pass; make *him* pass *you*. But the driver on
Denny's team moved over, and he hit the marbles, which is
what they call the bits of rubber that shed off the tires and
that accumulate on the track next to the established racing
line. He hit the marbles and the rear end snapped around;
he plowed into the wall at pretty close to top speed, and the
car shattered into a million little pieces.

The driver was unhurt, but the race was over for the team.
And Denny, who had spent a year working for his moment
to shine, found himself standing in the infield wearing the

fancy race suit they had given him for the race with the sponsor patches all over it and his own special helmet that he had fitted with all sorts of radio gear and vent adaptors and the special carbon fiber HANS device for protection, watching the opportunity of his lifetime get dragged off the track by the wrecker, strapped onto a flatbed, and driven off to salvage without his having sat in it for a single racing lap.

"And you don't get any of your money back," Mike said.

"I don't care about any of that," Denny said. "I should have been here."

"She came early. You can't know what's going to happen before it happens."

"Yes, I can," Denny said. "If I'm any good, I can."

"Anyway," Mike said, lifting his beer bottle, "to Zoë."

"To Zoë," Denny echoed.

To Zoë, I said to myself. *Whom I will always protect.*

7

When it was just Denny and me, he used to make up to ten thousand dollars a month in his spare time by calling people on the telephone, like the commercial said. But after Eve became pregnant, Denny took his job behind the counter at the fancy auto shop that serviced only expensive German cars. Denny liked his real job, but it ate up all of his free time, and he and I didn't get to spend our days together anymore.

Sometimes on weekends, Denny taught at a high-performance driver's education program run by one of the many car clubs in the area—BMW, Porsche, Alfa Romeo—and he often took me to the track with him, which I enjoyed very much. He didn't really like teaching at these events because he didn't get to drive; he just had to sit in the passenger seat and tell other people how to drive. And it hardly paid for the gas it cost him to get down to the track, he said. He fantasized about moving somewhere—to Sonoma or Phoenix or Connecticut or Las Vegas, or even Europe—and catching on with one of the big schools so he could drive more, but Eve said she didn't think she could ever leave Seattle.

Eve worked for some big retail clothing company because it provided us with money and health insurance, and also because she could buy clothes for the family at the employee discount. She went back to work a few months after Zoë was born, even though she really wanted to stay home with her baby. Denny offered to give up his own job to care for Zoë, but Eve said that wasn't practical; instead, she dropped Zoë off at the day-care center every morning and picked her up every night on her way home from work.

With Denny and Eve working and Zoë off at day care, I was left to my own devices. For most of the dreary days I was alone in the apartment, wandering from room to room, from nap spot to nap spot, sometimes spending my hours doing nothing more than staring out the window and timing the Metro buses that drove by on the street outside to see if I could decipher their schedule. I hadn't realized how much I enjoyed having everyone bustling around the house for those first few months of Zoë's life. I had felt so much a part of something. I was an integral figure in Zoë's entertainment: sometimes after a feeding, when she was awake and alert and strapped safely into her bouncy seat, Eve and

Denny would play Monkey in the Middle, throwing a ball of socks back and forth across the living room; I got to be the monkey. I leapt after the socks and then scrambled back to catch them, and then danced like a four-legged clown to catch them again. And when, against all odds, I reached the sock ball and batted it into the air with my snout, Zoë would squeal and laugh; she would shake her legs with such force, the bouncy chair would scoot along the floor. And Eve, Denny, and I would collapse in a pile of laughter.

But then everyone moved on and left me behind.

I wallowed in the emptiness of my lonely days. I would stare out the window and try to picture Zoë and me playing Enno-Fetch, a game I had invented but she later named, in which Denny or Eve would help her roll a sock ball or fling one of her toys across the room, and I would push it back to her with my nose, and she would laugh and I would wag my tail, and then we would do it again. Until one day when a fortunate accident happened that changed my life. Denny turned on the TV in the morning to check the weather report, and he forgot to turn the TV off.

Let me tell you this: The Weather Channel is not about weather; it is about the *world*! It is about how weather affects us all, our entire global economy, health, happiness, spirit. The channel delves with great detail into weather phenomena of all different kinds—hurricanes, cyclones, tornadoes, monsoons, hail, rain, lightning storms—and they especially delight in the confluence of multiple phenomena. Absolutely fascinating. So much so that when Denny returned from work that evening, I was still glued to the television.

"What are you watching?" he asked when he came in, asked it as if I were Eve or Zoë, as if it couldn't have been more natural to see me there or address me like that. But Eve was in the kitchen cooking dinner and Zoë was with her; it was just me. I looked at him and then back to the TV, which was reviewing the day's major event: flooding due to heavy rainstorms on the East Coast.

"The Weather Channel?" he scoffed, snatching up the remote and changing the channel. "Here."

He changed it to Speed Channel.

I had watched plenty of TV as I grew up, but only when a person was already watching: Denny and I enjoyed racing and the movie channels; Eve and I watched music videos and Hollywood gossip; Zoë and I watched children's shows. (I tried to teach myself to read by studying Sesame Street, but it didn't work. I achieved a degree of literacy, and I can still tell the difference between "pull" and "push" on a door, but after I figured out the shapes of the letters, I couldn't grasp which sounds each letter made and why.) But, suddenly, the idea of watching television *by myself* entered my life! If I had been a cartoon, the lightbulb over my head would have illuminated. I barked excitedly when I saw cars racing on the screen. Denny laughed.

"Better, right?"

Yes! Better! I stretched deeply, joyously, doing my best

downward-facing dog and wagging my tail—both gestures of happiness and approval. And Denny got it.

"I didn't know you were a television dog," he said. "I can leave it on for you during the day, if you want."

I want! I want!

"But you have to limit yourself," he said. "I don't want to catch you watching TV all day long. I'm counting on you to be responsible."

I am responsible!

While I had learned a great deal up until that point in my life—I was three years old already—once Denny began leaving the TV on for me, my education really took off. With the tedium gone, time started moving quickly again. The weekends, when we were all together, seemed short and filled with activity, and while Sunday nights were bittersweet, I took great comfort in knowing I had a week of television ahead.

I was so immersed in my education, I suppose I lost count of the weeks, so I was surprised by the arrival of Zoë's second birthday. Suddenly I was engulfed by a party in the apartment with a bunch of little kids she had met in the park and at her day-care center. It was loud and crazy and all the children let me play with them and wrestle on the rug, and I let them dress me up with a hat and a sweat jacket and Zoë called me her big brother. They got lemon cake all over the floor, and I got to be Eve's helper cleaning it up while Denny opened presents with the kids. I thought it nice that

Eve seemed so happy cleaning up this mess, when she some-times complained about cleaning the apartment when one of us made a mess. She even teased me about my crumb-cleaning skills and we raced, she with her Dustbuster and me with my tongue. After everyone had left and we had all completed our cleaning assignments, Denny had a surprise birthday present for Zoë. He showed her a photograph that she looked at briefly and with little interest. But then he showed the same photograph to Eve, and it made Eve cry. And then it made her laugh and she hugged him and looked at the photo again and cried some more. Denny picked up the photograph and showed it to me, and it was a photo of a house.

"Look at this, Enzo," he said. "This is your new yard. Aren't you excited?"

I guess I was excited. Actually, I was kind of confused. I didn't understand the implications. And then everyone started shoving things in boxes and scrambling around, and the next thing I knew, my bed was somewhere else entirely.

The house was nice. It was a stylish little Craftsman like I'd seen on *This Old House*, with two bedrooms and only one bathroom but with plenty of living space, situated very close to its neighbors on a hillside in the Central District. Many electrical wires draped from poles along the sidewalk out-side, and while our house looked neat and trim, a few doors down stood other houses with unkempt lawns and peeling paint and mossy roofs.

Eve and Denny were in love with the place. They spent almost the entire first night there rolling around naked in every room except Zoë's. When Denny came home from work, he would first say hello to the girls, then he would take me outside to the yard and throw the ball, which I happily retrieved. And then Zoë got big enough that she would run around and squeal while I pretended to chase her. And Eve would admonish her: "Don't run like that; Enzo will bite you." She did that frequently in the early years, doubt me like that. But one time, Denny turned on her quickly and said: "Enzo would never hurt her—ever!" And he was right. I knew I was different from other dogs. I had a certain willpower that was strong enough to overcome my more primal instincts. What Eve said was not out of line, as most dogs cannot help themselves; they see an animal running and they track it and they go after it. But that sort of thing doesn't apply to me.

Still, Eve didn't know that, and I had no way of explaining it to her, so I never played rough with Zoë. I didn't want Eve to start worrying unnecessarily. Because I had already smelled it. When Denny was away and Eve fed me and she leaned down to give me my bowl of food and my nose was near her head, I had detected a bad odor, like rotting wood, mushrooms, decay. Wet, soggy decay. It came from her ears and her sinuses. There was something inside Eve's head that didn't belong.

Given a facile tongue, I could have warned them. I could have alerted them to her condition long before they discovered it with their machines, their computers and super-vision scopes that can see inside the human head. They may think those machines are sophisticated, but in fact they are clunky and clumsy, totally reactive, based on a philosophy of symptom-driven medicine that is always a step late. My nose—yes, my little black nose that is leathery and cute—could smell the disease in Eve's brain long before even she knew it was there.

But I hadn't a facile tongue. So all I could do was watch and feel empty inside; Eve had assigned me to protect Zoë no matter what, but no one had been assigned to protect Eve. And there was nothing I could do to help her.

8

One summer Saturday afternoon, after we had spent the morning at the beach at Alki swimming and eating fish and chips from Spud's, we returned to the house red and tired from the sun. Eve put Zoë down for a nap; Denny and I sat in front of the TV to study.

He put on a tape of an enduro he had been asked to co-drive in Portland a few weeks earlier. It was an exciting race, eight hours long, in which Denny and his two co-drivers took turns behind the wheel in two-hour shifts, ultimately finishing first in class after Denny's eleventh-hour heroics, which included recovering from a near spin to overtake two class competitors.

Watching a race entirely from in-car video is a tremendous experience. It creates a wonderful sense of perspective that is often lost in a television broadcast with its many cameras and cars to follow. Seeing a race from the cockpit of a single car gives a true feeling of what it's like to be a driver: the grip on the steering wheel, the dash, the track, and the glimpse through the rearview mirror of other cars overtaking or being overtaken, the sense of isolation, the focus and determination that are necessary to win.

Denny started the tape at the beginning of his final stint, with the track wet and the sky heavy with dark clouds that threatened more rain. We watched several laps in silence. Denny drove smoothly and almost alone, as his team had fallen behind after making the crucial decision to pull into the pits and switch to rain tires; other racing teams had predicted the rain would pass and dry track conditions would return, and so had gained more than two laps on Denny's team. Yet the rain began again, which gave Denny a tremendous advantage.

Denny quickly and easily passed cars from other classes: underpowered Miatas that darted through the turns with their excellent balance; big-engine Vipers with their atrocious handling. Denny, in his quick and muscular Porsche Cup Car, slicing through the rain.

"How come you go through the turns so much faster than the other cars?" Eve asked.

I looked up. She stood in the doorway, watching with us.

"Most of them aren't running rain tires," Denny said.

Eve took a seat on the sofa next to Denny.

"But some of them are."

"Yes, some," he said.

We watched. Denny got up behind a yellow Camaro at the end of the back straight, and though it looked as if he could have taken the other car in turn 12, he held back. Eve noticed.

"Why didn't you pass him?" she asked.

"I know him. He's got too much power and would just pass me back on the straight. I think I take him in the next series of turns."

Yes. At the next turn-in, Denny was inches from the Camaro's rear bumper. He rode tight through the double-apex right-hand turn and then popped out at the exit to take the inside line for the next turn, a quick left, and he zipped right by.

"This part of the track is really slick in the rain," he said. "He has to back way off. By the time he gets his grip back, I'm out of his reach."

On the back straight again, the headlights illuminating the turn markers against a sky that was still not completely dark, the Camaro could be seen in Denny's panoramic racing rearview mirror, fading into the background.

"Did he have rain tires?" Eve asked.

"I think so. But his car wasn't set up right."

"Still. You're driving like the track isn't wet, and every-one else is driving like it is."

Turn 12 and blasting down the straight, we could see

brake lights of the competition flicker ahead; Denny's next victims.

"That which you manifest is before you," Denny said softly.

"What?" Eve asked.

"When I was nineteen," Denny said after a moment, "at my first driving school down at Sears Point, it was raining and they were trying to teach us how to drive in the rain. After the instructors were finished explaining all their secrets, all the students were totally confused. We had no idea what they were talking about. I looked over at the guy next to me—I remember him, he was from France and he was very fast. Gabriel Flouret. He smiled and he said: 'That which you manifest is before you.'"

Eve stuck out her lower lip and squinted at Denny.

"And then everything made sense," she said jokingly.

"That's right," Denny said seriously.

On the TV, the rain didn't stop; it kept coming. Denny's team had made the right choice; other teams were pulling off into the hot pits to change to rain tires.

"Drivers are afraid of the rain," Denny told us. "Rain amplifies your mistakes, and water on the track can make your car handle unpredictably. When something unpredictable happens you have to react to it; if you're reacting at speed, you're reacting too late. And so you *should* be afraid."

"I'm afraid just watching it," Eve said.

"If I intentionally make the car do something, then I can

predict what it's going to do. In other words, it's only unpredictable if I'm not . . . *possessing* . . . it."

"So you spin the car before the car spins itself?" she asked.

"That's it! If I initiate the action—if I get the car a little loose—then I know it's going to happen before it happens. Then I can react to it before even the car knows it's happening."

"And you can do that?"

Dashing past other cars on the TV screen, his rear end suddenly stepped out, his car got sideways but his hands were already turning to correct, and instead of his car snapping around into a full spin, he was off again, leaving the others behind. Eve sighed in relief, held her hand to her forehead.

"Sometimes," Denny said. "But all drivers spin. It comes from pushing the limits. But I'm working on it. Always working on it. And I had a good day."

She sat with us another minute, and then she smiled at Denny almost reluctantly and stood up.

"I love you," she said. "I love all of you, even your racing. And I know on some level that you are completely right about all this. I just don't think I could ever do it myself."

She went off into the kitchen; Denny and I continued watching the cars on the video as they drove around and around the circuit drenched in darkness.

I will never tire of watching tapes with Denny. He knows

so much, and I have learned so much from him. He said nothing more to me; he continued watching his tapes. But my thoughts turned to what he had just taught me. Such a simple concept, yet so true: that which we manifest is before us; we are the creators of our own destiny. Be it through intention or ignorance, our successes and our failures have been brought on by none other than ourselves.

I considered how that idea applied to my relationship with Eve. It was true that I carried some resentment toward her for her involvement in our lives, and I know that she sensed that fact and protected herself by remaining aloof. And even though our relationship had changed greatly since Zoë's arrival, there was still a distance between us.

I left Denny at the TV and walked into the kitchen. Eve was preparing dinner, and she looked at me when I entered.

"Bored with the race?" she asked casually.

I wasn't bored. I could have watched the race all that day and all the next. I was manifesting something. I lay down near the refrigerator, in a favorite spot of mine, and rested.

I could tell she felt self-conscious with me there. Usually, if Denny was in the house, I spent my time by his side; that I had chosen to be with her now seemed to confuse her. She didn't understand my intentions. But then she got rolling with dinner, and she forgot about me.

First she started some hamburger frying, which smelled good. Then she washed some lettuce and spun it dry. She sliced apples. She added onions and garlic to a pot and then a can of tomatoes. And the kitchen was rich with the smell of food. The smell of it and the heat of the day made me feel quite drowsy, so I must have nodded off until I felt her hands on me, until I felt her stroking my side, then scratching my belly, and I rolled over on my back to acknowledge her dominance; my reward was more of her comforting scratches.

"Sweet dog," she said to me. "Sweet dog."

She returned to her preparations, pausing only occasionally to rub my neck with her bare foot as she passed, which wasn't all that much, but meant a lot to me nonetheless.

I had always wanted to love Eve as Denny loved her, but I never had because I was afraid. She was my rain. She was my unpredictable element. She was my fear. But a racer should not be afraid of rain; a racer should embrace the rain. I, alone, could manifest a change in that which was around me. By changing my mood, my energy, I allowed Eve to regard me differently. And while I cannot say that I am a master of my own destiny, I can say that I have experienced a glimpse of mastery, and I know what I have to work toward.

9

A couple of years after we moved into the new house, something very frightening happened.

Denny got a seat for a race at Watkins Glen. It was another enduro, but it was with a well-established team, and he didn't have to find all the sponsorship money for his seat. Earlier that spring he had gone to France for a Formula Renault testing program. It was an expensive program he couldn't afford; he told Mike his parents paid for it as a gift, but I had my doubts. His parents lived very far away in a small town, and they had never visited in all the time I had been there. Not for the wedding, Zoë's birth, or anything. No matter. Wherever the funding came from, Denny had attended this program, and he had kicked ass because it was in France in the spring when it rains. When he told Eve about it, he said that one of the scouts who attend these things approached him in the paddock after a session and said, "Can you drive as fast in the dry as you can in the wet?" And Denny looked him straight in the eyes and replied, simply, "Try me."

That which you manifest is before you.

The scout offered Denny a tryout, and Denny went away for two weeks. Testing and tuning and practicing. It was a big deal. He did so well, they offered him a seat in the enduro race at Watkins Glen.

When he first left for New York, we all grinned at each other because we couldn't wait to watch the race on Speed Channel.

"It's so exciting." Eve would giggle. "Daddy's a professional race car driver!"

And Zoë, whom I love very much and would not hesitate to sacrifice my own life to protect, would cheer and hop into her little race car they kept in the living room and drive around in circles until we were all dizzy and then throw her hands into the air and proclaim, "I am the champion!"

I got so caught up in the excitement, I was doing idiotic dog things like digging up the lawn. Balling myself up and then stretching out long and thin on the floor with my legs straight and my back arched and letting them scratch my belly. And chasing things. I chased!

It was the best of times. Really.

And then it was the worst of times.

Race day came, and Eve woke up with a darkness upon her. A pain so insufferable she stood in the kitchen in the early hours, before Zoë was awake, and vomited with great intensity into the sink. She vomited as if she were turning herself inside out.

"I don't know what's wrong with me, Enzo," she said. And she rarely spoke to me candidly like that. Like how Denny talks to me, as if I'm his true friend, his soul mate. The last time she had talked to me like that was when Zoë was born.

But this time she did talk to me like I was her soul mate. She asked, "What's wrong with me?"

She knew I couldn't answer. Her question was totally rhetorical. That's what I found so frustrating about it: I had an answer.

I knew what was wrong, but I had no way to tell her, so I pushed at her thigh with my muzzle. I nosed in and buried my face between her legs. And I waited there, afraid.

"I feel like someone's crushing my skull," she said.

I couldn't respond. I had no words. There was nothing I could do.

"Someone's crushing my skull," she repeated.

And quickly she gathered some things while I watched. She shoved Zoë's clothes in a bag and some of her own and toothbrushes. All so fast. And she roused Zoë and stuffed her little kid-feet into her little-kid sneakers and—*bang*—the door slammed shut and—*snick, snick*—the deadbolt was thrown and they were gone.

And I wasn't gone. I was there. I was still there.

10

Ideally, a driver is a master of all that is around him, Denny says. Ideally, a driver controls the car so completely that he corrects a spin before it happens, he anticipates all possibilities. But we don't live in an ideal world. In our world, surprises sometimes happen, mistakes happen, incidents with other drivers happen, and a driver must react.

When a driver reacts, Denny says, it's important to remember that a car is only as good as its tires. If the tires lose traction, nothing else matters. Horsepower, torque, braking. All is moot when a skid is initiated. Until speed is scrubbed by good, old-fashioned friction and the tires regain traction, the driver is at the mercy of momentum. And momentum is a powerful force of nature.

It is important for the driver to understand this idea

and override his natural inclinations. When the rear of a car "steps out," the driver may panic and lift his foot off the accelerator. If he does, he will throw the weight of the car toward the front wheels, the rear end will snap around, and the car will spin.

A good driver will try to catch the spin by turning wheels in the direction the car is moving; he may succeed. However, at a critical point, the skid has completed its mission, which was to scrub speed from a car going too fast. Suddenly the tires find grip, and the driver has traction— unfortunately for him, with his front wheels turned sharply in the wrong direction. This induces a counterspin, as there is no balance to the car whatsoever. Thus, the spin in one direction, when overcorrected, becomes a spin in the other direction, and the secondary spin is much faster and more dangerous.

If, however, at the very first moment his tires began to break free, our driver had been experienced enough to resist his instinctive reaction to lift, he might have been able to apply his knowledge of vehicle behavior and, instead, *increase* the pressure on the accelerator, and at the same time ease out on the steering wheel ever so slightly. The increase in acceleration would have pushed his rear tires onto the track and settled his car. Relaxing the steering would have lessened the lateral g-forces at work. The spin would therefore have been corrected, but our driver would then have to deal with the secondary problem his correction has created:

by increasing the radius of the turn, he has put himself at risk of running off the track.

Alas! Our driver is not where he had hoped to be! Yet he is still in control of his car. He is still able to act in a positive manner. He still can create an ending to his story in which he completes the race without incident. And, perhaps, if his manifesting is good, he will win.

11

When I was locked in the house suddenly and firmly, I did not panic. I did not overcorrect or freeze. I quickly and carefully took stock of the situation and understood these things: Eve was ill, and the illness was possibly affecting her judgment, and she likely would not return for me; Denny would be home on the third day, after two nights.

I am a dog, and I know how to fast. It's a part of the genetic background for which I have such contempt. When God gave men big brains, he took away the pads on their feet and made them susceptible to salmonella. When he denied dogs the use of thumbs, he gave them the ability to survive without food for extended periods. While a thumb—*one thumb!*—would have been very helpful at that time, allowing me to *turn a stupid doorknob and escape*, the second best tool, and the one at my disposal, was my ability to go without nourishment.

For three days I took care to ration the toilet water. I wandered around the house sniffing at the crack beneath the pantry door and fantasizing about a big bowl of my kibble, scooping up the occasional errant dust-covered Cheerio Zoë had dropped in a corner somewhere. And I urinated and defecated on the mat by the back door, next to the laundry machines. I did not panic.

During the second night, approximately forty hours into my solitude, I think I began to hallucinate. Licking at the legs of Zoë's high chair where I had discovered some remnants of yogurt spilled long ago, I inadvertently sparked my stomach's digestive juices to life with an unpleasant groan, and I heard a sound coming from her bedroom. When I investigated, I saw something terrible and frightening. One of her stuffed animal toys was moving about on its own.

It was the zebra. The stuffed zebra that had been sent to her by her paternal grandparents, who may have been stuffed animals themselves for all that we saw them in Seattle. I never cared for that zebra, as it was something of my rival for Zoë's affection. Frankly, I was surprised to see it in the house, since it was one of Zoë's favorites and she carted it around at length and even slept with it, wearing little grooves in its coat just below the animal's velveteen head. I found it hard to believe Eve hadn't grabbed it when she threw together their bag, but I guess she was so freaked out or in such pain that she overlooked the zebra.

The now-living zebra said nothing to me at all, but when it saw me it began a dance, a twisting, jerky ballet, which culminated with the zebra repeatedly thrusting its gelded groin into the face of an innocent Barbie doll. That made me quite angry, and I growled at the molester zebra, but it simply smiled and continued its assault, this time picking on a stuffed frog, which it mounted from behind and rode bareback, its hoof in the air like a bronco rider, yelling out, "Yee-haw! Yee-haw!"

I stalked the bastard as it abused and humiliated each of Zoë's toys with great malice. Finally, I could take no more and I moved in, teeth bared for attack, to end the brutal burlesque once and for all. But before I could get the demented zebra in my fangs, it stopped dancing and stood on its hind legs before me. Then it reached down with its forelegs and tore at the seam that ran down its belly. Its own seam! It ripped the seam open until it was able to reach in and tear out its own stuffing. It continued dismantling itself, seam by seam, handful by handful, until it expelled whatever demon's blood had brought it to life and was nothing more than a pile of fabric and stuffing that undulated on the floor, beating like a heart ripped from a chest, slowly, slower, and then nothing.

Traumatized, I left Zoë's room, hoping that what I had seen was in my mind, a vision driven by the lack of glucose in my blood, but knowing, somehow, that it wasn't a vision; it was true. Something terrible had happened.

The following afternoon, Denny returned. I heard the taxi pull up, and I watched him unload his bags and walk them up to the back door. I didn't want to seem too excited to see him, and yet at the same time I was concerned about what I had done to the doormat, so I gave a couple of small barks to alert him. Through the window, I could see the look of surprise on his face. He took out his keys and opened the door, and I tried to block him, but he came in too quickly and the mat made a squishy sound. He looked down and gingerly hopped into the room.

"What the hell? What are you doing here?"

He glanced around the kitchen. Nothing was out of place, nothing was amiss, except me.

"Eve?" he called out.

But Eve wasn't there. I didn't know where she was, but she wasn't with me.

"Are they home?" he asked me.

I didn't answer. He picked up the phone and dialed.

"Are Eve and Zoë still at your house?" he asked without saying hello. "Can I speak to Eve?"

After a moment, he said, "Enzo is here."

He said, "I'm trying to wrap my head around it myself. You left him here?"

He said, "This is insane. How could you not remember that your dog is in the house?"

He said, "He's been here the whole time?"

He said very angrily, "Shit!"

And then he hung up the phone and shouted in frustration, a big long shout that was very loud. He looked at me after that and said, "I am *so* pissed off."

He walked through the house quickly. I didn't follow him; I waited by the back door. A minute later he returned.

"This is the only place you used?" he asked, pointing at the mat. "Good boy, Enzo. Good work."

He got a garbage bag out of the pantry and scooped the sopping mat into it, tied it closed, and put it on the back porch. He mopped up the area near the door.

"You must be starving."

He filled my water bowl and gave me some kibble, which I ate too quickly and didn't enjoy, but at least it filled the empty space in my stomach. In silence, fuming, he watched me eat. And very soon, Eve and Zoë arrived on the back porch.

Denny threw open the door.

"Unbelievable," he said bitterly. "You are unbelievable."

"I was sick," Eve said, stepping into the house with Zoë hiding behind her. "I wasn't thinking."

"He could have died."

"He didn't die."

"He *could* have died," Denny said. "I've never heard of anything so stupid. Careless. Totally unaware."

"I was sick!" Eve snapped at him. "I wasn't thinking!"

"You don't think, people die. Dogs die."

"I can't do this anymore," she cried, standing there shaking like a thin tree on a windy day. Zoë scurried around her and disappeared into the house. "You always go away, and I have to take care of Zoë and Enzo all by myself, and I can't do it! It's too much! I can barely take care of myself!"

"You should have called Mike or taken him to a kennel or *something*! Don't try to kill him."

"I didn't try to kill him," she whispered.

I heard weeping and looked over. Zoë stood in the door to the hallway, crying. Eve pushed past Denny and went to Zoë, kneeling before her.

"Oh, baby, we're sorry we're fighting. We'll stop. Please don't cry."

"My animals," Zoë whimpered.

"What happened to your animals?"

Eve led Zoë by the hand down the hall. Denny followed them. I stayed where I was. I wasn't going near that room where the dancing sex-freak zebra had been. I didn't want to see it.

Suddenly, I heard thundering footsteps. I cowered by the back door as Denny hurtled through the kitchen toward me. He was puffed up and angry and his eyes locked on me and his jaw clenched tight.

"You stupid dog," he growled, and he grabbed the back of my neck, taking a huge fistful of my fur and jerking. I went limp, afraid. He'd never treated me like this before.

He dragged me through the kitchen and down the hall, into Zoë's room where she sat, stunned, on the floor in the middle of a huge mess. Her dolls, her animals, all torn to shreds, eviscerated, a complete disaster. Total carnage. I could only assume that the evil demon zebra had reassembled itself and destroyed the other animals after I had left. I should have eliminated the zebra when I had my chance. I should have eaten it, even if it had killed me.

Denny was so angry that his anger filled up the entire room, the entire house. Nothing was as large as Denny's anger. He reared up and roared, and with his great hand, he struck me on the side of the head. I toppled over with a yelp, hunkering as close to the ground as possible. "Bad dog!" he bellowed and he raised his hand to hit me again.

"Denny, no!" Eve cried. She rushed to me and covered me with her own body. She protected me.

Denny stopped. He wouldn't hit her. No matter what. Just as he wouldn't hit me. He *hadn't* hit me, I know, even though I could feel the pain of the blow. He had hit the demon, the evil zebra, the dark creature that came into the house and possessed the stuffed animal. Denny believed the evil demon was in me, but it wasn't. I saw it. The demon had possessed the zebra and left me at the bloody scene with no voice to defend myself—I had been framed.

"We'll get new animals, baby," Eve said to Zoë. "We'll go to the store tomorrow."

As gently as I could, I slunk toward Zoë, the sad little

girl on the floor, surrounded by the rubble of her fantasy world, her chin tucked into her chest, tears on her cheeks. I felt her pain because I knew her fantasy world intimately, as she allowed me to see the truth of it, and often included me in it. Through our role-playing—silly games with significant telltales—I saw what she thought about who she really was, her place in life. How she worshipped her father and always hoped to please her mother. How she trusted me but was afraid when I made faces at her that were too expressive and defied what she'd learned from the adult-driven World Order that denies animals the process of thought. I crawled to her on my elbows and placed my nose next to her thigh, tanned from the summer sun. And I raised my eyebrows slightly as if to ask if she could ever forgive me for not protecting her animals.

She waited a long time to give me her answer, but she finally gave it. She placed her hand on my head and let it rest there. She didn't scratch me. It would be a while before she allowed herself to do that. But she did touch me, which meant she forgave me for what had happened, though the wound was still too raw and the pain was still too great for her to forget.

Later, after everyone had eaten and Zoë was put to bed in her room that had been cleaned of the carnage, I found Denny sitting on the porch steps with a drink of hard liquor, which I thought was strange because he hardly ever drank hard liquor. I approached cautiously, and he noticed.

"It's okay, boy," he said. He patted the step next to him and I went to him. I sniffed his wrist and took a tentative lick. He smiled and rubbed my neck.

"I'm really sorry," he said. "I lost my mind."

The patch of lawn behind our house was not big, but it was nice in the evening. It was rimmed by a dirt strip covered with sweet-smelling cedar chips where they planted flowers in the spring, and they had a bush in the corner that made flowers that attracted the bees and made me nervous whenever Zoë played near it, but she never got stung.

Denny finished his drink with a long swallow and shivered involuntarily. He produced a bottle from nowhere—I was surprised I hadn't noticed it—and poured himself another. He stood up and took a couple of steps and stretched to the sky.

"We got first place, Enzo. Not 'in class.' We took first place overall. You know what that means?"

My heart jumped. I knew what it meant. It meant that he was the champion. It meant he was the best!

"It means a seat in a touring car next season, that's what it means," Denny said to me. "I got an offer from a real, live racing team. Do you know what an offer is?"

I loved it when he talked to me like that. Dragging out the drama. Ratcheting up the anticipation. I've always found great pleasure in the narrative tease. But then, I'm a dramatist. For me, a good story is all about setting up expectations and delivering on them in an exciting and surprising way.

"Getting an offer means I can drive if I come up with my share of sponsorship money for the season—which is reasonable and almost attainable—and if I'm willing to spend the better part of six months away from Eve and Zoë and you. Am I willing to do that?"

I didn't say anything because I was torn. I knew I was Denny's biggest fan and most steadfast supporter in his racing. But I also felt something like what Eve and Zoë must have felt whenever he went away: a hollow pit in my stomach at the idea of his absence. He must have been able to read my mind, because he gulped at his glass and said, "I don't think so, either." Which was what I was thinking.

"I can't believe she left you like that," he said. "I know she had a virus, but still."

Did he really believe that, or was he lying to himself? Or maybe he just believed it because Eve wanted him to believe it. No matter. Had I been a person, I could have told him the truth about Eve's condition.

"It was a bad virus," he said more to himself than to me. "And she couldn't think."

And suddenly I was unsure: had I been a person, had I been able to tell him the truth, I'm not sure he would have wanted to hear it.

He groaned and sat back down and filled his glass again.

"I'm taking those stuffed animals out of your allowance," he said with a chuckle. He looked at me then, took my chin with his hand.

"I love you, boy," he said. "And I promise I'll never do that again. No matter what. I'm really sorry."

He was blathering, he was drunk. But it made me feel so much love for him, too.

"You're tough," he said. "You can do three days like that because you're one tough dog."

I felt proud.

"I know you'd never do anything deliberately to hurt Zoë," he said.

I laid my head on his leg and looked up at him.

"Sometimes I think you actually understand me," he said. "It's like there's a person inside there. Like you know everything."

I do, I said to myself. *I do*.

12

Eve's condition was elusive and unpredictable. One day she would suffer a headache of crushing magnitude. Another day, debilitating nausea. A third would open with dizziness and end with a dark and angry mood. And these days were never linked together consecutively. Between them would be days or even weeks of relief, life as usual. And then Denny would get a call at work, and he would run to Eve's assistance, drive her home from her job, impose on a friend to follow in her car, and spend the rest of the day watching helplessly.

The intense and arbitrary nature of Eve's affliction was far beyond Denny's grasp. The wailings, the dramatic screaming fits, the falling on the floor in fits of anguish. These are things that only dogs and women understand because we tap into the pain directly, we connect to pain directly from its source, and so it is at once brilliant and brutal and clear, like white-hot metal spraying out of a fire hose, we can appreciate the aesthetic while taking the worst of it straight in the face. Men, on the other hand, are all filters and deflectors and timed release. For men, it's like athlete's foot: spray the special spray on it, they say, and it goes away. They have no idea that the manifestation of their affliction—the fungus between their hairy toes—is merely a symptom, an indication of a systemic problem. A candida bloom in their bowels, for instance, or some other upset to their system. Suppressing the symptom does nothing but force the true problem to express itself on a deeper level at some other time. Go see a doctor, he said to her. Get some medication. And she howled to the moon in reply. He never understood, as I did, what she meant when she said that medication would only mask the pain, not make it go away, and what's the point of that. He never understood when she said that if she went to a doctor, the doctor would only invent a disease that would explain why he couldn't help her. And there was so much time between episodes. There was so much hope.

Denny was frustrated by his impotence, and in that regard, I could understand his point of view. It's frustrating for me to be unable to speak. To feel that I have so much to say, so many ways I can help, but I'm locked in a sound-proof box, a game show isolation booth from which I can see out and I can hear what's going on, but they never turn on my microphone and they never let me out. It might drive a person mad. It certainly has driven many a dog mad. The good dog that would never hurt a soul but is found one day having eaten the face of his master as she slept deeply under the influence of sleeping pills? There was nothing wrong with that dog except that his mind finally snapped. As awful as it sounds, it happens; it's on the TV news regularly.

Myself, I have found ways around the madness. I work at my human gait, for instance. I practice chewing my food slowly like people do. I study the television for clues on behavior and to learn how to react in certain situations. In my next life, when I am born again as a person, I will practically be an adult the moment I am plucked from the womb, with all the preparation I have done. It will be all I can do to wait for my new human body to mature to adulthood so I may excel at all the athletic and intellectual pursuits I hope to enjoy.

Denny avoided the madness of his personal sound-booth hell by driving through it. There was nothing he could do to make Eve's distress go away, and once he realized that, he made a commitment to do everything else better.

Often things happen to race cars in the heat of the race. A square-toothed gear in a transmission may break, suddenly leaving the driver without all of his gears. Or perhaps a clutch fails. Brakes go soft from overheating. Suspensions break. When faced with one of these problems, the poor driver crashes. The average driver gives up. The great drivers drive through the problem. They figure out a way to continue racing. Like in the Luxembourg Grand Prix in 1989, when the Irish racer Kevin Finnerty York finished the race victoriously and later revealed that he had driven the final twenty laps of the race with only two gears! To be able to possess a machine in such a way is the ultimate show of determination and awareness. It makes one realize that the physicality of our world is a boundary to us only if our will is weak; a true champion can accomplish things that a normal person would think impossible.

Denny cut back his hours at work so he could take Zoë to her preschool. In the evenings after dinner, he read to her and helped her learn her numbers and letters. He took over all the grocery shopping and cooking. He took over the cleaning of the house. And he did it all excellently and without complaint. He wanted to relieve Eve of any burden, any job that could cause stress. What he couldn't do, though, with all of the extra he was doing, was continue to engage her in the same playful and physically affectionate way I had grown used to seeing. It was impossible for him to do everything; clearly, he had decided that the care of her organism would receive the topmost priority. Which I believe was the correct thing for him to do under the circumstances. Because he had me.

I see green as gray. I see red as black. Does that make me a bad potential person? If you taught me to read and provided for me the same computer system as someone has provided for Stephen Hawking, I, too, would write great books. And yet you don't teach me to read, and you don't give me a computer stick I can push around with my nose to point at the next letter I wish typed. So whose fault is it that I am what I am?

Denny did not stop loving Eve, he merely delegated his love-giving to me. I became the provider of love and comfort by proxy. When she ailed and he took charge of Zoë and whisked her out of the house to see one of the many wonderful animated films they make for children so that she might not hear the cries of agony from her mother, I stayed behind. He trusted me. He would tell me, as he and Zoë packed their bottles of water and their special sandwich cookies without hydrogenated oils that he bought for her at the good market, he would say, "Go take care of her for me, Enzo, please."

And I did. I took care of her by curling up at her bedside, or, if she had collapsed on the floor, by curling up next to her there. Often, she would hold me close to her, hold me tight to her body, and when she did, she would tell me things about the pain.

I cannot lie still. I cannot be alone with this. I need to scream and thrash, because it stays away when I scream. When I'm silent, it finds me, it tracks me down and pierces me and says, "Now I've got you! Now you belong to me!"

Demon. Gremlin. Poltergeist. Ghost. Phantom. Spirit. Shadow. Ghoul. Devil. People are afraid of them so they relegate their existence to stories, volumes of books that can be closed and put on the shelf or left behind at a bed and breakfast; they clench their eyes shut so they will see no evil. But trust me when I tell you that the zebra is real. Somewhere, the zebra is dancing.

The spring finally ground around to us through an exceptionally wet winter, full of gray days and rain and an edgy cold I rarely found rejuvenating. Over the winter, Eve ate poorly and became drawn and pale. When her pain came, she often went for days without eating a bite of food. She never exercised, so her thinness had no tone, slack skin over brittle bones; she was wasting away. Denny was concerned, but Eve never heeded his pleas for her to consult a doctor. A mild case of depression, she would say. They'll try to give her pills and she doesn't want pills. And one evening after dinner, which was a special one, though I don't remember if it was a birthday or an anniversary, Denny suddenly appeared naked in the bedroom and Eve was naked on the bed.

It seemed so odd to me because they hadn't mounted or even played with each other in such a long time. But there they were. He positioned himself over her and she said to him, "The field is fertile."

"You aren't really, are you?" he asked.

"Just say it," she replied after a moment, her eyes having dimmed, having been sucked deep into their sockets and swallowed by the puffy skin, suggesting anything but fertility.

"I embrace the fertility," he said. But their exchange seemed weak and unenthusiastic. She made noise, but she was pretending, I could tell, because in the middle of it she looked at me and shook her head and waved me off. Respectfully, I withdrew to another room and drifted into a light sleep. And, if I recall correctly, I dreamed of the crows.

13

They sit in the trees and on the electric wires and on the roofs and they watch everything, the sinister little bastards. They cackle with a dark edge, like they're mocking you, cawing constantly, they know where you are when you're in the house, they know where you are when you're outside; they're always waiting. The smaller cousin of the raven, they are resentful and angry, bitter at being genetically dwarfed by their brothers. The raven, it is said, is the next step up the evolutionary ladder from man. The raven created man, after all, according to the legends of the Northwest Coast natives. (It's interesting to note here that the deity that corresponds with the raven in Plains Indian folklore is the coyote, which is a dog. So it seems to me we are all smashed together at the top of the spiritual food chain.) So if the raven created man, and the crow is the raven's cousin, where does the crow fit in?

The crow fits in the garbage. Very smart, very sly, they are best when they apply their evil little genius to uncapping a garbage can or pecking through some kind of enclosure to get at scrap food. They are scum, creatures of cluster, they call them a murder when they are in a group. A good word, because when they are together, you want to kill them.

I never chase a crow. They hop away, taunting, trying to dupe you into a chase in which you will become injured. Trying to get you stuck somewhere far away, so they can have their way with the garbage. It's true. Sometimes when I have nightmares, I dream of crows. A murder of them. Attacking me ruthlessly, cruelly tearing me to shreds. It is the worst.

When we first moved to our house, something happened with the crows, and that's why I know they hate me. It's bad to have enemies. Denny always picked up my leavings in small green biodegradable bags. It's part of what people do as a penance for their need to keep dogs under such strict supervision. They must extract our excrement from between the grass blades with a plastic bag that has been turned inside out. They must grab it with their fingers and handle it. Even though there's a plastic barrier, they never enjoy the task because they can smell it and their sense of smell lacks the sophistication to discern the subtlety of the layers of scent and their meaning.

Denny collected the small crap-filled bags and kept

them in a plastic grocery bag. Occasionally he would dispose
of the larger bag in a garbage can in the park up the street.
I guess he didn't want to pollute his own garbage can with
bags of my feces. I don't know.

The crows, who pride themselves on being cousins of the
raven and therefore being very smart, love going after a bag
of groceries. And they have, on many occasion, gone after a
bag on the porch left outside when Denny or Eve brought
home more than a few at a time. They can get in and out so
fast, maybe find some cookies or something and fly away.

On one occasion, when I was young, the crows spotted
Eve bringing home the groceries and they crowded nearby,
clustering in a tree just on the edge of the property, so many
of them. They were silent, not wanting to draw attention to
themselves, but I knew they were there. Eve had parked in
the alley, and she made several trips with bags from the car
to the porch, then from the porch into the house. The crows
watched. And they noticed that Eve had left a bag behind.

Well. They are smart, I have to give them credit, for they
didn't move in right away. They watched and waited until
Eve went upstairs and undressed and got into the bathtub,
as she sometimes did in the afternoon when she had a day
off from her work. They watched and were sure that the
glass-paned kitchen door was closed and locked so thieves
and rapists couldn't get in, and so I couldn't get out. Then
they made their move.

They swooped in, several of them, and picked up the bag

with their beaks. One of them goaded me by walking up to the glass and trying to get me to bark. Normally, I would have resisted the urge, just to spite them, but knowing what I knew, I barked a few times, enough to make it convincing. They didn't go far. They wanted to taunt me with it. They wanted me to watch them enjoy the treats in the bag, so they stopped inside the yard, on the grass, the whole group of them. They danced around in circles and made faces at me and flapped their wings and called for their friends. They tore open the plastic and they dove in with all of their beaks to eat the wonderful food and delicious items that were hidden inside, and they ate. They gulped, those stupid birds; they ate from the bag and they swallowed with glee. And they choked on giant mouthfuls of my shit.

My shit!

Oh, the looks on their faces! The stunned silence. The indignation! The shaking of heads, and then they flew off en masse to the neighbor up the street with the dribbling fountain so they could wash their beaks.

They came back, then. Clean and mad. Hundreds of them. Maybe thousands. They stood on the back porch and on the back lawn, so thick with crows it was like a massive, undulating layer of tar and feathers, all of their beady eyes trained on me, staring at me, as if to say, Come out, little doggie, and we'll peck your eyeballs out!

I didn't go out. And they soon left. But when Denny got home from work that day, he looked in the back. Eve was cooking dinner, and Zoë was still little, in a high chair. Denny looked outside and said, "Why is there so much bird crap on the deck?" I knew. Given a Stephen Hawking computer, I could have made a good joke of it.

He went out and turned on the hose and washed the deck. And he collected the torn poop bags with puzzlement but no inquiry. The trees and telephone wires and electrical wires were heavy with those birds, all of them watching. I didn't go out with him. And when he wanted to go throw the ball, I pretended I was sick and climbed onto my bed and slept.

It was a good laugh, watching those dumb birds who think they're so smart with their beaks full of dog shit. But, as with all things, there were repercussions: since that time, my nightmares have always contained angry crows.

A murder of them.

14

The clues were all there, I simply hadn't read them correctly. Over the winter, he had played a video racing game obsessively, which wasn't like him. He had never gotten into racing games. But that winter, he played the game every night after Eve went to bed. And he raced on American circuits only. St. Petersburg and Laguna Seca. Road Atlanta and Mid-Ohio. I should have known just from seeing the tracks he was racing. He wasn't playing a video game, he was studying the circuits. He was learning turn-in points and braking points. I'd heard him talk about how accurate the backgrounds are on these video games, how drivers have found the games can be quite helpful for getting acquainted with new circuits. But I never thought—

And his diet: no alcohol, no sugar, no fried foods. His exercise regimen: running several days a week, swimming at the Medgar Evers Pool, lifting weights in the garage of the big guy down the street who started lifting when he was in prison. Denny had been preparing himself. He was lean and strong and ready to do battle in a race car. And I had missed all the signs. But then, I believe I had been duped. Because when he came downstairs with his track bag packed that day in March and his suitcase on wheels and his special helmet-and-HANS-device bag, Eve and Zoë seemed to know all about his leaving. He had told *them*. He hadn't told *me*.

The parting was strange. Zoë was both excited and nervous, Eve was somber, and I was utterly confused. *Where was he going?* I raised my eyebrows, lifted my ears, and cocked my head; I used every facial gesture at my disposal in an attempt to glean information.

"Sebring," he said to me, reading my mind the way he does sometimes. "I took the seat in the touring car, didn't I tell you?"

The touring car? But that was something he said he could never do! We agreed on that!

I was at once elated and devastated. A race weekend is at least three nights away, sometimes four when the event is on the opposite coast, and there are eleven races over an eight-month period. He would be away so much of the time! I was worried about the emotional well-being of those of us left behind.

But I am a racer at heart, and a racer will never let something that has already happened affect what is happening now. The news that he had taken the touring car seat and was flying to Sebring to race on ESPN 2 was extremely good. He was finally doing what he should be doing when he was supposed to do it. He wasn't waiting or worrying about everyone else. He was looking out for himself. A race car driver must be very selfish. It is a cold truth: even his family must come second to the race.

I wagged my tail enthusiastically, and he smiled at me with a twinkle in his eye. He knew that I understood everything he said.

"Be good, now," he chided me playfully. "Watch over the girls."

He hugged little Zoë and kissed Eve gently, but as he turned away from her she launched herself into his chest and grabbed him tight. She buried herself in his shoulder, her face red with congested tears.

"Please come back," she said, her words muffled by his mass.

"Of course I will."

"Please come back," she repeated.

He soothed her.

"I promise I'll come back in one piece," he said.

She shook her head, which was still pressed against his body.

"I don't care how many pieces," she said. "Just promise you'll come *back*."

He quickly glanced at me, as if I could clarify what she

was really asking. Did she mean come back alive? Or come back and not leave her? Or something else entirely? He didn't know.

I, however, knew exactly what she meant. Eve wasn't worried about Denny not returning, she was worried about herself. She knew that something was wrong with her, though she didn't know what, and she was afraid it would return in some terrible way when Denny was not with us. I was concerned as well, the memory of the zebra still in my head. I couldn't explain this to Denny, but I could resolve to remain steadfast in his absence.

"I promise," he said, hopefully.

After he had gone, Eve closed her eyes and took a deep breath. When she opened her eyes again, she looked at me, and I could see that she had resolved something for herself as well.

"I insisted he do it," she said to me. "I think it will be good for me; it will make me stronger."

That was the first race of the series, and the race didn't go well for Denny, though it went fine for Eve, Zoë, and me. We watched it on TV, and Denny qualified in the top third of the field. But shortly into the race, he had to pit because of a cut tire; a crew member had trouble mounting the new wheel, and by the time Denny returned to the race, he was a lap down and never recovered. Twenty-fourth place.

The second race came only a few weeks after the first, and, again, Eve, Zoë, and I managed fine. For Denny, the results of the race were very much the same as the first: spilled fuel that resulted in a stop-and-go penalty, costing Denny a lap. Thirtieth place.

Denny was extremely frustrated.

"I like the guys," he told us at dinner when he was home for a stretch. "They're good people, but they're not a good pit crew. They're making mistakes, killing our season. If they would just give me a chance to finish, I'd finish well."

"Can't you get a new crew?" Eve asked.

I was in the kitchen, next to the dining room. I never stayed in the dining room when they ate, out of respect. No one likes a dog under the table looking for crumbs when they're eating. So I couldn't see them, but I could hear them. Denny picking up the wooden salad bowl and serving himself more salad. Zoë pushing her chicken nuggets around on the plate.

"Eat them, honey," Eve said. "Don't play with them."

"It's not the quality of the man," Denny tried to explain. "It's the quality of the *team*."

"How do you fix it?" Eve asked. "You're spending so much time away, it seems like a waste. What's the point of racing if you can't finish? Zoë, you've only had two bites. *Eat*."

The crunching of romaine. Zoë drinking from her sippy cup.

"Practice," Denny said. "Practice, practice, practice."

"When will you practice?"

"They want me to go down to Infineon next week, work with the Apex Porsche people. Work hard with the pit crew so there are no more mistakes. The sponsors are getting frustrated."

Eve fell silent.

"Next week is your week off," she said finally.

"I won't be gone long. Three or four days. Good salad. Did you make the dressing yourself?"

I couldn't read their body language because I couldn't see them, but there are some things a dog can sense. Tension. Fear. Anxiety. These states of being are the result of a chemical release inside the human body. They are totally physiological, in other words. Involuntary. People like to think they have evolved beyond instinct, but in fact, they still have fight-or-flight responses to stimuli. And when their bodies respond, I can smell the chemical release from their pituitary glands. For instance, adrenaline has a very specific odor, which is not so much smelled but tasted. I know a person can't understand that concept, but that's the best way to describe it: the taste of an alkaline on the back of my tongue. From my position on the kitchen floor, I could taste Eve's adrenaline. Clearly, she had steeled herself for Denny's racing absences; she was not prepared for his impromptu practices in Sonoma, and she was angry and afraid.

I heard chair legs scrape as a chair was pushed back. I heard plates being stacked, flatware nervously gathered.

"Eat your nuggets," Eve said again, this time sternly.

"I'm full," Zoë declared.

"You haven't eaten anything. How can you be full?"

"I don't like nuggets."

"You're not leaving the table until you eat your nuggets."

"I DON'T LIKE NUGGETS!" Zoë shrieked, and suddenly the world was a very dark place.

Anxiety. Anticipation. Excitement. Antipathy. All these emotions have a distinctive smell, many of which were exuding from the dining room at that moment.

After a long silence, Denny said, "I'll make you a hot dog."

"No," Eve said. "She'll eat the nuggets. She likes nuggets, she's just being difficult. Eat!"

Another pause, and then the sound of a child gagging.

Denny almost laughed. "I'll make her a hot dog," he said again.

"She's going to eat the goddamn nuggets!" Eve shouted.

"She doesn't like the nuggets. I'll make her a hot dog," Denny replied firmly.

"No, you won't! She likes the nuggets, she's just doing this because you're here. I'm not making a new dinner every time she decides she doesn't like something. She asked for the fucking nuggets, now she'll eat the fucking nuggets!"

Fury has a very distinctive smell, too.

Zoë started to cry. I went to the door and looked in. Eve was standing at the head of the table, her face red and pinched. Zoë was sobbing into her nuggets. Denny stood to make himself seem bigger. It's important for the alpha to be bigger. Often just posturing can get a member of the pack to back down.

"You're overreacting," he said. "Why don't you go lie down and let me finish up here."

"You always take her side!" Eve barked.

"I just want her to have a dinner she'll eat."

"Fine," Eve hissed. "I'll make her a hot dog, then."

Eve whirled from the table and almost crushed me when she burst into the kitchen. She threw open the freezer door and snatched a package of hot dogs, turned on the faucet and held the package under the running water. She grabbed a knife from the block and stabbed into the package, and that's when the evening turned from one filled with forgettable arguments to one marked by undeniable and permanent evidence. As if the knife had a will of its own and wanted to get involved in the fracas, the blade leapt from the wet, frozen package and sliced deep and clean into the fleshy webbing of Eve's left palm, between her thumb and fingers.

The knife clattered in the sink, and Eve grabbed her hand with a wail. Watery drops of blood speckled the backsplash. Denny was there in a moment with a dishcloth.

"Let me see it," he said, peeling the blood-soaked cloth from her hand, which she held by the wrist as if it were no longer a part of her body but some alien creature that had attacked her.

"We should take you to the hospital," he said.

"No!" she bellowed. "No hospital!"

"You need stitches," he said, examining the gushing wound.

She didn't answer immediately, but her eyes were filled

with tears. Not from pain, but from fear. She was so afraid of doctors and hospitals. She was afraid that she might go in and they would never let her out.

"Please," she whispered to Denny. "Please. No hospital."

He groaned and shook his head.

"I'll see if I can close it," he said.

Zoë stood next to me, silent, eyes wide, holding a chicken nugget, watching. Neither of us knew what to do.

"Zoë, baby," Denny said. "Can you find the butterfly closures for me in the hall closet? We'll get Mommy all patched up, okay?"

Zoë didn't move. How could she? She knew she was the cause of Mommy's pain. It was her blood that Eve was bleeding.

"Zoë, please," Denny said, lifting Eve to her feet. "Blue and white box, red letters. Look for the 'B' word. *Butterfly.*"

Zoë headed off to find the box. Denny guided Eve to the bathroom and closed the door. I heard Eve cry out in pain.

When Zoë returned with the box of bandages, she didn't know where her parents had gone, so I walked her to the bathroom door and barked. Denny opened the door a crack and took the bandages.

"Thanks, Zoë. I'll take care of Mommy, now. You can go play or watch TV."

He closed the door.

Zoë looked at me for a moment with concern in her eyes, and I wanted to help her. I walked toward the living room and looked back. She still hesitated, so I went to get her. I nudged her and tried again; this time she followed me. I sat before the television and waited for her to turn it on, which she did. And we watched *Kids Next Door*. And then Denny and Eve appeared.

They saw us watching TV together, and they seemed somehow relieved. They sat next to Zoë and watched along with us, not saying a word. When the show was over, Eve pressed the mute button on the remote.

"The cut isn't very bad," she said to Zoë. "If you're still hungry, I can make you a hot dog. . . ."

Zoë shook her head.

And then Eve started sobbing. Sitting on the couch, exposed to the world, she collapsed into herself; I could see her energy implode.

"I'm so sorry," she cried.

Denny put his arm around her shoulder and held her.

"I don't want to be like this," she sobbed. "It's not me. I'm so sorry. I don't want to be mean. It's not who I am."

Beware, I thought. The zebra hides everywhere.

Zoë grabbed her mother and held tight, which unleashed a flood of tears from both of them, and they were joined by Denny, who hovered over them like a firefighting helicopter, dumping his bucket of tears on the fire.

I left. Not because I felt they wanted their privacy, believe me. I left because I felt that they had resolved their issues and all was good in the world.

And, also, I was hungry.

I wandered into the dining room and scanned the floor for droppings. There wasn't much. But in the kitchen I found something good. A nugget.

Zoë must have dropped it after Eve cut herself. It looked like a fair snack to me, something to tide me over until they got over their cuddly moment and remembered to feed me. I sniffed the nugget, and I recoiled in disgust. It was bad! I sniffed again. Rancid. Foul. Disease laden! The nuggets had been in the freezer too long, or out of the freezer too long. Or both, I concluded, having witnessed what little regard people pay to their grocery sacks. This nugget—and probably all the others on the plate—had definitely turned.

I felt bad for Zoë: all she'd had to do was say that the nuggets didn't taste right, and this incident would have been avoided. But Eve would have found a way to hurt herself anyway, I suppose. They needed this. This moment. It was important to them as a family, and I understood that.

In racing, they say that your car goes where your eyes go. The driver who cannot tear his eyes away from the wall as he spins out of control will meet that wall; the driver who looks down the track as he feels his tires break free will regain control of his vehicle.

Your car goes where your eyes go. Simply another way of saying that which you manifest is before you.

I know it's true; racing doesn't lie.

15

When Denny went away the following week, we went to Eve's parents' house so they could take care of us. Eve's hand was bandaged up, which indicated to me that the cut was worse than she had let on. But it didn't slow her down much.

Maxwell and Trish, the Twins, lived in a very fancy house on a large parcel of wooded land on Mercer Island, with an amazing view of Lake Washington and Seattle. And for having such a beautiful place to live, they were among the most unhappy people I've ever met. Nothing was good enough for them. They were always complaining about how things could be better or why things were as bad as they were. When we arrived, they started in about Denny right away. *He doesn't spend enough time with Zoë. He's neglecting your relationship. His dog needs a bath.* Like *my* hygiene had anything to do with it.

"What are you going to do?" Maxwell asked her.

They were standing around in the kitchen while Trish cooked dinner, making something that Zoë would inevitably hate. It was a warm spring evening, so the Twins were wearing polo shirts with their slacks. Maxwell and Trish were drinking Manhattans with cherries, Eve, a glass of wine. She had rejected the painkiller offered to her, which was left over from the hernia operation Maxwell had undergone a few months before.

"I'm going to get in shape," Eve said. "I feel fat."

"But you're so thin," Trish said.

"You can feel fat even if you're thin. I feel out of shape."

"Oh."

"I mean about Denny," Maxwell said.

"What do I need to do about Denny?" Eve asked.

"*Something!* What is he contributing to your family? *You* make all the money!"

"He's my husband and he's Zoë's father, and I love him. What else does he need to contribute to our family?"

Maxwell snorted and slapped the counter. I flinched.

"You're scaring the dog," Trish pointed out. She rarely called me by name. They do that in prisoner of war camps, I've heard. Depersonalization.

"I'm just frustrated," Maxwell said. "I want the best for my girls. Whenever you come to stay here, it's because he's gone racing. It's not good for you."

"This season is really important for his career," Eve said,

trying to remain steadfast. "I wish I were able to be more involved, but I'm doing the best I can, and he appreciates that. What I don't need is you going after me for it."

"I'm sorry," Maxwell said, holding up his hands in surrender. "I'm sorry. I just want what's best for you."

"I know, Daddy," Eve said, and she leaned forward and kissed his cheek. "I want what's best for me, too."

She took her wine outside into the backyard, and I lingered. Maxwell opened the refrigerator and retrieved a jar of the hot peppers he liked to eat. He was always eating peppers. He opened the jar and squeezed his fingers inside, extracted a long pepperoncini, and crunched into it.

"Do you see how frail she's gotten?" Trish asked. "Like a whippet. But she *feels* fat."

He shook his head. "My daughter, with a mechanic—no, not a mechanic. A *customer service technician*. Where did we go wrong?"

"She's always made her own choices," Trish said.

"But at least her choices made sense. She majored in art history, for Christ's sake. She ends up with him?"

"The dog is watching you," Trish said after a moment. "Maybe he wants a pepper."

Maxwell's expression changed.

"Want a treat, boy?" he asked, holding out a pepperoncini.

That wasn't why I had been watching him. I was watching him to better glean the meaning of his words. Still, I was hungry, so I sniffed at the pepper.

"They're good," he prompted. "Imported from Italy."

I took the pepper from him and immediately felt a prickly sensation on my tongue. I bit down, and a burning liquid filled my mouth. I quickly swallowed and thought I was done with the discomfort—surely the acid in my stomach would cancel out the acid of the pepper—but that's when the pain really began. My throat felt as if it had been scraped raw. My stomach churned. I immediately left the room and the house. Outside the back door, I lapped at my bowl of water, but it did little to help. I made my way to a nearby shrub and lay down in its shade and rested until the burning went away.

When they took me out that night—Trish and Maxwell did, as Zoë and Eve had long been asleep—they stood at the back porch and repeated their silly mantra, "Get busy, boy, get busy!" Still feeling somewhat queasy, I ventured away from the house farther than I usually did, crouched in my stance, and shat. After I did my business, I saw that my stool was loose and watery, and when I sniffed at it, it was unusually foul-smelling. I knew I was safe and the ordeal had passed; still, since that time I have been wary of trying new foods that might upset my system, and I have never accepted food from someone I didn't fully trust.

16

The weeks tripped by with tremendous haste, as if digging into the fall were the most important mission of all. There was no lingering on accomplishment: Denny got his first victory in Laguna in early June, he pegged a podium finish—third place—at Road Atlanta, and he finished eighth in Denver. That week with the boys in Sonoma had worked out the kinks with the crew, and it was all on Denny's shoulders. And his shoulders were broad.

That summer, when we gathered around the dinner table, there was something to talk about. Trophies. Photographs. Replays on television late at night. Suddenly people were hanging around, coming over for dinner. Not just Mike from work—where they were happy to accommodate Denny's crazy schedule—but others, too. NASCAR veteran

Derrike Cope. Motorsports Hall of Famer Chip Hanauer. We were even introduced to Luca Pantoni, a very powerful man at Ferrari headquarters in Maranello, Italy, who was in Seattle visiting Don Kitch Jr., Seattle's premier racing tutor. I never broke my rule about the dining room, I have too much integrity for that. But I sat upon the threshold, I assure you. My toenails edged over the line so that I could be that much closer to greatness. I learned more about racing in those few weeks than I had in all my prior years of watching video and television; to hear the estimable Ross Bentley, coach of champions, speak about breathing—*breathing!*—was absolutely stunning.

Zoë chattered away constantly, always something to say, always something to show. She would sit on Denny's knee with her big eyes absorbing every word of the conversation, and at an appropriate moment she would declare some racing truth Denny had taught her—"slow hands in the fast stuff, fast hands in the slow stuff," or something like that—and all the big men would be suitably impressed. I was proud of her in those moments; since I was unable to impress the racing men with my own knowledge, the next best thing was to experience it vicariously through Zoë.

Eve was happy again: she took what she called "mat" classes and gained muscle tone, and often alerted Denny to the needs of her fertile field, sometimes with great urgency. Her health had greatly improved with no explanation: no more headaches, no more nausea. She continued to have trouble with her injured hand, oddly, and sometimes she used a wrist support to help her grip when cooking. Still, from what I heard in the bedroom late at night, her hands retained all of the necessary flexibility and suppleness to make Denny and herself very happy.

Yet for every peak there is a valley. Denny's next race was pivotal, as a good finish would solidify his position as rookie of the year. In that race, at Phoenix International Raceway, Denny got tagged in the first turn.

This is a rule of racing: No race has ever been won in the first corner; many have been lost there.

He got caught in a bad spot. Someone tried to late-brake him going into the corner and locked it up. Tires don't work if they aren't rolling. In full-out skid, the hard charger slammed into Denny's left front wheel, destroying the car's alignment. The toe was skewed so badly that his car crabbed up the track, scrubbing seconds off his lap time.

Alignment, late-braking, locking up, toe-in: mere jargon. These are simply the terms we use to explain the phenomena around us. What matters is not how precisely we can explain the event, but the event itself and its consequence, which was that Denny's car was broken. He finished the race, but he finished DFL. That's what he called it when he told me about it. A new category. There's DNS: Did Not Start. There's DNF: Did Not Finish. And there's DFL: Dead Fucking Last.

"It just doesn't seem fair," Eve said. "It was the other driver's fault."

"If it was anybody's fault," Denny said, "it was mine for being where I could get collected."

This is something I'd heard him say before: getting angry at another driver for a driving incident is pointless. You need to watch the drivers around you, understand their skill, confidence, and aggression levels, and drive with them accordingly. Know who is driving next to you. Any problems that may occur have ultimately been caused by you, because you are responsible for where you are and what you are doing there.

Still, fault or no, Denny was crushed. Zoë was crushed. Eve was crushed. I was decimated. We had come so close to greatness. We had smelled it, and it smelled like roast pig. Everybody likes the smell of roast pig. But what is worse, smelling the roast and not feasting, or not smelling the roast at all?

August was hot and dry, and the grass all around the neighborhood was brown and dead. Denny spent his time doing math. By his figuring, it was still possible for him to finish in the top ten in the series and likely win rookie of the year, and either result would assure him of getting another ride the following year.

We sat on the back porch basking in the early evening sun, the smell of Denny's freshly baked oatmeal cookies wafting from the kitchen. Zoë running in the sprinkler. Denny massaging Eve's hand gently, giving it life. I was on the deck doing my best impression of an iguana: soaking up all the heat I could to warm my blood, hoping that if I absorbed enough, it would carry me through the winter, which would likely be harsh, cold, dark, and bitter, as a hot Seattle summer usually portends.

"Maybe it isn't meant to be," Eve said.

"It'll happen when it happens," Denny told her.

"But you're never here anymore when I'm ovulating."

"So come with me next week. Zoë will love it; we'll stay where they have a pool. She loves anything with a pool. And you can come to the track for the race."

"I can't go to the track," Eve said. "Not now. I mean, I wish I could, I really do. But I've been feeling good lately, you know? And . . . I'm afraid. The track is so loud and it's hot, and it smells like rubber and gas, and the radio blasts static into my ears, and everyone's shouting at each other so they can be heard. It might give me a—I might react badly to it."

Denny smiled and sighed. Even Eve cracked a smile.

"Do you understand?" she asked.

"I do," Denny answered.

I did, too. Everything about the track. The sounds, the smells. Walking through the paddock and feeling the energy, the heat of race motors emanating from each pit. The electricity that ripples up and down the paddock when the announcer calls the next race group to pre-grid. Watching the frantic scramble of a standing start, and then imagining the possibilities, putting together the story of what's going on when the cars are out of sight on other parts of the race circuit until they come around to start/finish again in an entirely different order, dodging and drafting and making runs and diving into the next turn that can flip everything upside down again. Denny and I fed off it; it gave us life. But I totally understood that what filled us with energy could be toxic to someone else, especially Eve.

"We could use a turkey baster," Denny said, and Eve laughed hard, harder than I'd seen her laugh in a long time. "I could leave you with a cupful of potential babies in the refrigerator," he said, and she laughed even harder. I didn't get the joke, but Eve thought it was hysterical.

She got up and went into the house, reappearing a moment later with the turkey baster from the kitchen. She scrutinized it with a devious smile, ran her fingers along its length.

"Hmm," she said. "Maybe."

They giggled together and looked out to the lawn and I looked with them and we all watched Zoë, her wet hair clinging to her shoulders in glistening locks. Her childish bikini and tanned feet. Pure joy as she ran circles around the sprinkler, her shrieks and squeals and laughs echoing through the Central District streets.

17

Your car goes where your eyes go.

We went to Denny Creek, not because it was named after Denny—it wasn't—but because it was such an enjoyable hike, Zoë clumping along in her first pair of waffle stompers, me cut loose of my leash. Summer in the Cascades is always pleasant, cool under the canopy of cedars and alders, the beaten path packed down, making long strides easy; off the beaten path—where dogs prefer—a soft and spongy bed of fallen needles that rot and feed the trees with a steady trickle of nutrients. And the smell!

The smell would have given me an erection if I'd still had testicles. Richness and fertility. Growth and death and food and decay. Waiting. Just waiting for someone to smell it, lingering close to the ground in layers, each distinct scent with its own aromatic weight, its own place. A good nose like mine can separate each odor, identify, enjoy. I rarely let myself go, practicing to be restrained like men are, but that summer, considering the joy of all that we had, Denny's success and Zoë's exuberance and even Eve, who was light and free, I ran through those woods that day wildly, like a crazy dog, diving through the bushes, over the fallen trees, giving gentle chase to chipmunks, barking at the jays, rolling over and scratching my back on the sticks and leaves and needles and earth.

We made our way along the path, up the hills and down, over the roots and past the rock outcroppings, eventually arriving at the Slippery Slabs, as they are called, where the creek runs over a series of broad, flat rocks, pooling at some points, streaming at others. Children love the Slippery Slabs as they slide and slice through the sluices and slate. And so we arrived and I drank the water, cold and fresh, the last of that year's snow melt. Zoë and Denny and Eve stripped down to their swimsuits and bathed gently in the waters. Zoë was old enough to safely navigate parts herself, and Denny took the lower and Eve took the upper and they slid Zoë down the stream of water, Eve giving a push and Zoë slipping down. The rocks had traction when dry, but when wet, there was a film on them that made them quite slick. Down she would go, squealing and squirming, splashing into the frigid pool at Denny's feet; he would snatch her up and whisk her back to Eve, who would slide her down again. And again.

People, like dogs, love repetition. Chasing a ball, lapping a course in a race car, sliding down a slide. Because as much as each incident is similar, so it is different. Denny rushed up the slab and handed off Zoë. He returned to his spot by the pool. Eve lowered Zoë into the water; she screamed and flung herself in play, slid down the slab to be caught by Denny again.

Until once. Eve dipped Zoë into the water, but instead of screaming and splashing, Zoë suddenly pulled her toes from the icy water, upsetting Eve's balance. Eve shifted her weight and somehow managed to release Zoë safely onto the dry rock, but her move was too abrupt, too sudden—an overcorrection. Her foot touched the creek, and she didn't realize how slippery those rocks were, slippery slabs like glass.

Her legs went out from underneath her. She reached out, but her hand grasped only the air; her fist closed, empty. Her head hit the rock with a loud crack and bounced. It hit and bounced and hit again, like a rubber ball.

We stood, it seemed like for a long time, waiting to see what was going to happen. Eve lay unmoving, and there was Zoë, again the cause, not knowing what to do. She looked at her father, who quickly bounded up to them both.

"Are you okay?"

Eve blinked hard, painfully. There was blood in her mouth.

"I bit my tongue," she said woozily.

"How's your head?" Denny asked.

"—Hurts."

"Can you make it back to the car?"

With me in the lead herding Zoë, Denny steered Eve. She wasn't staggering, but she was lost, and who knows where she would have ended up if someone hadn't been with her. It was early evening when we got to the hospital in Bellevue.

"You probably have a minor concussion," Denny said. "But they should check it out."

"I'm okay," Eve repeated over and over. But clearly she wasn't okay. She was dazed and slurring her words and she kept nodding off but Denny would wake her up, saying something about not falling asleep when you have a concussion.

They all went inside and left me in the car with the windows open a crack. I settled into the pocketlike passenger seat of Denny's BMW 3.0 CSi and forced myself to sleep; when I sleep, I don't feel the urge to urinate nearly as badly as when I am awake.

18

In Mongolia, when a dog dies, he is buried high in the hills so people cannot walk on his grave. The dog's master whispers into the dog's ear his wishes that the dog will return as a man in his next life. Then his tail is cut off and put beneath his head, and a piece of meat or fat is placed in his mouth to sustain his soul on its journey; before he is reincarnated, the dog's soul is freed to travel the land, to run across the high desert plains for as long as it would like.

I learned that from a program on the National Geographic Channel, so I believe it is true. Not all dogs return as men, they say; only those who are ready.

I am ready.

19

It was hours before Denny returned, and he returned alone. He let me out, and I barely could scramble from the seat before unleashing a torrent of urine on the lamppost in front of me.

"Sorry, boy," he said. "I didn't forget about you."

When I had finished, he opened a package of peanut butter sandwich crackers he must have gotten from a vending machine. I love those crackers the best. It's the salt and the butter in the crackers mixed with the fat in the peanuts. I tried to eat slowly, savoring each bite, but I was too hungry and swallowed them so quickly I barely got to taste them. What a shame to waste something so wonderful on a dog. Sometimes I hate what I am so much.

We sat on the berm for quite a long time, not speaking or

anything. He seemed upset, and when he was upset, I knew the best thing I could do was be available for him. So I lay next to him and waited.

Parking lots are weird places. People love their cars so much when they are moving, but they hurry away from them so quickly when they stop moving. People are loath to sit in a parked car for long. They are afraid someone might judge them for it, I think. The only people who sit in parked cars are police and stalkers, and sometimes taxi drivers on a break, but usually only when they're eating. Whereas me, I can sit in a parked car for hours and nobody thinks to ask. Odd. I could be a stalker dog, and then what would happen? But in that hospital parking lot, with its very black blacktop, warm like a sweater just removed, and its very white white lines painted with surgical care, people parked their cars and *ran* from them. Sprinted into the building. Or scurried out of the building and into their cars, quick to drive away with no mirror adjustment, no assessment of gauges, like a getaway car.

Denny and I sat at length and watched them, the comers and goers, and did nothing more than breathe; we did not need conversation to communicate with each other. After a while, a car pulled into the parking lot and parked near us. It was beautiful, a 1974 Alfa Romeo GTV in pine green with a factory-installed fabric sunroof, in mint condition. Mike got out slowly and walked toward us.

I greeted him, and he gave me a perfunctory pat on the

head. He continued over to Denny and sat down in my spot on the berm. I tried to muster some joy because the mood was definitely down, but Mike pushed me away when I went to nuzzle him.

"I appreciate this, Mike," Denny said.

"Hey, man, no problem. What about Zoë?"

"Eve's dad took her to their house and put her to bed."

Mike nodded. The crickets were louder than the traffic from the nearby Interstate 405, but not by much. We listened to them, a concert of crickets, wind, leaves, cars, and fans on the roof of the hospital building.

Here's why I will be a good person. Because I listen. I cannot speak, so I listen very well. I never interrupt, I never deflect the course of the conversation with a comment of my own. People, if you pay attention to them, change the direction of one another's conversations constantly. It's like having a passenger in your car who suddenly grabs the steering wheel and turns you down a side street. For instance, if we met at a party and I wanted to tell you a story about the time I needed to get a soccer ball in my neighbor's yard but his dog chased me and I had to jump into a swimming pool to escape, and I began telling the story, you, hearing the words "soccer" and "neighbor" in the same sentence, might interrupt and mention that your childhood neighbor was Pelé, the famous soccer player, and I might be courteous and say, Didn't he play for the Cosmos of New York? Did you grow up in New York? And you might reply that, no, you grew up in Brazil on the streets of Três Corações with Pelé, and I might say, I thought you were from Tennessee, and you might say not originally, and then go on to outline your genealogy at length. So my initial conversational gambit— that I had a funny story about being chased by my neighbor's dog—would be totally lost, and only because you had to tell me all about Pelé. Learn to *listen*! I beg of you. Pretend you are a dog like me and listen to other people rather than steal their stories.

I listened that night and I heard.

"How long will they keep her?" Mike asked.

"They might not even do a biopsy. They might just go in and get it. Malignant or not, it's still causing problems. The headaches, the nausea, the mood swings."

"Really," Mike deadpanned. "Mood swings? Maybe *my* wife has a tumor."

It was a joke line, a throwaway, but Denny didn't have a sense of humor that night. He said sharply, "It's not a tumor, Mike. It's a *mass*. It's not a tumor until they test it."

"Sorry," Mike said. "I was . . . Sorry." He grabbed me by the scruff and gave me a shake. "Really rough," he said. "I'd be freaking out right now if I were you."

Denny stood up tall. For him. He wasn't a tall guy. He was a Formula One guy. Well proportioned and powerful, but scaled down. A flyweight.

"I *am* freaking out," he said.

Mike nodded thoughtfully.

"You don't look it. I guess that's why you're such a good driver," he said, and I looked at him quickly. That was just what I was thinking.

"You don't mind stopping by my place and getting his stuff?"

Denny took out his key ring, picked through the bundle.

"The food is in the pantry. Give him a cup and a half. He gets three of those chicken cookies before he goes to bed— take his bed, it's in the bedroom. And take his dog. Just say, 'Where's your dog?' and he'll find it, sometimes he hides it."

He found the house key and held it out for Mike, letting the other keys dangle.

"It's the same for both locks," he said.

"We'll be fine," Mike said. "Do you want me to bring you some clothes?"

"No," Denny said. "I'll go back in the morning and pack a bag if we're staying."

"You want me to bring these back?"

"I have Eve's inside."

No words, then, just crickets, wind, traffic, fans blowing on the roof, a distant siren.

"You don't have to keep it inside," Mike said. "You can let go. We're in a parking lot."

Denny looked down at his shoes, the same old three-quarter boots he liked to hike in; he wanted a new pair, I knew because he'd told me, but he didn't want to spend the money he said, and I think he held out hope that someone would give him a pair of boots for a birthday or Christmas or something. But no one ever did. He had a hundred pair of driving gloves, but no one ever thought to give him a new pair of hiking boots. I *listen*.

He looked up at Mike.

"This is why she didn't want to go to the hospital."

"What?" Mike asked.

"This is what she was afraid of."

Mike nodded, but clearly he didn't understand what Denny was saying.

"What about your race next week?" he asked.

"I'll call Jonny tomorrow and tell him I'm out for the season," Denny said. "I have to be *here*."

Mike took me to our house to get my things. I was humiliated when he said, "Where's your dog?" I didn't want to admit that I still slept with a stuffed animal. But I did. I loved that dog, and Denny was right, I did hide it during the day because I didn't want Zoë to assimilate it into her collection and also because when people saw it they wanted to play tug and I didn't like tugging with my dog. And also, I was afraid of the virus that had possessed the zebra.

But I got my dog out of his hiding spot under the sofa and we climbed back into Mike's Alfa and went to his house. His wife, who wasn't really a wife but a man who was wife-like, asked how it all went and Mike brushed him off right away and poured himself a drink.

"That guy is bottled so tight," Mike said. "He's gonna have an aneurism or something."

Mike's wife picked up my dog that I had dropped on the floor.

"We have to take this, too?" he asked.

"Listen," Mike sighed, "everyone needs a security blanket. What's wrong with that?"

"It stinks," Mike's wife said. "I'll wash it."

And he put it in the washing machine! My dog! He took the first toy that Denny ever gave me and stuck it into the washing machine . . . with soap! I couldn't believe it. I was stunned. No one had ever handled my dog in such a way!

I watched through the glass window of the machine as it spun around and around, sloshing with the suds, I watched it. And they laughed at me. Not meanly. They thought I was a dumb dog—all people do. They laughed and I watched and when it came out, they put it in the dryer with a towel, and I waited. And when it was dry, they took it out and gave it to me. Tony, Mike's wife, took it out and it was warm, and he handed it to me and said, "Much better, right?"

I wanted to hate him then. I wanted to hate the world. I wanted to hate my own dog, a goofy stuffed animal that Denny gave me when I was just a puppy. I was so angry with how our family had been suddenly torn apart, Zoë stuck with the Twins, Eve sick in a hospital, me shuttled off like a foster child. And now my dog, washed clean of smell. I wanted to push everyone away and go live by myself with my ancestors on the high desert plains of Mongolia and guard the sheep and the ewes from the wolves.

When Tony handed me my dog, I took it in my mouth out of respect. I took it to my bed because that's what Denny would have wanted me to do. And I curled up with it.

And the irony? I liked it.

I liked my stuffed dog better clean than smelly, which was something I never would have imagined, but which gave me something I could hold on to. Some belief that the center of our family could not be fractured by a chance occurrence, an accidental washing, an unexpected illness. Deep in the kernel of our family existed a bond; Denny, Zoë, Eve, me, and even my stuffed dog. However things might change around us, we would always be together.

20

I was not privy to much, being a dog. I was not allowed into the hospital to hear the hushed conversations, the diagnosis, the prognosis, the analysis, to witness the doctor with the blue hat and blue gown whispering his misgivings, revealing the clues they all should have seen, unraveling the mysteries of the brain. No one confided in me. I was never consulted. Nothing was expected of me except that I do my business outside when called upon to do so, and that I stop barking when told to stop barking.

Eve stayed in the hospital for a long time. Weeks. Because there was so much for Denny to do, caring for both me and Zoë, as well as visiting Eve in the hospital whenever possible, he decided that the best plan was to implement a template system, rather than our usual spontaneous way of living. Whereas before, he and Eve sometimes took Zoë to dinner at a restaurant, without Eve, we always ate at home. Whereas before, Denny sometimes fed Zoë breakfast at a coffee shop, without Eve, breakfast was always eaten at home. The days consisted of a series of regimented events: Zoë ate her cereal while Denny made her a sack lunch consisting of a peanut butter and banana sandwich on whole grain bread, potato chips, the good cookies, and a small bottle of water. Denny then dropped Zoë at her summer camp, and continued on to work. At the end of the workday, Denny retrieved Zoë from camp and returned home to cook dinner while Zoë watched cartoons. After dinner, Denny gave me my food and then took Zoë to visit Eve. Later, they returned, Denny bathed Zoë, read her a story, and tucked her into bed. Denny then attended to whatever tasks needed attending, such as paying bills or arguing with the health insurance company about cost overruns and payment schedules and so forth. Weekends were spent largely at the hospital. It was not a very colorful way to live. But it was efficient. And considering the seriousness of Eve's illness, efficient was the best we could expect. My walks were infrequent, my trips to the dog park nonexistent. Little attention was paid to me by Denny or Zoë. But I was ready to make that sacrifice in the interest of Eve's well-being and to preserve the family dynamic. I vowed not to be a squeaky wheel in any way.

After two weeks of this pattern, Maxwell and Trish

offered to keep Zoë for a weekend, so as to afford Denny a bit of a respite. They told him he looked sickly, that he should take a vacation from his troubles, and Eve agreed. "I don't want to see you this weekend," she said to him, at least that's what he told Zoë and me. Denny was ambivalent about the idea, I could tell as he packed Zoë's overnight bag. He was hesitant to let Zoë go. But he did let her go, and then he and I were alone. And it felt very strange.

We did all the things we used to do. We went jogging. We ordered delivery pizza for lunch. We spent the afternoon watching the fantastic movie *Le Mans*, in which Steve McQueen endures tragedy and pain in the ultimate test of courage and personal fortitude. We watched one of Denny's tapes featuring an onboard view of the grand Nürburgring racetrack in Germany, filmed in the track's heyday when the likes of Jackie Stewart and Jim Clark raced its lengthy twenty-two-kilometer, 174-turn *Nordschleife*, or Northern Loop. After that, Denny took me to the Blue Dog Park that was a few blocks away and he threw the ball for me. But even for that venture, our energy was wrong; a dog with darkness about him got after me and was at my throat with bared teeth everywhere I moved, so I couldn't retrieve the tennis ball but was forced to stay close by Denny's side.

It all felt wrong. The absence of Eve and Zoë was wrong. There was something missing in everything we did. After we had both eaten dinner, we sat together in the kitchen, fidgeting. There was nothing for us to do but fidget. Because while we were going through the motions, doing what we always used to do, there was no joy in it whatsoever.

Finally, Denny stood. He took me outside, and I urinated for him. He gave me my usual bedtime cookies, and then he said to me, "You be good."

He said, "I have to go see her."

I followed him to the door; I wanted to go see her, too.

"No," he said to me. "You stay here. They won't let you into the hospital."

I understood; I went to my bed and lay down.

"Thanks, Enzo," he said. And then he left.

He returned a few hours later, in the darkness, and he silently climbed into his bed with a shiver before the sheets got warm. I lifted my head and he saw me.

"She's going to be okay," he said to me. "She's going to be okay."

21

She made me wear the bumblebee wings she had worn the previous Halloween. She dressed herself in her pink ballet outfit with the tulle skirt and the leotard and stockings. We went out into the backyard and ran around together until her pink feet were stained with dirt.

Zoë and me, playing in the backyard on a sunny afternoon. It was the Tuesday after her weekend with Maxwell and Trish, and by then she had thankfully lost the sour vinegar smell that clung to her whenever she spent time at the Twins' house. Denny had left work early and picked up Zoë so they could go shopping for new sneakers and socks. When they got home, Denny cleaned the house while Zoë and I played. We danced and laughed and ran and pretended we were angels.

She called me over to the corner of the yard by the spigot. On the wood chips lay one of her Barbie dolls. She kneeled down before it.

"You're going to be okay," she said to the doll. "Everything is going to be okay."

She unfolded a dishcloth that she'd brought from the house. In the dishcloth were scissors, a Sharpie pen, and masking tape. She pulled off the doll's head. She took the kitchen scissors and cut off Barbie's hair, down to the plastic nub. She then drew a line on the doll's skull, all the while whispering softly, "Everything's going to be okay."

When she was done, she tore off a piece of masking tape and put it on the doll's head. She pressed the head back onto the neck stub and laid the doll down. We both stared at it. A moment of silence.

"Now she can go to heaven," Zoë said to me. "And I'll live with Grandma and Grandpa."

I was disheartened. Clearly, the weekend of respite Maxwell and Trish had offered Denny was a false one. I had no clear evidence, and yet I could sense it. For the Twins, it had been a working weekend, an effort to establish an agenda. They were already sowing the seeds of their story, spinning the yarn of their propaganda, prophesying a future they hoped would come true.

22

Soon, Labor Day weekend came, and after that, Zoë was enrolled in school. "Real school," as she called it. Kindergarten.
And she was so excited to go. She picked out her clothes the
night before her first day, bell-bottom jeans and sneakers and
a bright yellow blouse. She had her backpack, her lunch box,
her pencil case, her notebook. With great ceremony, Denny
and I walked with her a block from our house to the corner
of Martin Luther King Jr. Way, and we waited for the bus
that would take her to her new elementary school. We waited
with a few other kids and parents from the neighborhood.

When the bus trundled over the hill, we were all so excited.

"Kiss me now," she said to Denny.

"Now?"

GARTH STEIN

"Not when the bus is here. I don't want Jessie to see."

Jessie was her best friend from preschool, who was going to be in the same kindergarten class.

Denny obliged and kissed her before the bus had stopped.

"After school, you go to Extended Day," he said. "Like we practiced yesterday at orientation. Remember?"

"Daddy!" she scolded.

"I'll pick you up after Extended Day. You wait in the classroom, and I'll come and get you."

"Daddy!"

She made a stern face at him, and for a second I could have sworn she was Eve. The flashing eyes. The flared nostrils. The balanced stance and arms akimbo, the head cocked, ready for battle. She quickly turned and climbed onto the bus, and as she walked down the aisle, she turned and waved at us both before she took her seat next to her friend.

The bus pulled away and headed for school.

"Your first?" another father asked Denny.

"Yeah," Denny replied. "My only. You?"

"My third," the man said. "But there's nothing like your first. They grow up so fast."

"That they do," Denny said with a smile; we turned and walked home.

114

23

Everything they said made sense, but none of it added up properly in my mind. It was an evening on which Denny took me along to the hospital to visit Eve, though I didn't get to go inside. After the visit, Zoë and I waited in the car while Maxwell and Trish joined Denny for a conference on the pavement. Zoë was immersed in a book of mazes, something she loved to do; I listened carefully to the conversation. Maxwell and Trish did all of the talking.

"Of course, there has to be a nurse on duty, around the clock."

"They work in shifts—"

"They work in shifts, but still, the one on duty takes breaks."

"So someone needs to be there to help."

"And since we're always around."

"We have nowhere to go—"

"And you have to work."

"So it's best."

"Yes, it's best."

Denny nodded without conviction. He got into the car, and we drove off.

"When's Mommy coming home?" Zoë asked.

"Soon," Denny said.

We were crossing the floating bridge, the one Zoë used to call the "High 90," when she was younger.

"Mommy's going to stay with Grandma and Grandpa for a while," Denny said. "Until she feels better. Is that okay with you?"

"I guess," Zoë said. "Why?"

"It'll be easier for—" He broke off. "It'll be easier."

A few days later, a Saturday, Zoë, Denny, and I went to Maxwell and Trish's house. A bed had been set up in the living room. A large hospital bed that moved up and down and tilted and did all sorts of things by touching a remote control, and that had a broad footboard from which hung a clipboard, and that came stocked with a nurse, a crinkly older woman who had a voice that sounded like she was singing whenever she spoke and who didn't like dogs, though I had no objection to her whatsoever. Immediately, the nurse started fretting about me. To my dismay, Maxwell concurred and Denny was preoccupied, so I was shoved outside into the backyard; thankfully, Zoë came to my rescue.

"Mommy's coming!" Zoë told me.

She was very excited and wore the madras dress that she liked because it was so pretty, and I found her excitement infectious so I joined in with it, I embraced the festivity, a real homecoming. Zoë and I played; she threw a ball for me and I did tricks for her, and we rolled together in the grass. It was a wonderful day, the family all together again. It felt very special.

"She's here!" Denny called from the back door, and Zoë and I rushed to see; this time I was allowed inside. Eve's mother entered the house first, followed by a man in blue slacks and a yellow shirt with a logo on it who wheeled in a white figure with dead eyes, a mannequin in slippers. Maxwell and Denny lifted the figure and placed it in the bed and the nurse tucked it in and Zoë said, "Hi, Mommy," and all this happened before it even entered my consciousness that this strange figure was not a dummy, not a mock-up used for practice, but Eve.

Her head was covered with a stocking cap. Her cheeks were sunken, her skin, sallow. She lifted her head and looked around.

"I feel like a Christmas tree," she said. "In the living room, everyone standing around me expecting something. I don't have any presents."

Uncomfortable chuckles from the onlookers.

And then she looked at me directly.

"Enzo," she said. "Come here."

I wagged my tail and approached cautiously. I hadn't seen her since she went into the hospital, and I wasn't prepared for what I saw. It seemed to me the hospital had made her much sicker than she really was.

"He doesn't know what to think," Denny said for me.

"It's okay, Enzo," she said.

She dangled her hand off the side of the bed, and I bumped it with my nose. I didn't like any of this, all the new furniture, Eve looking limp and sad, people standing around like Christmas without the presents. None of it seemed right. So even though everyone was staring at me, I shuffled over to Zoë and stood behind her, looking out the windows into the backyard, which was dappled with sunlight.

"I think I've offended him by being sick," she said.

That was not what I meant at all. My feelings were so complicated, I have difficulty explaining them with any clarity even today, after I have lived through it and had time to reflect upon it. All I could do was move to her bedside and lie down before her like a rug.

"I don't like seeing me like this either," she said.

The afternoon was interminable. Finally the dinner hour came, and Maxwell, Trish, and Denny poured themselves cocktails and the mood lifted dramatically. An old photo album of Eve as a child was taken out from hiding and everyone laughed while the smell of garlic and oil floated from the kitchen where Trish cooked the food. Eve took off her cap and we marveled at her shaved head and grotesque scars. She showered with the help of the nurse, and when she emerged from the bathroom in one of her own dresses and not the hospital gown and robe, she looked almost normal, though there was a darkness behind her eyes, a look of resignation. She tried to read Zoë a book, but she said she couldn't focus well enough, so Zoë tried her best to read to Eve, and her best was fairly good. I wandered into the kitchen, where Denny was again conferencing with Trish and Maxwell.

"We really think Zoë should stay with us," Maxwell said, "until . . ."

"Until . . ." Trish echoed, standing at the stove with her back to us.

So much of language is unspoken. So much of language is comprised of looks and gestures and sounds that are not words. People are ignorant of the vast complexity of their own communication. Trish's robotic repeating of the single word "until" revealed everything about her state of mind.

"Until *what*?" Denny demanded. I could hear the irritation in his voice. "How do you know what's going to happen? You're condemning her to something before you even know."

Trish dropped her frying pan onto the burner with a loud clatter and began to sob. Maxwell wrapped his arms around her and enveloped her in his embrace. He looked over at Denny.

"Please, Denny. We have to face the reality of it. The

doctor said six to eight months. He was quite definite."

Trish pulled away from him and steadied herself, sniffed in her tears.

"My baby," she whispered.

"Zoë is just a child," Maxwell continued. "This is valuable time—the *only* time she has to spend with Eve. I can't *imagine*—I can't *believe for a second*—that you would possibly object."

"You're such a caring person," Trish added.

I could see that Denny was stuck. He had agreed to have Eve stay with Maxwell and Trish, and now they wanted Zoë, too. If he objected, he would be keeping a mother and a daughter apart. If he accepted their proposal, he would be pushed to the periphery, he would become an outsider in his own family.

"I understand what you're saying—" Denny said.

"We knew you would," Trish interrupted.

"But I'll have to talk to Zoë about it to see what she wants."

Trish and Maxwell looked at each other uneasily.

"You can't seriously consider asking a little girl what she wants," Maxwell snorted. "She's *five*, for God's sake! She can't—"

"I'll talk to Zoë to see what she wants," Denny repeated firmly.

After dinner, he took Zoë into the backyard, and they sat together on the terrace steps.

"Mommy would like it if you stayed here with her and Grandma and Grandpa," he said. "What do you think about that?"

She turned it over in her head.

"What do *you* think about it?" she asked.

"Well," Denny said, "I think maybe it's the best thing. Mommy has missed you so much, and she wants to spend more time with you. It would just be for a little while. Until she's better and can come home."

"Oh," Zoë said. "I still get to take the bus to school?"

"Well," Denny said, thinking. "Probably not. Not for a while. Grandma or Grandpa will drive you to school and pick you up, I think. When Mommy feels better, you both will come home, then you can take the bus again."

"Oh."

"I'll come and visit every day," Denny said. "And we'll spend weekends together, and sometimes you'll stay with me, too. But Mommy really wants you with her."

Zoë nodded somberly.

"Grandma and Grandpa really want me, too," she said.

Denny was clearly upset, but he was hiding it in a way that I thought little kids didn't understand. But Zoë was very smart, like her father. Even at five years old, she understood.

"It's okay, Daddy," she said. "I know you won't leave me here forever."

He smiled at her and took her little-kid hand and held it in his own and kissed her on the forehead.

"I promise I will never do that," he said.

It was agreed then, perhaps to neither of their satisfaction, that she would stay.

I marveled at them both; how difficult it must be to be a person. To constantly subvert your desires. To worry about doing the right thing, rather than doing what is most expedient. At that moment, honestly, I had grave doubts as to my ability to interact on such a level. I wondered if I could ever become the human I hoped to be.

As the night wound down, I found Denny sitting in the stuffed chair next to Eve's bed, nervously tapping his hand against his leg.

"This is crazy," Denny said. "I'm going to stay, too. I'll sleep on the couch."

"No, Denny," Eve said. "You'll be so uncomfortable—"

"I've slept on plenty of couches in my life. It's fine."

"Denny, please—"

There was something about the tone of her voice, something pleading in her eyes, that made him stop.

"Please go home," she said.

He scratched the back of his neck and looked down.

"Zoë is here," he said. "Your folks are here. You've told me you want Enzo to stay with you tonight. But you send me away? What did I do?"

She sighed deeply. She was very tired and seemed like she hadn't the energy to explain it to Denny. But she tried.

"Zoë won't remember," she said. "I don't care what my

parents think. And Enzo—well, Enzo understands. But I don't want *you* to see me like this."

"Like what?"

"Look at me," she said. "My head is shaved. My face looks old. My breath smells like I'm rotting inside. I'm ugly—"

"I don't care what you look like," he said. "I see you. I see who you really are."

"*I* care what I look like," she said, trying to muster her old Eve smile. "When I look at you, I see my reflection in your eyes. I don't want to be ugly in front of you."

Denny turned away as if to shield his eyes from her, as if to take away the mirrors. He looked out the window into the backyard, which was lit with lights along the patio's edge and more lights that were suspended in the trees, illuminating our lives. Out there, beyond the light, was the unknown. Everything that wasn't us.

"I'll pack Zoë's things and come back in the morning," he said, finally, without turning around.

"Thank you, Denny," Eve said, relieved. "You can take Enzo. I don't want you to feel abandoned."

"No," he said. "Enzo should stay. He misses you."

He kissed Eve good night, tucked Zoë into bed, and then he left me with Eve. I wasn't sure why she wanted me around, but I understood why she wanted Denny to go: as he fell asleep that night, she wanted him to dream of her as she used to be, not as she currently was; she didn't want Denny's vision of her to be corrupted by her presence. What she didn't understand was Denny's ability to look beyond her physical condition. He was focusing on the next turn. Perhaps if she had had the same ability, things would have turned out differently for her.

The house grew quiet and dark, Zoë in bed, Maxwell and Trish in their room with their TV blinking under the door. Eve was settled into her bed in the living room with the nurse sitting in a dark corner playing a page of her word-search book, in which she circled the hidden messages. I lay next to Eve's bed.

Later, Eve was asleep and the nurse nudged me with her foot. I lifted my head and she held a finger to her lips and told me to be a good dog and follow her, which I did. She led me through the kitchen, through the laundry room to the back of the house and she opened the door that led to the garage.

"In you go," she said. "We don't want you disturbing Mrs. Swift during the night."

I looked at her, puzzled. Disturb Eve? Why would I do that?

She took my hesitation as rebellion; she snatched my collar and gave it a jerk. She shoved me into the dark garage and closed the door. I heard her slippers tread away, back into the house.

I was not afraid. All I knew was how dark it was in the garage.

It wasn't too cold, and it wasn't overly unpleasant, if you

don't mind a concrete floor and the smell of engine oil in an absolutely pitch-black room. I'm sure there were no rats, as Maxwell kept a clean garage for his valuable cars. But I had never slept in a garage before.

The time clicked by. Literally. I watched it click by on an old electric clock that Maxwell kept on the workbench he never used. It was one of those old clocks with the numbers on little plastic tabs that rotate around a spindle, illuminated by a small bulb, the only source of light in the room. Each minute was two clicks, the first when the little plastic half-number was released, the second when the half-number settled, revealing an entirely new number. *Click-click*, and a minute went by. *Click-click*, and another. And that's how I passed my time in my prison, counting the clicks. And daydreaming about the movies I've seen.

My two favorite actors are, in this order: Steve McQueen and Al Pacino. *Bobby Deerfield* is a very underappreciated film, as is Pacino's performance in it. My third favorite actor is Paul Newman, for his excellent car-handling skills in the film *Winning*, and because he is a fantastic racer in his own right and owns a Champ Car racing team, and finally, because he purchases his palm fruit oil from renewable sources in Colombia and thereby discourages the decimation of vast tracts of rain forest in Borneo and Sumatra. George Clooney is my fourth favorite actor because he's exceptionally clever at helping cure children of diseases on reruns of *ER*, and because he looks a little like me around the eyes. Dustin Hoffman is my fifth favorite actor, mostly because he did such great things for the Alfa Romeo trademark in *The Graduate*. Steve McQueen, though, is my first, and not only because of *Le Mans* and *Bullitt*, two of the greatest car movies ever made. But also because of *Papillon*. Being a dog, I know what it's like to be locked in a prison cell without hope, every day waiting for the sliding door to open and for a metal bowl of undernourishing slop to be shoved through the slot.

Hours into my nightmare, the garage door opened, and Eve was there in her nightgown, silhouetted by the nightlight in the kitchen.

"Enzo?" she questioned.

I said nothing but I emerged from the darkness, relieved to see her again.

"Come with me."

She led me back to the living room and she took a cushion from the sofa and placed it next to her bed. She told me to lie on it, and I did. Then she climbed into the bed and pulled up the sheets to her neck.

"I need you with me," she said. "Don't go away again."

But I hadn't gone away! I had been abducted!

I could feel the sleep pressing down on her.

"I need you with me," she said. "I'm so afraid. I'm so afraid."

It's okay, I said. *I'm here.*

She rolled to the edge of the bed and looked down at me, her eyes glazed.

"Get me through tonight," she said. "That's all I need. Protect me. Don't let it happen tonight. Enzo, please. You're the only one who can help."

I will, I said.

"You're the only one. Don't worry about that nurse; I sent her home."

I looked over to the corner, and the crinkly old woman was gone.

"I don't need her," she said. "Only you can protect me. Please. Don't let it happen tonight."

I didn't sleep at all that night. I stood guard, waiting for the demon to show his face. The demon was coming for Eve, but he would have to get past me first, and I was ready. I noted every sound, every creak, every change in air density, and by standing or shifting my weight, I silently made it clear to the demon that he would have to contend with me if he intended to take Eve.

The demon stayed away. In the morning, the others awoke and cared for Eve, and I was able to relinquish my guard duties and sleep.

"What a lazy dog," I heard Maxwell mutter as he passed me.

And then I felt Eve's hand on my neck, stroking.

"Thank you," she said. "Thank you."

24

For the first few weeks of our new arrangement—Denny and I lived in our house, while Eve and Zoë lived with the Twins—Denny visited them every single evening after work, while I stayed home alone. By Halloween, Denny's pace had slowed, and by Thanksgiving, he visited them only twice during the week. Whenever he came home from the Twins' house, he reported to me how good Eve looked and how much better she was getting and that she would be coming home soon. But I saw her, too, on the weekends, when he would take me to visit, and I knew. She wasn't getting better, and she wouldn't be coming home any time soon.

Every weekend, without fail, both Denny and I visited with Eve on Saturday when we picked up Zoë, and again on

Sunday when we delivered her home after our sleepover; we frequently took our Sunday meal with the extended family. I spent the occasional night with Eve in her living room, but she never needed me as much as she had that first night when she was so afraid. Zoë's time with us should have been filled with joy, but she didn't seem altogether happy. How could she be, living with her mother, who was dying, and not with her father, who was very much alive?

Zoë's schooling had briefly become a point of contention. Shortly after she began staying with Maxwell and Trish, they asked to transfer Zoë to a school on Mercer Island, as traveling back and forth across the I-90 floating bridge twice a day was a burden for them. But Denny put down his foot, knowing how much Zoë loved her Madrona school. He insisted she remain there, as he was her father and legal guardian, and also, he maintained, since both Zoë and Eve would be moving home in the near future.

Frustrated by Denny's intractability, Maxwell offered to pay for Zoë's schooling if she enrolled in a private school located on Mercer Island. Their conversations were frequent and intense. But even in the face of Maxwell's persistence, Denny proved that he had a bit of the Gila monster in him—though I don't know whether on his mother's side or his father's side—as his jaws never slackened. Eventually he prevailed, and Maxwell and Trish were forced to commute twice daily across the lake.

"If they're really doing it for Zoë and Eve," Denny said to

me once, "it shouldn't bother them to drive fifteen minutes across the lake. It's really not that far."

Denny missed Eve tremendously, I know, but he missed Zoë just as much. I could see it most on those days when he kept Zoë overnight and we got to walk her to her bus stop. Usually a Monday or a Thursday. On those mornings, our house seemed filled with electricity so that neither Denny nor I needed the alarm clock to wake, but instead waited anxiously in the darkness until the hour came to rouse Zoë. We didn't want to miss a single minute we could spend with her. On those mornings, Denny was a different person altogether. The way he so lovingly packed her sack lunches, often writing a note on a piece of notepaper, a thought or a joke he hoped she would find at lunch and might make her smile. The way he took such care with her peanut butter and banana sandwiches, slicing the banana so that each slice was exactly the same thickness. (I got to eat the extra banana on those occasions, which I enjoyed. I love bananas almost as much as I love pancakes, my favorite food.)

After Zoë drove away on the yellow bus those days, the other father with the three children would sometimes offer to buy us a coffee, and sometimes we would accept and we would all walk to Madison to the nice bakery and drink coffee at the sidewalk tables. Until once, when the other father said, "Your wife works?" Obviously, he was trying to explain to himself Eve's absence.

"No," Denny replied. "She's recovering from brain cancer."

The man dipped his head sadly upon hearing the situation.

After that day, whenever we went to the bus stop, the man made himself busy talking to other people or checking his cell phone. We never spoke to him again.

25

In February, the black pit of winter, we went on a trip to north-central Washington, to an area called the Methow Valley. It is important for United States citizens to celebrate the birthdays of their greatest presidents, so all the schools were closed for a week; Denny, Zoë, and I went to a cabin in the snowy mountains to celebrate. The cabin was owned by a relative of Eve's whom I had never met. It was quite cold, too cold for me, though on the warmer afternoons I enjoyed running in the snow. I much preferred to lie by the base-board heater and let the others do their exercises, skiing and snowshoeing and all of that. Eve, who was too weak to travel, and her parents were not there. But many others were, all of whom were relatives of some kind or another. We were only there, I overheard, because Eve had thought it was very important for Zoë to spend time with these people, since she, Eve, someone said, would die very soon.

I didn't like that whole line of reasoning. First, that Eve would be dying soon. And second, that Zoë needed to spend time with people she had never met because Eve would soon die. They might have been perfectly pleasant people, in their puffy pants and fleece vests and sweaters that smelled of sweat. I don't know. But I wondered why they had waited for Eve's illness to make themselves available for companionship.

There were a great many of them, and I had no idea who was connected to whom. They were all cousins, I understood, but there were certain generational gaps that were confusing to me, and some of the people were without parents but were with uncles and aunts instead, and some might have just been friends. Zoë and Denny kept mostly to themselves, but they still participated in certain group events like horseback riding in the snow, sledding, and snowshoeing. The group meals were convivial, and though I was determined to remain aloof, one of the cousins was always willing to slip me a treat at mealtime. And no one ever kicked me out from under the very large dining table where I lingered during dinner, even though I was breaking my own personal code; a certain sense of lawlessness pervaded the house, what with children staying awake late into the night and adults sleeping at all hours of the day like dogs. Why shouldn't I have partaken in the debauchery?

Conflicted though I was, each night something special happened that I liked very much. Outside the house—which had many identical rooms, each with many identical beds to house the multitude—was a stone patio with a large hearth. Apparently in the summer months, it was used for outdoor cooking, but it was used in the winter as well. I didn't care for the stones, which were very cold and were sprinkled with salt pellets that hurt when they got wedged between my pads, but I loved the hearth. Fire! Cracking and hot, it blazed in the evenings after dinner, and they all gathered, bundled in their great coats, and one had a guitar and gloves without fingertips and he played music while they all sang. It was well below freezing, but I had my place next to the hearth. And the stars we could see! Billions of them, because the night was so intensely dark, and the sounds in the distance, the snap of a snow-burdened tree branch giving way to the wind. The barking of coyotes, my brethren, calling each other to the hunt. And when the cold overpowered the heat from the hearth, we all shuffled into the house and into our separate rooms, our fur and jackets smelling of smoke and pine sap and flaming marshmallows.

It was on one of the evenings while sitting around the fire that I noticed Denny had an admirer. She was young, the sister of someone, whom Denny apparently had met years earlier at a Thanksgiving or an Easter, because his first comment to her and the others was about how much she had grown since he had seen her last. She was a teenager who had a full set of breasts for milking and hips wide enough for childbirth and so was, for all intents and purposes, an adult, but who still acted like a child, always asking for permission to do things.

This girl-not-yet-a-woman was named Annika, and she was very crafty and always knew how to position herself and time her movements to force a meeting with Denny. She sat next to him around the fire. She sat across from him at meals. She always managed to be in the backseat of someone's Suburban when he was in the backseat. She laughed too loudly at every comment he made. She loved his hair after he took off his sweaty ski cap. She proclaimed an extreme admiration for his hands. She doted on Zoë. She became emotional at the mention of Eve. Denny was ignorant of her advances; I don't know if it was deliberate or not, but he certainly acted as if he hadn't a clue.

Who is Achilles without his tendon? Who is Samson without Delilah? Who is Oedipus without his clubfoot? Mute by design, I have been able to study the art of rhetoric unfettered by ego and self-interest, and so I know the answers to these questions.

The true hero is flawed. The true test of a champion is not whether he can triumph, but whether he can overcome obstacles—preferably of his own making—in order to triumph. A hero without a flaw is of no interest to an audience or to the universe, which, after all, is based on conflict and opposition, the irresistible force meeting the unmovable object. Which is also why Michael Schumacher, clearly one of the most gifted Formula One drivers of all time, winner of more races, winner of more championships, holder of more pole positions than any other driver in Formula One history, is often left off of the race fan's list of favorite champions. He is unlike Ayrton Senna, who often employed the same devious and daring tactics as Schumacher, but did so with a wink and therefore was called charismatic and emotional rather than what they call Schumacher: remote and unapproachable. Schumacher has no flaws. He has the best car, the best-financed team, the best tires, the most skill. Who can rejoice in his wins? The sun rises every day. What is to love? Lock the sun in a box. Force the sun to overcome adversity in order to rise. *Then* we will cheer! I will often admire a beautiful sunrise, but I will never consider the sun a champion for having risen. So. For me to relate the history of Denny, who is a true champion, without including his missteps and failings would be doing a disservice to all involved.

As the end of the week drew near, the weather reports on the radio changed, and Denny became quite tense. It was almost time to return to Seattle, and he wanted to leave, get back on the highway and drive the five hours over the mountain passes to our house on the other side, which, though cold and dark and wet, was mercifully without six feet of base snow and subfreezing temperatures. He needed to get back to work, he said. And Zoë needed time to adjust to the school schedule. And . . .

And Annika needed to get back, too. A student at the Holy Names Academy, she needed to return so that she could consult with fellow students and prepare some kind of project they were working on that concerned sustainable living. She spoke of it with urgency, but only after she understood that Denny was planning on heading west before any of the other cousins. Only after she realized that if her needs and Denny's needs coincided, she might win for herself five hours next to him in his car, five hours of watching his hands hold the steering wheel, five hours of seeing his tousled hat head, of inhaling his intoxicating pheromones.

The morning of our departure came, and the storm had settled in and the windows of the cabin were pelted with a freezing rain the likes of which I had never experienced. Denny fretted for most of the morning. The radios announced the closure of Stevens Pass because of the storm. Traction devices were required on Snoqualmie Pass.

"Stay! Stay!"

That's what they said, the insipid cousins. I hated them all. They smelled rank. Even when they showered, they put on their same sweaters without washing them and their sour odor returned to them like a boomerang.

We ate lunch quickly and then we left, stopping at a gas station along the way to purchase chains for our tires. The drive south was horrific. The freezing rain accumulated on the windshield faster than the wipers could push it away, and every few tedious miles, Denny would stop the car and get out to scrape away the icy glaze. It was dangerous driving, and I didn't like it at all. I rode in the back with Zoë; Annika rode in the front. I could see Denny's hands were gripping the steering wheel far too tightly. In a race car the hands must be relaxed, and Denny's always are when I see the in-car videos from his races; he often flexes his fingers to remind himself to relax his grip. But for that excruciating drive down the Columbia River, Denny held the wheel in a death grip.

I felt very badly for Zoë, who was clearly frightened. The rear of the car moved more suddenly than the front, and so she and I experienced more of the slipping and sliding sensation generated by the ice. Thinking of how scared Zoë must have been, I worked myself into a state of agitation, and I let myself get carried away. Before I knew it, I was in a full-blown panic. I pushed at the windows. I tried to clamber into the front seat, which was totally counterproductive. Denny finally barked, "Zoë, please settle Enzo down!"

She grabbed me around the neck and held me tightly. I fell against her as she lay back, and she started singing a song in my ear, one I remembered from her past, "Hello, little Enzo, so glad to see you. . . ." She had just started preschool when she learned that song. She and Eve used to sing it together. I relaxed and let her cradle me. "Hello, little Enzo, so glad to see you, too . . ."

I would like to tell you that I am such a master of my destiny that I contrived the entire situation, that I made myself crazy so Zoë could calm me on this trip, and thus would be distracted from her own agitation. Truth be told, however, I have to admit I was glad she was holding me; I was very afraid, and I was grateful for her care.

The line of cars trudged steadily but slowly. Many cars were stopped on the side of the road to wait out the storm. The weathermen and -women on the radio said waiting would be worse, however, as the front was stalled, the ceiling was low, and when the warm air arrived as anticipated, the ice would turn to rain and the flooding would begin.

When we reached the turnoff for Highway 2, there was an announcement on the radio that Blewett Pass was closed because of a jackknifed tractor-trailer rig. We would have to make a long detour to reach I-90 near George, Washington. Denny anticipated faster travel on I-90 because of its size, but it was worse, not better. The rains had begun, and the median was more like a spillway than a grassy divide between east and west. Still, we continued our journey because there was little else we could do.

After seven hours of grueling travel and still two hours away from Seattle in good driving weather, Denny had Annika call her parents on her cell phone and ask them to find a place for us to stay somewhere near Cle Elum. But they called back soon and told us that all the motels were full because of the storm. We stopped at a McDonald's, and Denny purchased food for us to eat—I got chicken nuggets—then we pressed onward to Easton.

Outside Easton, where snow was piled on the sides of the highway, Denny stopped his car alongside dozens of other cars and trucks in the chain-up area and ventured into the freezing rain. He lay down on the pavement and installed the tire chains, which took half an hour, and when he climbed back into the car, he was soaking wet and shivering.

"You poor thing," Annika said, and she rubbed his shoulders to warm him.

"They're going to close the pass soon," Denny said. "That trucker heard it on the radio."

"Can't we wait here?" Annika asked.

"They expect flooding. If we don't make it over the pass tonight, we might be stuck for days."

It was nasty and horrible, snowy and icy and freezing rain, but we pushed on, our little old BMW chugging up the mountain until we reached the summit where they have the ski lifts, and then everything changed. There was no snow, no ice, just rain. We rejoiced in the rain!

Shortly, Denny stopped the car to remove the chains, which took another half hour and got him soaking again, and then we were going downhill. The windshield wipers flipped back and forth as quickly as they could, but they didn't help much. The visibility was terrible. Denny held the wheel tightly and squinted into the darkness, and we eventually reached North Bend and then Issaquah and then the floating bridge across Lake Washington. It was near midnight—the five-hour drive having taken more than ten—

when Annika called her parents and told them we had made it safely to Seattle. They were relieved. They told her—and she related to us—that the news had reported flash-flooding conditions that caused a rock slide closing westbound I-90 near the summit.

"We must have just missed it," Denny said. "Thank God."

Beware the whimsy of Fate, I said to myself. She is a mean bitch of a lab.

"No, no," Annika said into her phone. "I'll stay with Denny. He's too exhausted to keep driving, and Zoë is sleeping in the backseat; she should be put to bed. Denny said he's happy to drive me home in the morning."

This made Denny turn and look at her questioningly, wondering if he had actually said anything like that. Of course, I knew he hadn't. Annika smiled at him and winked. She ended her call and slipped her phone into her bag. "We're almost there," she said, looking ahead out the windshield, her breaths shallow with anticipation.

Why he didn't take action at that moment. Why he didn't get right back on the freeway and drive up to Edmonds, where her family lived. Why he said nothing. I'll never know. Perhaps, on some level, he needed to connect with someone who reminded him of the passion he and Eve used to share. Perhaps.

Back at the house, Denny carried Zoë to her room and put her to sleep. He turned on the television, and we watched the footage of Snoqualmie Pass being shut down by the authorities, only for a few days, they predicted hopefully, though possibly for a week or more. Denny went into the bathroom and shed his wet clothes; he returned wearing sweatpants and an old T-shirt. He pulled a beer from the refrigerator and opened it.

"Can I take a shower?" Annika asked.

Denny seemed startled. With all of the heroics he had been up to, he had almost forgotten about her.

He showed her where the towels were, how to work the handheld shower temperature thing, and then he closed the door.

He got the extra sheets and pillows and blankets, unfolded the couch in the living room, and made the temporary bed for Annika. When he was done, he went into his bedroom and sat on the end of his own bed.

"I'm fried," he said to me, and then he fell backward so he was lying on the bed, his hands on his chest, his feet still on the floor, his knees dangling over the edge of the bed, and the rest of him asleep even though the lights in the room were still on. I lay on the floor near him and fell asleep as well.

I opened my eyes and saw her standing over him. Her hair was wet and she wore Denny's bathrobe. She said nothing. She watched him sleep for several minutes, and I watched her. It was spooky behavior. Creepy. I didn't like it. She opened her robe, exposing a sliver of pale white flesh and a tattoo of a sunburst encircling her belly button. She didn't speak. She shrugged off her robe and stood naked, her large breasts with their brown nipples pointing at him. Still, he was unconscious. Asleep.

She reached down and slipped her small hands into the band of his sweatpants. She pulled his pants down to his knees.

"Don't," he muttered, his eyes still closed.

He had driven for more than ten hours across a harrowing course of snow and ice and flooding. He had nothing left with which to fend off an attack.

She pulled his pants down to his ankles, then lifted one foot and then the other to remove them completely. She looked at me.

"Shoo," she said.

I didn't shoo. I was too angry. And yet I didn't attack, either. Something was holding me back. The zebra keeps dancing.

She gave me a dismissive look and turned her attention toward Denny.

"Don't," he said, sleepily.

"Shhh," she soothed. "It's all good."

I have faith. I will always have faith in Denny. So I have to believe what she did to him was without his consent, without his knowledge. He had nothing to do with it. He was a prisoner of his body, which had no more energy, and she took advantage of him.

Still, I could no longer stand by and watch. I'd been

in a position to prevent the demon from destroying Zoë's toys, and I had failed. I could not fail this new test. I barked sharply, aggressively. I growled, I snapped, and Denny suddenly awakened; his eyes popped open, and he saw the naked girl and he leapt away from her.

"What the hell?" he shouted.

I continued to bark. The demon was still in the room.

"Enzo!" he snapped. "That's enough!"

I stopped barking, but I kept my eye on her in case she were to assault him once again.

"Where are my pants?" Denny asked frantically, standing on the bed. "What were you doing?"

"I love you so much," she said.

"I'm married!"

"It's not like it's having sex," she said.

And she crawled onto the bed, reaching for him, so I barked again.

"Make the dog go away," she said.

"Annika, stop!"

Denny grabbed her wrists; she squirmed playfully.

"Stop!" he shouted, jumping off the bed, grabbing his sweatpants from the floor, and pulling them on quickly.

"I thought you liked me," Annika said, her mood abruptly darkening.

"Annika—"

"I thought you *wanted* me."

"Annika, put this on," he said, holding out her robe. "I

can't talk to a fifteen-year-old nude woman. It's not legal. You shouldn't be here. I'll take you home."

She clutched the robe to herself.

"But, Denny . . ."

"Annika, please, put on the robe."

Denny tightened the strings on his sweatpants.

"Annika, this isn't happening right now. This isn't something that happens. I don't know why you thought—"

"You!" she wailed and she started crying. "You flirted with me all week. You teased me. You kissed me."

"I kissed you on the cheek," Denny said. "It's normal for relatives to kiss on the cheek. It's called affection, not love."

"But I love you!" she howled, and then she was in an all-out crying fit, her eyes squeezed shut, her mouth contorted. "I love *you*!" she kept saying over and over. "I love *you*!"

Denny was trapped. He wanted to console her, but whenever he moved closer, she dropped her hands, which were clutching the crumpled robe to her chest, and suddenly her massive breasts, heaving with grief, were exposed to him and he had to retreat. This happened several times, like a funny toy, a monkey with cymbals or something. He approached to comfort her, she dropped her hands, her breasts shot out at him, and he flew back. It's possible I was witnessing a living interpretation of an antique pornographic penny bank, similar to one I saw in a movie called *The Stunt Man*, which depicted a bear copulating with a girl on a swing.

Finally, Denny had to put a stop to it.

"I'm going to leave the room," he said. "You will put on the robe and make yourself decent. When you're ready, come into the living room, and we can discuss it further."

And he turned around and marched away. I followed. And then we waited. And we waited. And we waited.

Finally she came out wearing the robe, her eyes swollen with tears. She didn't say a word, but she went straight to the bathroom. A few moments later, she emerged wearing her clothes.

"I'll take you home," Denny said.

"I called my father," Annika said, "from the bedroom."

Denny froze. I suddenly sensed apprehension in the room.

"What did you tell him?" he asked.

She looked at him for a long time before she answered. If her intention was to make him anxious, it worked.

"I told him to come pick me up," she said. "The bed is too uncomfortable here."

"Good," Denny sighed. "Good thinking."

She didn't respond, but continued to stare at him.

"If I gave you the wrong impression, I'm sorry," Denny said, looking away. "You're a very attractive woman, but I'm married and you're so young. This isn't a viable . . ."

He trailed off. Words not spoken.

"Affair," she said, firmly.

"Situation," he whispered.

She picked up her handbag and her duffel and walked

to the foyer. We could all see the headlights when they appeared in front of the house. Annika threw open the door and jogged down the walk to the street. Denny and I watched from the doorway as she tossed her bags in the back of the Mercedes, climbed into the front seat. Her father, in his pajamas, waved and then drove away.

26

That year we had a cold spell in each winter month, and when the first warm day of spring finally arrived in April, the trees and flowers and grasses burst to life with such intensity that the television news had to proclaim an allergy emergency. The drugstores literally ran out of antihistamines. The pharmaceutical companies—those who profit from the misery of others—could have asked for no greater income-generating scenario than a cold, wet winter full of flu shots and NyQuil, followed by a hot spring and record-breaking pollen counts. (I believe that people were not so allergic to their environment until they began polluting themselves and their world with so many drugs and toxins. But then, nobody asked me.) So while the rest of the world was focused on the inconvenience of hay fever, the people in my world had other things to do: Eve continued with the inexorable process of dying, Zoë spent too much time with her grandparents, and Denny and I worked at slowing the beating of our hearts so we wouldn't feel so much pain.

Still, Denny allowed for an occasional diversion, and that April, one presented itself. He had gotten a job offer from one of the racing schools he worked for: they had been hired to provide race car drivers for a television commercial, and they asked Denny to be one of the drivers. The racecourse was in California, a place called Thunderhill Raceway Park. I knew it was happening in April because Denny talked about it quite a bit; he was very excited. But I had no idea that he planned to drive himself there, a ten-hour trip. And I had even less of an idea that he planned on taking me with him.

Oh, the joy! Denny and me and our BMW, driving all day and into the evening like a couple of banditos running from the law, like partners in crime. It had to be a crime to lead such a life as we led, a life in which one could escape one's troubles by racing cars!

The drive down wasn't very special: the middle of Oregon is not noted for its scenic beauty, though other parts of Oregon are. And the mountain passes in northern California were still somewhat snowy, which made me cringe with the memory of Annika and how she had taken advantage of Denny. Luckily, the snow of the Siskiyous was confined to the shoulders of the highway, and the road surface was bare and wet. And then we fell out of the sky and into the verdant fields north of Sacramento.

Stunning. Absolutely stunning, the vastness of a world so intense with growth and birth, in the season of life between the dormant winter and the baking heat of summer. Vast, rolling hills covered with newly sprung grass and great swaths of wildflowers. Men working the land in their tractors, churning the soil, releasing a heady brew of smells: moisture and decay, fertilizer and diesel fumes. In Seattle we live among the trees and the waterways, and we feel we are rocked gently in the cradle of life. Our winters are not cold and our summers are not hot and we congratulate ourselves for choosing such a spectacular place to rest our heads and raise our chickens. But around the Thunderhill Raceway Park, spring is *spring*! There is no better evidence of the season.

And the track. Relatively new, well cared for, challenging with twists and elevation changes and so much to look at. The morning after we arrived, Denny took me jogging. We jogged the entire track. He was doing it to familiarize himself with the surface. You can't really see a track from inside a race car traveling at one hundred fifty miles per hour or more, he said. You have to get out and *feel* it.

Denny explained to me what he was looking for. Bumps in the pavement that might upset one's suspension. Visible seams that he might use as braking zone markers or turn-in points. He touched the pavement at the apex of the turns and felt the condition of the asphalt—were the small stones worn smooth? Could he find better grip slightly off the established racing line? And there were tricks to the camber of certain turns, places where the track appeared level from inside a car but were actually graded ever so slightly—usually by design to allow rainwater to run off the track and not puddle dangerously.

After we had traveled the entire track and studied all three miles and fifteen turns, we returned to the paddock. Two large semi trucks had arrived. Several men in racing-crew uniforms erected tents and canopies, and laid out an elaborate food service, while other men unloaded six beautifully identical Aston Martin DB5 automobiles, the kind made famous by James Bond. Denny introduced himself to a man who carried a clipboard and walked with the gait of someone in charge. His name was Ken.

"Thanks for your dedication," Ken said, "but you're early."

"I wanted to walk the track," Denny explained.

"Feel free."

"I already did, thanks."

Ken nodded and looked at his watch.

"It's too early for race engines," he said, "but you can take your street exhaust out if you want. Just keep it sane."

"Thanks," Denny said, and he looked at me and winked.

We went over to a crew truck, and Denny caught the arm of a crew member.

"I'm Denny," he said. "One of the drivers."

The man shook his hand and introduced himself as Pat.

"You've got time," he said. "Coffee is over there."

"I'm going to take my Bimmer out for a few easy laps. Ken said it was okay. I was wondering if you had a tie-down I could borrow."

"What do you need a tie-down for?" Pat asked.

Denny glanced at me quickly, and Pat laughed.

"Hey, Jim," he called to another man. "This guy wants to borrow a tie-down so he can take his dog for a joy ride."

They both laughed, and I was a little confused.

"I have something better," the Jim guy said. He went around to the cab of the truck and returned a minute later with a bedsheet.

"Here," he said. "I can always wash it at the hotel if he shits himself."

Denny told me to get in the front seat of his car and sit, which I did. They wrapped the sheet over me, pressing me to the seat, leaving only my head sticking out. They somehow secured the sheet tightly from behind.

"Too tight?" Denny asked.

I was too excited to reply. He was going to take me out in his car!

"Take it easy on him until you see if he has a stomach for it," Pat said. "Nothing worse than cleaning dog puke out of your vents."

"You've done this before?"

"Oh, yeah," he said. "My dog used to love it."

Denny walked around to the driver's side. He took his

helmet out of the backseat and squeezed it onto his head. He got in the car and put on his seat belt.

"One bark means slower, two means faster, got it?"

I barked twice, and that surprised him and Pat and Jim, who were both leaning in the passenger window.

"He wants to go faster already," Jim said. "You've got yourself a good dog there."

The paddock at Thunderhill Raceway Park is tucked between two long parallel straights; the rest of the course fans out from the paddock area like butterfly wings. We cruised very slowly through the hot pit area and to the track entrance.

"We're going to take it easy," Denny said, and off we went.

Being on a track was a new experience for me. No buildings, no signs, no sense of proportion. It was like running through a field, gliding over a plain. Denny shifted smoothly, but I noticed he drove more aggressively than he did on the street. He revved the car much higher, and his braking was much harder.

"I'm finding my visuals," he explained to me. "Turn-in points, braking. Some guys drive more by feel. They get in a rhythm and trust it. But I'm very visual. It makes me feel comfortable to have references. I already have dozens of reference points on this track even though I've never driven it, seven or eight specific things I've noted on each turn from our track walk."

Around the turns we went. He noted his apexes and exits for my benefit. Down the straights we picked up speed. We weren't going very fast, maybe sixty, but I really felt the speed around the turns when the tires made a hollow, ghostly sound, almost like an owl. I felt special, being with Denny on the racetrack. He had never taken me on a track before. I felt sure and relaxed; being held firmly to the seat was comforting. The windows were open, and the wind was fresh and cold. I could have driven like that all day.

After three laps he looked over at me.

"Brakes are warm," he said. "Tires are warm."

I didn't understand what he was getting at.

"You want to try a hot lap?"

A hot lap? I barked twice. Then I barked twice again. Denny laughed.

"Sing out if you don't like it," he said, "one long howl." He firmly pressed the accelerator to the floor.

There is nothing like it. The sensation of speed. Nothing in the world can compare.

It was the sudden acceleration, not Jim's bedsheet, that kept me pinned to the seat as we gathered speed and flew down the first straight.

"Hold on, now," Denny said, "we're taking this at speed."

Fast, we went, hurtling, faster, I watched the turn approach, scream at us until we were practically past it and then he was off the accelerator and hard on the brakes. The nose of the car dove and then I was thankful for the sheet because without it I would have been thrown against the windshield. Slow, slow, slow the brake pads held the rotors as tightly as they could, burning from the friction, the heat being thrown off the calipers, the energy dissipating. And then he cranked the wheel left and so smoothly but without pause he was back on the gas and we were pushing through the turn, the g-forces shoving us toward the outside of the car but the tires holding us in place, they were not hooting, those tires, no. The owl was dead. The tires were screeching, they were shouting, howling, crying in pain, *ahhhhh!* He relaxed on the wheel at the apex and the car drifted toward the exit and he was full on the gas and we flew—*flew!*—out of that turn and toward the next and the next after that. Fifteen turns at Thunderhill. Fifteen. And I love them all equally. I adore them all. Each one is different, each with its own particular sensation, but each so magnificent! Around the track we went, faster and faster, lap after lap.

"You okay?" he asked, looking over at me as we sped nearly one hundred twenty miles per hour down the back straight.

I barked twice.

"I'm gonna use up my tires if you keep me out here," he said. "One more lap."

Yes, one more lap. One more lap. Forever, one more lap. I live my life for one more lap. I *give* my life for one more lap! Please, God, please give me *one more lap*!

And that lap was spectacular. I lifted my eyes as Denny

instructed. "Big eyes, far eyes," he said to me. Those reference points, the visuals he had identified when we walked the track, moved by so quickly it took me some time to realize that he was not even seeing them. He was *living* them! He had programmed the map of the racecourse into his brain and it was there like a GPS navigational system; when we slowed for a turn, his head was up and looking at *the next turn*, not at the apex of the turn we were driving. The turn we were in was simply a state of existence for Denny. It was where we were, and he was happy to be there, and I could feel the joy emanating from him, the love of life. But his attention—and his *intention*—was far ahead, to the next turn and the one beyond that. With every breath he adjusted, he reassessed, he corrected, but he did it all subconsciously; I saw, then, how in a race he could plot now to pass another driver three or four laps later. His thinking, his strategies, his mind; all of Denny unfolded for me that day.

After a cool-down lap, we pulled into the paddock and the entire crew was waiting. They surrounded the car and their hands released me from my harness and I leapt to the tarmac.

"Did you like it?" one of them asked me and I barked, Yes! I barked and jumped high in the air.

"You were hauling ass out there," Pat said to Denny. "We've got a real racer on the set."

"Well, Enzo barked twice," Denny explained with a laugh. "Two barks means faster!"

They laughed, and I barked twice again. Faster! The feeling. The sensation. The movement. The speed. The car. The tires. The sound. The wind. The track surface. The apex. The exit. The shift point. The braking zone. The ride. It's all about the ride!

There is nothing more to tell about that trip because nothing could possibly be more incredible than those few hot laps that Denny gave to me. Until that moment I *thought* that I loved racing. I intellectualized that I would enjoy being in a race car. Until that moment I didn't *know*. How could anyone know until he sits in a car at race speed and takes turns at the limits of adhesion, brakes a hair from lockup, the engine begging for the redline?

I floated through the rest of our trip. I dreamed of going out again at speed, but I suspected—as it turned out, correctly so—that more track time for me was unlikely. Still, I had my memory, my experience I could relive in my mind again and again. Two barks means faster. Sometimes, to this day, in my sleep I bark twice because I am dreaming of Denny driving me around Thunderhill, the two of us laying down a hot lap, and I bark twice to say faster. One more lap, Denny! *Faster!*

27

Six months came and six months left and Eve was still alive. Then seven months. Then eight. On the first of May, Denny and I were invited to the Twins' for dinner, which was unusual because it was a Monday night, and I never went with Denny on a weeknight visit. We stood awkwardly in the living room with the empty hospital bed while Trish and Maxwell prepared dinner. Eve was absent.

I wandered down the hallway to investigate, and I found Zoë playing quietly by herself in her room. Her room in Maxwell and Trish's house was much larger than her room at home, and it was filled with all the things a little girl could want: dolls and toys and frilly bed skirts and clouds painted on the ceiling. She was immersed in her dollhouse and didn't notice me enter.

I spotted a sock ball on the floor, which must have fallen when the clean clothes were being loaded into her dresser, and I pounced on it. I playfully dropped it at Zoë's feet, nudged it with my nose, and then dropped down to my elbows, leaving my haunches tall and my tail upright: universal sign language for "Let's play!" But she ignored me.

So I tried again. I snatched up the socks, flung them in the air, batted them with my snout, retrieved them for myself, and dropped them again at Zoë's feet, and downwardly I faced. I was all prepared for a fun game of Enno-Fetch. She wasn't. She pushed the socks aside with her foot.

I barked expectantly, one last attempt. She turned and looked at me seriously.

"That's a baby game," she said. "I have to be a grown-up now."

My little Zoë, a grown-up at her tender age. A sad thought.

Disappointed, I walked slowly to the door and looked back at her over my shoulder.

"Sometimes bad things happen," she said to herself. "Sometimes things change, and we have to change, too."

She was speaking someone else's words, and I'm not sure she believed them or even understood them. Perhaps she was committing them to memory because she hoped they would hold the key to her uncertain future.

I returned to the living room and waited with Denny until, finally, Eve emerged from the hallway where the bedroom and bathrooms were. The nurse who spent her breaks obsessively knitting with metal needles that drove me mad with their scraping and scratching was helping Eve walk. And Eve was brilliant. She was wearing a gorgeous dress, long and navy blue and cut just so. She wore the lovely string of small freshwater pearls from Japan that Denny had given her for their fifth anniversary, and her makeup and her hair, which had grown enough so she could arrange it into some kind of a hairdo, was done that way, and she was beaming. Even though she needed help for her runway walk, she was walking the runway, and Denny gave her a standing ovation.

"Today is the first day I am not dead," Eve said to us. "And we're having a party."

To live every day as if it had been stolen from death, that is how I would like to live. To feel the joy of life, as Eve felt the joy of life. To separate oneself from the burden, the angst, the anguish that we all encounter every day. To say I am alive, I am wonderful, I am. I am. That is something to aspire to. When I am a person, that is how I will live my life.

The party was festive. Everyone was happy, and those who were not happy pretended that they were with such conviction that we all were convinced. Even Zoë came alive with her usual humor, apparently forgetting for a time her need to be a grown-up. When the hour came for us to leave, Denny kissed Eve deeply.

"I love you so much," he said. "I wish you could come home."

"I want to come home," she replied. "I *will* come home."

She was tired, so she sat on the sofa and called me to her; I let her rub my ears. Denny was helping Zoë get ready for her bedtime, while the Twins, for once, were keeping a respectful distance.

"I know Denny's disappointed," she said to me. "They're all disappointed. Everyone wants me to be the next Lance Armstrong. And if I could just grab it and hold it in front of me, maybe I could be. But I can't hold it, Enzo. It's bigger than me. It's everywhere."

In the other room we could hear Zoë playing in the bath, Denny laughing with her, as if they had no worries in the world.

"I shouldn't have allowed it to be this way," she said regretfully. "I should have insisted on going home so we could all be together. That's my fault; I could have been stronger. But Denny would say we can't worry about what's already happened, so . . . Please take care of Denny and Zoë for me, Enzo. They're so wonderful when they're together."

She shook her head to rid herself of her sad thoughts and looked down at me.

"Do you see?" she asked. "I'm not afraid of it anymore. I wanted you with me before because I wanted you to protect me, but I'm not afraid of it anymore. Because it's not the end."

She laughed the Eve laugh that I remembered.

"But you knew that," she said. "You know everything."

Not everything. But I knew she had been right about her

situation: while doctors are able to help many people, for her, they could only tell her what couldn't be done. And I knew that once they identified her disease for her, once everyone around her accepted her diagnosis and reinforced it and repeated it back to her time and again, there was no way she could stop it. The visible becomes inevitable. Your car goes where your eyes go.

We took our leave, Denny and I. I didn't sleep in the car on the ride home as I usually did. I watched the bright lights of Bellevue and Medina flicker by, so beautiful. Crossing the lake on the floating bridge and seeing the glow of Madison Park and Leschi, the buildings of downtown peeking out from behind the Mount Baker ridge; the city sharp and crisp, all the dirt and age hidden by the night.

If I ever find myself before a firing squad, I will face my executioners without a blindfold, and I will think of Eve. Of what she said. It is not the end.

She died that night. Her last breath took her soul, I saw it in my dream. I saw her soul leave her body as she exhaled, and then she had no more needs, no more reason; she was released from her body, and, being released, she continued her journey elsewhere, high in the firmament where soul material gathers and plays out all the dreams and joys of which we temporal beings can barely conceive, all the things that are beyond our comprehension, but even so, are not beyond our attainment if we choose to attain them, and believe that we truly can.

28

In the morning, Denny didn't know about Eve, and I, having awakened in a fog from my dream, barely suspected. He drove me over to Luther Burbank Park on the eastern shore of Mercer Island. Since it was a warm spring day, it was a good choice of dog parks, as it afforded lake access so Denny could throw the ball and I could swim after it. The park was empty of other dogs; we were by ourselves.

"We'll move her back home," Denny said to me as he threw the ball. "And Zoë. We should all be together. I miss them."

I swam out into the cold lake and retrieved the ball.

"This week," he said. "This week I'll bring both of them home."

And he threw the ball again. I waded over the rocky bottom until my body gained buoyancy and then I paddled out to the ball, bobbed for it in the lake, and returned. When I dropped the ball at Denny's feet and looked up, I saw that he was on his cell phone. After a moment he nodded and hung up.

"She's gone," he said, and then he sobbed loudly and turned away, crying into the crook of his arm so I couldn't see.

I am not a dog who runs away from things. I had never run away from Denny before that moment, and I have never run away since. But in that moment, I had to run.

There was something about it. I don't know. The setting of the dog park, perched on the eastern bank of Mercer Island like that, so ready. The split rail fence, not a containment fence in any way. The entire scene begs for a dog to run, to flee from his captivity, to lash out against the establishment. And so I ran.

Off to the south, I burst off down the short path through the gap in the split rail and out onto the big field, then I broke west. Over the asphalt path and down the other side to the amphitheater I found what I was looking for, untamed wilderness. I needed to go wilding. I was upset, sad, angry— something! I needed to do something! I needed to feel myself, understand myself and this horrible world we are all trapped in, where bugs and tumors and viruses worm their way into our brains and lay their putrid eggs that hatch and eat us alive from the inside out. I needed to do my part to crush it, stamp out what was attacking me, my way of life. So I ran.

The twigs and vines whipped my face. The rough earth hurt my feet. But I ran until I saw what I needed to see. A squirrel. Fat and complacent. Eating from a bag of Fritos. Stupidly shoving chips into its mouth, and I found in the darkest part of my soul a hatred I had never felt before. I didn't know where it came from but it was there and I charged that squirrel. It looked up too late. It noticed me long after it should have if it had wanted to live, and I was on it. I was on that squirrel and it had no chance. I was ruthless. My jaws slapped down on it, cracking its back, my teeth ripped into its fur, and I shook it to death after that, for good measure, I shook it until I heard its neck snap in two. And then I ate it. I ripped it open with my fangs, my incisors, tore into it, and blood was on me, all the blood, hot and rich, I drank its life and I ate its entrails and pulverized its bones and swallowed. I crushed its skull and ate its head. I devoured the squirrel. I *had* to do it. I missed Eve so much I couldn't be a human anymore and feel the pain that humans feel. I had to be an animal again. I devoured, I gorged, I gulped, I did all the things I shouldn't have done. My trying to live to human standards had done nothing for Eve; I ate the squirrel for Eve.

I slept in the bushes. Sometime later I emerged, myself again. Denny found me and he said nothing. He led me to the car. I got in the backseat and fell asleep again immediately. With the taste of blood from the squirrel I had murdered fresh in my mouth, I slept. And while I slept I dreamed of the crows.

I chased them; I caught them; I killed them. I did it for Eve.

29

For Eve, her death was the end of a painful battle. For Denny it was the beginning.

What I did in the park was selfish because it was about satisfying my basest needs. It was also selfish because it prevented Denny from going to Zoë right away. He was angry with me for having delayed him in the park. But to postpone, even for a short time, what he was to find at the home of the Twins might have been the most merciful thing I could have done for him.

When I awoke from my slumber, we were at Maxwell and Trish's house. In the driveway was a windowless white van with a fleur-de-lis insignia on the driver's door. Denny parked in such a way as to not block the vehicle, and then he led me around the side of the house to the hose bib in back.

He turned on the hose and rinsed the blood from my muzzle in a rough and joyless manner; it was not a bath, it was a scrubbing.

"What did you get into out there?" he asked me.

When I was cleaned of dirt and blood, he released me and I shook myself dry. He went to the French doors on the patio and knocked. After a moment, Trish appeared. She opened the door and embraced Denny. She was crying.

After a long time, during which Maxwell and Zoë also appeared, Denny ended the embrace and asked, "Where is she?"

Trish pointed. "We told them to wait for you," she said.

Denny stepped into the house, touching Zoë's head as he passed. After he disappeared, Trish looked at Maxwell.

"Let him have a minute," she said.

And they, with Zoë, stepped outside and closed the French door so that Denny could be alone with Eve for the last time, even though she was no longer living.

In the emptiness that was all around me, I noticed an old tennis ball in the plantings; I picked it up and dropped it at Zoë's feet. I didn't know what I was doing, if I had a specific intention. Was I trying to lighten the mood? I don't know, but I felt I had to do something. So there the ball bounced to a stop at her bare feet.

She looked down at the ball but did nothing with it.

Maxwell noticed what I had done, and he noticed Zoë's lack of reaction. He picked up the ball and, with a mighty heave, threw it so far into the woods behind the house that I lost sight of it and could only barely hear it crash through the leaves of bushes on its way back to earth. It was quite an impressive toss, the pale tennis ball sailing through the air against the clear blue sky. What amount of psychic pain was expended on that ball, I had no idea.

"Fetch, boy," Maxwell said to me sardonically, and then he turned back to the house.

I didn't fetch, but waited with them until Denny returned. When he did, he went to Zoë immediately, picked her up, and held her tightly. She squeezed his neck.

"I'm so sad," he said.

"Me, too."

He sat on one of the teak deck chairs with Zoë on his knee. She buried her face in his shoulder and stayed like that.

"The people from Bonney-Watson will take her now," Trish said. "We'll bury her with our family. It's what she wanted."

"I know," he said, nodding. "When?"

"Before the end of the week."

"What can I do?"

Trish looked at Maxwell.

"We'll take care of the arrangements," Maxwell said. "But we did want to speak with you about something."

Denny waited for Maxwell to continue, but he didn't.

"You haven't eaten breakfast, Zoë," Trish said. "Come with me and I'll fix you an egg."

Zoë didn't budge until Denny tapped her shoulder and nudged her off of his lap.

"Go get some food with Grandma," he said.

Zoë obediently followed Trish into the house.

When she was gone, Denny leaned back with his eyes closed and sighed heavily, his face lifted to the sky. He stayed like that for a long time. Minutes. He was a statue. While Denny was immobile, Maxwell shifted his weight from one foot to the other and back. Several times Maxwell began speaking but stopped himself. He seemed somehow reluctant.

"I knew it was coming," Denny said, finally, his eyes still closed. "But still . . . I'm surprised."

Maxwell nodded to himself.

"That's what concerns Trish and me," he said.

Denny opened his eyes and looked at Maxwell.

"Concerns you?" he asked, taken aback.

"That you haven't made preparations."

"Preparations?"

"You have no plan."

"Plan?"

"You keep repeating the last thing I've said," Maxwell observed after a pause.

"Because I don't understand what you're talking about," Denny said.

"That's what concerns us."

Denny, still sitting, leaned forward and screwed up his face at Maxwell.

"What exactly are you concerned about, Maxwell?" he asked.

Then Trish was there.

"Zoë is eating an egg and toast, and watching TV in the kitchen," she announced. She looked at Maxwell expectantly.

"We've just started," Maxwell said.

"Oh," Trish said, "I thought . . . What have you said so far?"

"Why don't you take it from the top, Trish," Denny said. "Maxwell is having some difficulty with the opening. You're concerned . . ."

Trish glanced around, apparently disappointed that their concerns hadn't already been resolved.

"Well," she began, "Eve's passing is obviously a terrible tragedy. Still, we've been anticipating it for many months. Maxwell and I have discussed at great length our lives—the lives of *all* of us—in the aftermath of Eve's death. We discussed it with Eve, as well, just so you know. And we believe that the best situation for all parties involved would be for us to have custody of Zoë, to raise her in a warm and stable family situation, to provide her with the kind of upbringing and, well, not to be gauche, but *privileges* we can provide for her. We think it will be best. We hope you understand that this is in no way a commentary on you as a person or your fathering abilities. It is simply what is in Zoë's best interest."

Denny looked from one of them to the other, a perplexed look still on his face, but he said nothing.

I was perplexed, too. It was my understanding that Denny had allowed Eve to live with the Twins so they could spend time with their dying daughter, and that he had allowed Zoë to live with the Twins so she could spend time with her dying mother. As I understood it, once Eve died, Zoë would be with us. The idea of a transition period made some sense to me: Eve had died the previous night; to spend the following day—or even few days—with her grandparents made sense. But, custody?

"What do you think?" Trish asked.

"You can't have custody of Zoë," Denny said simply.

Maxwell sucked in his cheeks, crossed his arms, and tapped his fingers against his biceps, which were clad in a dark polyester knit.

"I know this is hard for you," Trish said. "But you have to agree that we have the advantages of parental experience, available free time, and fiscal abundance that will ensure Zoë's education through whatever level she might choose to pursue, and a large home in a safe neighborhood that has many young families and many children her age."

Denny thought for a moment.

"You can't have custody of Zoë," he said.

"I told you," Maxwell said to Trish.

"If you could just sleep on it," Trish said to Denny. "I'm sure you will see that what we're doing is right. It's best for all. You can pursue your racing career, Zoë can grow up in a loving and supportive environment. It's what Eve wanted."

"How do you know that?" Denny asked quickly. "She told you?"

"She did."

"But she didn't tell me."

"I don't know why she wouldn't have," Trish said.

"She didn't," Denny said firmly.

Trish forced a smile.

"Will you sleep on it?" she asked. "Will you think about what we've said? It will be much easier."

"No, I will not sleep on it," Denny said, rising from the chair. "You can't have custody of my daughter. Final answer."

The Twins sighed simultaneously. Trish shook her head in dismay. Maxwell reached into his back pocket and removed a business envelope.

"We didn't want it to have to be this way," he said, and he handed the envelope to Denny.

"What's this?" Denny asked.

"Open it," Maxwell said.

Denny opened the envelope and removed several sheets of paper. He glanced at them briefly.

"What does this mean?" he asked again.

"I don't know if you have a lawyer," Maxwell said. "But if you don't, you should get one. We're suing for custody of our granddaughter."

Denny flinched like he had been punched in the gut. He

fell back into the deck chair, his hands still clinging to the documents.

"I finished my egg," Zoë announced.

None of us had noticed her return, but there she was. She climbed onto Denny's lap.

"Are *you* hungry?" she asked. "Grandma can make you an egg, too."

"No," he said apologetically. "I'm not hungry."

She thought a moment. "Are you still sad?" she asked.

"Yes," he said after a pause. "I'm still very sad."

"Me, too," she agreed, and she laid her head on his chest.

Denny looked at the Twins. Maxwell's long arm hung on Trish's narrow shoulders like some kind of heavy chain. And then I saw something change in Denny. I saw his face tighten with resolve.

"Zoë," he said, standing her up. "You run inside and pack your things, okay?"

"Where are we going?" she asked.

"We're going home now."

Zoë smiled and started off, but Maxwell stepped forward.

"Zoë, stop right there," he said. "Daddy has some errands he has to run. You'll stay with us for now."

"How dare you!" Denny said. "Who do you think you are?"

"I'm the one who's been raising her for the past eight months," Maxwell said, his jaw set.

Zoë looked from her father to her grandfather. She didn't

know what to do. No one knew what to do. It was a standoff. And then Trish stepped in.

"Run inside and put your dolls together," she said to Zoë, "while we talk a little more."

Zoë reluctantly withdrew.

"Let her stay with us, Denny," Trish pleaded. "We can work this out. I *know* we can work it out. Let her stay with us while the lawyers come up with some kind of compromise. You were fine with her staying here before."

"You begged me to let her stay here," Denny said to her.

"I'm sure we can work this out."

"No, Trish," he said. "I'm taking her home with me."

"And who's going to take care of her when you're at work?" Maxwell snapped, shaking with anger. "When you're off at your races for days at a time? Who will take care of her if, God forbid, she were to get sick? Or would you just ignore it, hide it from the doctors until she was on the verge of death, like you did with Eve?"

"I didn't hide Eve from the doctors."

"And yet she never saw anyone—"

"She refused!" Denny cried out. "She refused to see anyone!"

"You could have forced her," Maxwell shouted.

"No one could force Eve to do anything Eve didn't want to do," Denny said. "*I* certainly couldn't."

Maxwell clenched his fists tightly. The tendons in his neck bulged.

"And that's why she's dead," he said.

"What?" Denny asked incredulously. "This is a joke! I'm not continuing this conversation."

He glared at Maxwell and started toward the house.

"I regret the day she met you," Maxwell muttered after him.

Denny stopped at the door and called inside.

"Zoë, let's go now. We can stop by later to get your dolls."

Zoë emerged looking confused, holding an armful of stuffed animals.

"Can I take these?" she asked.

"Yes, honey. But let's go now. We'll come back later for the rest."

Denny ushered her toward the path that led around to the front of the house.

"You're going to regret this," Maxwell hissed at Denny as he passed. "You have no idea what you're getting yourself into."

"Let's go, Enzo," Denny said.

We walked around to the driveway and got into our car. Maxwell followed us and watched Denny strap Zoë into her car seat. Denny started the engine.

"You're going to regret this," Maxwell said again. "Mark my words."

Denny pulled the driver's-side door closed with a slam that shook the car.

"Do I have a lawyer?" he said to himself. "I work at the

most prestigious BMW and Mercedes service center in Seattle. Who does he think he's dealing with? I have a good relationship with all the best lawyers in this town. *And* I have their home phone numbers."

We pulled out of the driveway with a spray of gravel at Maxwell's feet, and as we took off up the idyllic, twisty Mercer Island road, I couldn't help but notice that the white van was gone. And with it, Eve.

30

With experience, a driver adjusts his understanding of how a car feels when it is near its limits. A driver becomes comfortable driving on the edge, so when his tires begin to lose adhesion, he can easily correct, pause, and recover. Knowing where and when he can push for a little extra becomes ingrained in his being.

When the pressure is intense and the race is only half completed, a driver who is being chased relentlessly by a competitor realizes that he might be better off pushing from behind than pulling from the front. In that case, the smart move is to yield his lead to the trailing car and let the other driver pass. Relieved of his burden, our driver can tuck in behind and make the new leader drive his mirrors.

Sometimes, however, it is important to hold one's

position and not allow the pass. For strategic reasons, psychological reasons. Sometimes a driver simply has to prove that he is better than his competition.

Racing is about discipline and intelligence, not about who has the heavier foot. The one who drives smart will always win in the end.

31

Zoë insisted on going to school the next day, and when Denny said he would pick her up at dismissal time, she complained that she wanted to play with her friends in the after-school program. Denny reluctantly agreed.

"I'll pick you up a little earlier than I usually do," he said when we dropped her off. He must have been afraid that the Twins would try to steal her away.

From Zoë's school, we drove up Union to Fifteenth Avenue and found a parking spot directly across from Victrola Coffee. Denny tied my leash to a bicycle stand and went inside; he returned a few minutes later with coffee and a scone. He untied me and told me to sit underneath an outdoor table, which I did. A quarter of an hour later, we were joined by someone else. A large but compact man composed of circles: round head, round torso, round thighs, round hands. There was no hair on the top of his head, but a lot on the sides. He was wearing very wide jeans and a large gray sweatshirt with a giant purple W on it.

"Good morning, Dennis," the man said. "Please accept my sincere condolences for your devastating loss."

He leaned down and forcefully embraced Denny, who sat awkwardly, hands in his lap, looking out to the street.

"I—" Denny started, then stopped himself as the man released him and stood upright. "Of course," Denny said uncomfortably.

The man nodded slightly, ignoring Denny's confused reply, and then wedged himself between the metal arms of the other sidewalk chair by our table; he was not fat, and in fact, he might have been considered muscular in some circles, yet he was very large.

"Good-looking dog," he said. "He has some terrier in him?"

I lifted my head. Me?

"I don't know exactly," Denny said. "Probably."

"Good-looking animal," the man mused.

I was impressed that he noticed me at all.

"Oh, she pulls a good latte," the man said, slurping his coffee drink.

"Who?" Denny asked.

"My little barista in there. The one with the plump lips, the pierced eyebrow, and the dark chocolate eyes . . ."

"I didn't notice."

"You've got a lot on your mind," the man said. "This consultation will cost you an oil change. My gull-wing is very thirsty. An oil change, whether or not you decide to retain me."

"Fine."

"Let me see the paperwork."

Denny handed him the envelope Maxwell had given him. The man took it and removed the papers.

"They said Eve told them she wanted Zoë to be raised by them."

"I don't care about that," the man said.

"Sometimes she was on so many drugs, she would have said anything," Denny said desperately. "She may have said it, but she couldn't have *meant* it."

"I don't care what anyone said or why they said it," the man said sharply. "Children are not chattel. They cannot be given away or traded in the marketplace. Everything that happens will be done in the best interest of the child."

"That's what they said," Denny said. "Zoë's best interest."

"They're educated," the man said. "Still, the mother's final wishes are irrelevant. How long were you married?"

"Six years."

"Any other children?"

"No."

"Any secrets?"

"None."

The man drank his latte and leafed through the papers. He was a curious man, full of twitches and extra movements. It took me several minutes to realize that when he touched his hand to his hip pocket, which he did frequently, it was because he had some kind of buzzing device hidden away, and by touching it he could stop its buzzing. This man's attention was in many places at once. And yet, when he locked eyes with Denny, I could sense the totality of his focus. Denny could, too, I knew, because in those moments, Denny's tension slackened perceptibly.

"Are you in a drug treatment program?" the man asked.

"No."

"Are you a registered sex offender?"

"No."

"Have you ever been convicted of a felony? Spent any time in jail?"

"No."

The man stuffed the papers back in the envelope.

"This is nothing," he said. "Where is your daughter now?"

"She wanted to go to school. Should I have kept her home?"

"No, that's good. You're being responsive to her needs. That's important. Listen, this is not something you should be overly concerned with. I'll demand a summary judgment. I can't see why we won't get it. The child will be yours free and clear."

Denny bristled.

"By 'the child' you mean my daughter, Zoë?"

"Yes," the man said, sizing up Denny. "I mean your daughter, Zoë. This is Washington State, for Christ's sake! Unless you're cooking meth in your kitchen, the child is always awarded to the biological parent. No question."

"Okay," Denny said.

"Don't panic. Don't get mad. Be polite. Call them and give them my information. Tell them all correspondence has to be directed to me as your attorney. I'll call their lawyers and let them know the big dog is in your corner. My feeling is they're looking for a soft spot; they're hoping you'll go away quietly. Grandparents are like that. Grandparents are convinced they're better parents than their own kids, whose lives they've already fucked up. The problem is, grandparents are pains in the ass because they have money. Do they have money?"

"Plenty."

"And you?"

"Oil changes for life," Denny said with a forced smile.

"Oil changes ain't going to cut it, Dennis. My rate is four-fifty an hour. I need a twenty-five-hundred-dollar retainer. Do you have it?"

"I'll get it," Denny said.

"When? Today? This week? Next week?"

Denny looked at him hard.

"This is my daughter, Mark. I promise on my soul you'll

get every dollar you have coming to you. She's my daughter. Her name is Zoë. And I would appreciate it if you would use her name, or at least a gender-correct pronoun, when you refer to her."

Mark sucked in his cheeks and nodded.

"I totally understand, Dennis. She's your daughter, and her name is Zoë. And I understand that you're a friend and I trust you. I apologize for even questioning. Sometimes I get people . . ." He paused. "Me to you, Dennis? We're talking about seven or eight grand to make this thing go away. You can do that, right? Of course you can. I waive my retainer for you, my friend." He stood up and the chair almost stood with him, but he shucked himself out of it before it embarrassed him in front of the Victrola crowd. "This is a totally bogus custody suit. I can't even imagine why they would bother to file it. Call the in-laws—*your* in-laws—and tell them everything goes through me. I'll have the paralegal on this today—*my* paralegal. I really have a problem with my pronouns, don't I? Thanks for pointing it out. Trust me, they didn't see this coming. They're playing you for a sucker, and you aren't a sucker, are you, champ?"

He cuffed Denny on the chin.

"Be cool with them," Mark said. "Don't get angry. Be cool, and everything is in little Zoë's best interest, got it? Always say everything is for her. Got it?"

"Got it," Denny said.

The man paused solemnly.

"How are you holding up, friend?"

"I'm fine," Denny said.

"Taking time off? A head-clearing walk with . . . What's his name?"

"Enzo."

"Good name. Good-looking dog."

"He's upset," Denny said. "I'm taking him to work with me today. I don't feel comfortable leaving him home alone."

"Maybe you should take some time off," Mark said. "Your wife just passed away. Plus this nonsense. Craig will give you some time off, and if he doesn't, I'll call him and rattle his cage with the threat of a workplace harassment suit."

"Thanks, Mark," Denny said. "But I can't stay home right now. It reminds me too much—"

"Ah."

"I need to work. I need to do something. Keep moving."

"Understood," Mark said. "Say no more."

He gathered his bag.

"I have to admit," he said, "watching you win that race on TV was pretty sweet. Where was that? Last year?"

"Watkins Glen," Denny said.

"Yeah. Watkins Glen. That was sweet. The wife had some people over and I was barbecuing and I turned on the little TV in the kitchen and the guys were watching . . . sweet."

Denny smiled, but it was without conviction.

"You're a good man, Dennis," Mark said. "I'll take care of this. Of all the things you have to worry about, this is not one of them. You let *me* worry about this part. You take care of your daughter, okay?"

"Thanks."

Mark trundled off down the street, and when he had rounded the corner, Denny looked at me and held his hands out in front of himself. They were shaking. He didn't say anything, but he looked at his hands trembling and then he looked at me, and I knew what he was thinking. He was thinking that if he just had a steering wheel to hold on to, his hands wouldn't shake. If he had a steering wheel to hold on to, everything would be all right.

32

I spent most of the day hanging out in the garage with the guys who fix the cars because the owners of the shop didn't like it when I was in the lobby where the customers could see me.

I knew all the guys in the garage. I didn't go to work very often, but I'd been there enough that they all knew me and gave me a hard time by doing things like throwing wrenches across the shop and trying to get me to fetch them, and when I refused, they'd laugh and comment on how smart I was. There was one tech guy in particular, Fenn, who was really nice, and every time he walked by me he would ask: "Are you done yet?" At first I had no idea what he was talking about, but I finally figured out that one of the shop's owners, Craig, spent most of his time asking if the techs were finished with their cars, and Fenn was just passing it on down the line to the only one who ranked below him. Me.

"Are you done yet?"

I felt strangely anxious that day, in a very human way. People are always worried about what's happening next. They often find it difficult to stand still, to occupy the now without worrying about the future. People are not generally satisfied with what they have; they are very concerned with what they are *going* to have. A dog can almost power down his psyche and slow his anticipatory metabolism, like David Blaine attempting to set the record for holding his breath at the bottom of a swimming pool—the tempo of the world around him simply changes. On a normal dog day, I can sit still for hours on end with no effort. But that day I was anxious. I was nervous and worried, uneasy and distracted. I paced around and never felt settled. I didn't care for the sensation, yet I realized it was possibly a natural progression of my evolving soul, and therefore I tried my best to embrace it.

One of the garage bays was open, and a sticky drizzle fogged the air. Skip, the big funny man with the long beard, dutifully washed the cars that were ready for pickup, even though it was raining.

"Rain isn't dirty, *dirt* is dirty," he repeated to himself, a Seattle car-washing mantra. He squeezed his clump of sponge, and soapy water rushed like a river down the windshield of

an immaculately cared-for British racing green BMW 2002.
I lay, head between my forelegs, just inside the threshold of
the garage, watching him work.

The day seemed like it would never end, until the Seattle
police car showed up and two policemen got out.

"Can I offer you gentlemen a wash?" Skip called to them.

The men seemed confused by the question. They ex-
changed a glance.

"It's raining," one of them said.

"Rain isn't dirty," Skip said cheerfully. "*Dirt* is dirty."

The policemen looked at him strangely, as if they didn't
know if he was mocking them.

"No, thanks," one of them said as they walked to the
lobby door and went inside.

I nosed through the swinging door in the garage bay and
into the file room. I wandered up behind the counter, which
Mike was attending.

"Afternoon, officers," I heard Mike say. "A problem with
your car?"

"Are you Dennis Swift?" one of them asked.

"I am not," Mike replied.

"Is he here?"

Mike hesitated. I could smell his sudden tension.

"He may have left for the day," Mike said. "Let me check.
Can I tell him who's calling?"

"We have a warrant for his arrest," one of the policemen
said.

"I'll see if he's still in the back."

Mike turned and stumbled into me.

"Enzo. Clear out, boy."

He looked up at the police nervously.

"Shop dog," he said. "Always in the way."

I followed him into the back, where Denny was at the computer, logging invoices for the people who wanted their cars by the end of the day.

"Den," Mike said. "There are a couple of cops out front with a warrant."

"For?" Denny asked, not even looking up from the screen, tap-tap-tapping away at his invoices.

"You. For your arrest."

Denny stopped what he was doing.

"For what?" he asked.

"I didn't get the details. But they're uniform SPD and they don't look like male strippers and today isn't your birthday anyway, so I don't think it's a prank."

Denny stood up and started for the lobby.

"I told them you might have left for the day," Mike said, indicating the back door with his chin.

"I appreciate the thought, Mike. But if they've got a warrant, they probably know where I live. Let me find out what this is all about."

Like a train, the three of us snaked through the file room and up to the counter.

"I'm Denny Swift."

The police nodded.

"Could you step out from behind the counter, sir?" one of them asked.

"Is there a problem? Can you tell me what this is all about?"

There were half a dozen people sitting in the lobby waiting for their invoices to be prepared; they all looked up from their reading material.

"Please step out from behind the counter," the policeman said.

Denny hesitated for a moment, and then followed his instructions.

"We have a warrant for your arrest," one of the men said.

"For what?" Denny asked. "Can I see it? There must be some mistake."

The cop handed Denny a sheaf of paper. Denny read it.

"You're joking," he said.

"No, sir," the cop said, taking back the papers. "Please place your hands on the counter and spread your legs."

Denny's boss, Craig, came out of the back.

"Officers?" he said, approaching them. "I don't believe this is necessary, and if it is, you can do it outside."

"Sir, hold!" the policeman said sternly, pointing a long finger at Craig.

But Craig was right. The whole thing was designed to be prejudicial. It was the lobby of a place of business.

People were there, waiting for their BMWs and Mercedes gull-wings and other fancy cars. The police didn't have to do what they did in front of those people. They were customers. They trusted Denny, and now he was a criminal? What the police were doing wasn't right. There must have been a better way. But they had guns and batons. They had pepper spray and Tasers. And the SPD has always been notoriously nervous.

Denny followed their instructions and placed his hands on the counter and spread his legs; the cop patted him down thoroughly.

"Please turn around and place your hands behind your back," the cop said.

"You don't need handcuffs," Craig said angrily. "He's not running anywhere!"

"Sir!" the cop barked. "Hold!"

Denny turned around and placed his hands behind his back. The officer cuffed him.

"You have the right to remain silent," the cop said. "Anything you say can and will be held against you—"

"How long is this going to take?" Denny asked. "I have to pick up my daughter."

"I suggest you make other arrangements," the other police officer said.

"I can pick her up, Denny," Mike said.

"You're not on the list of approved pickup people."

"So who should I call?"

"... an attorney will be appointed to you ..."

"Call Mark Fein," Denny said, desperate. "He's in the computer."

"Do you understand these rights as I have read them to you?"

"Do you need me to bail you out?" Craig asked. "Whatever you need—"

"I have no idea what I need," Denny said. "Call Mark. Maybe he can pick up Zoë."

"Do you understand the rights as I have read them?"

"I understand!" Denny snapped. "Yes. I understand!"

"What are you being arrested for?" Mike asked.

Denny looked to the officers, but they said nothing. They waited for Denny to answer the question. They were well trained in the sophisticated methods of breaking down a subject—make him voice his own crime.

"Rape of a child in the third degree," Denny said.

"Felony rape," one of the cops clarified.

"But I didn't rape anyone," Denny said to the cop. "Who's behind this? What child?"

There was a long pause. The people in the lobby were rapt. Denny was standing before them all, his hands bound behind his back, they could all see how he was a prisoner now, he had no use of his hands now, he could not race a car now. All attention was on the police and their blue-gray shirts with the epaulets and their black guns, sticks, wands, and leather packets wrapped around their waists. It was true drama. Everyone wanted to know the answer to the question. *What child?*

"The one you raped," the cop replied simply.

I despised him for what he was doing, but I had to admire his dramatic flair; without another word, the police took Denny away.

33

Much of what happened to Denny regarding the custody suit concerning Zoë as well as the criminal charges of rape of a child in the third degree was not witnessed by me. These events spanned close to three years of our lives, as one of the tactics of Maxwell and Trish was to drag out the process in order to deplete Denny of money and destroy his will, as well as to play off of his desire to see Zoë mature in a loving and supportive environment. I was denied access to much information. I was not invited to attend any of the legal proceedings, for instance. I was allowed to attend only a few of the meetings Denny had with his attorney, Mark Fein, specifically, those that occurred at Victrola Coffee (because Mark Fein had a fancy for the barista with the pierced eyebrow and the dark chocolate eyes). I did not accompany Denny to the police station after his arrest. I was not present for his booking, his arraignment, or his subsequent lie detector testing.

Much of what I will tell you about the ordeal that followed Eve's death is a reconstruction based on information compiled by me from secondhand knowledge, overheard conversations, and established legal practices as I have gleaned from various television shows, most especially the *Law & Order* series and its spin-offs, *Special Victims Unit*, *Criminal Intent*, and the much maligned *Trial by Jury*. Further details regarding police methodology and terminology are based on two of the very best television shows in the history of the genre: *The Rockford Files*, starring James Garner, who also starred in the excellent racing film, *Grand Prix*; and of course, the greatest of all police dramas, *Columbo*, starring the fabulous and exceptionally clever Peter Falk in the title role. (My sixth favorite actor is Peter Falk.) And, finally, my knowledge of the courtroom is based solely on the work of the greatest of all courtroom dramatists, Sidney Lumet, whose many films, including *The Verdict* and *12 Angry Men*, have influenced me tremendously, and, as a side note, I would say that his casting of Al Pacino in *Dog Day Afternoon* was nothing short of inspired.

My intent, here, is to tell our story in a dramatically truthful way. While the facts may be less than accurate, please understand that the emotion is true. The intent is true. And, dramatically speaking, intention is everything.

34

They took him to a small room with a large table and many chairs. The walls were perforated with windows that looked out to the surrounding office, which was filled with police detectives doing their police work at their desks, just like on *Law & Order*. Wooden blinds filtered the blue light that crept into the room, rippling the table and floor with long shadows.

No one bothered him. A bad cop didn't pull his ears or hit him with a telephone directory or smash his fingers in the door or smack his head against the chalkboard, as often happens on television. No. After being booked and finger-printed and photographed, he was put in the room, alone, and left there, as if the police had forgotten him entirely. He sat by himself. He sat for hours with nothing. No coffee, no water, no restrooms, no radio. No distractions. His crime and his punishment and himself. Alone.

Did he despair? Did he silently berate himself for allowing himself to be in that situation? Or did he finally realize what it is like to be me, to be a dog? Did he understand, as those interminable minutes ticked by, that being alone is not the same as being lonely? That being alone is a neutral state; it is like a blind fish at the bottom of the ocean: without eyes, and therefore without judgment. Is it possible? That which is around me does not affect my mood; my mood affects that which is around me. Is it true? Could Denny have possibly appreciated the subjective nature of loneliness, which is something that exists only in the mind, not in the world, and, like a virus, is unable to survive without a willing host?

I like to think that he was alone for that time, but that he wasn't lonely. I like to think that he thought about his condition, but he did not despair.

And then Mark Fein burst into the East Precinct on Seattle's Capitol Hill; he burst in and began shouting. That is Mark Fein's blustery style. Bombastic. Boisterous. Bold. Bellicose. Mark Fein is a capital letter B. He is shaped like the letter, and he acts like the letter. Brash. Brazen. Bullish. Bellowing. He blew down the door, bull-rushed the desk, blasted the sergeant on duty, and bailed out Denny.

"What the fuck is this all about, Dennis?" Mark demanded on the street corner.

"It's nothing," Denny said, uninterested in the conversation.

"The fuck it is! A fifteen-year-old? Dennis! The fuck it's nothing!"

"She's lying."

"Is she? Did you have intercourse with this girl?"

"No."

"Did you penetrate any of her orifices with your genitals or any other object?"

Denny stared at Mark Fein and refused to answer.

"This is part of a plan, do you see that?" Mark said, frustrated. "I couldn't figure why they would file a bogus custody suit, but this changes everything."

Still, Denny said nothing.

"A pedophile. A sex offender. A statutory rapist. A child molester. Do these terms fit anywhere in the concept of 'the best interest of a child'?"

Denny ground his teeth; his jaw muscles bulged.

"My office, eight thirty tomorrow morning," Mark said. "Don't be late."

Denny burned.

"Where's Zoë?" he demanded.

Mark Fein dug his heel into the pavement.

"They got to her before I could," he said. "The timing on this was not an accident."

"I'm going to get her," Denny said.

"Don't!" Mark snapped. "Let them be. Now is not the

time for heroics. When you're stuck in quicksand, the worst thing you can do is struggle."

"So now I'm stuck in quicksand?" Denny asked.

"Dennis, you are in the quickest of all possible sand right now."

Denny wheeled around and started off.

"And don't leave the state," Mark called after him. "And, Jesus Christ, Dennis, don't even *look* at another fifteen-year-old girl!"

But Denny had already rounded the corner and was gone.

35

Hands are the windows to a man's soul.

Watch in-car videos of race drivers enough, and you'll see the truth of this statement. The rigid, tense grip of one driver reflects his rigid, tense driving style. The nervous hand-shuffle of another driver proves how uncomfortable he is in the car. A driver's hands should be relaxed, sensitive, aware. Much information is communicated through the steering wheel of a car; too tight or too nervous a grip will not allow the information to be communicated to the brain.

They say that senses do not operate alone, but rather are combined together in a special part of the brain that creates a picture of the body as a whole: sensors in the skin tell the brain about pressure, pain, heat; sensors in the joints and tendons tell the brain about the body's position in space; sensors in the ears track balance; and sensors in internal organs indicate one's emotional state. To voluntarily restrict one channel of information is foolish for a racer; to allow information to flow unfettered is divine.

Seeing Denny's hands shake was as upsetting for me as it was for him. After Eve's death, he glanced at his hands often, held them before his eyes as if they weren't really his hands at all, held them up and watched them shake. He tried to do it so no one would see. "Nerves," he would say to me whenever he caught me watching his manual examination. "Stress." And then he would tuck them into his pants pockets and keep them there, out of sight.

When Mike and Tony brought me home later that night, Denny was waiting on the dark porch with his hands in his pockets.

"Not only do I not want to talk about it," he said to them, "Mark told me not to. So."

They stood on the walk, looking up at him.

"Can we come in?" Mike asked.

"No," Denny replied, and then, aware of his abruptness, attempted to explain. "I don't feel like company right now."

They stared at him for a moment.

"You don't have to talk about what's going on," Mike said. "But it's good to *talk*. You can't keep everything inside. It's not healthy."

"You're probably right," Denny said. "But it's not how I operate. I just need to . . . assimilate . . . what's going on, and then I'll be able to talk. But not now."

Neither Mike nor Tony moved. It was like they were deciding if they would respect Denny's request to be left alone, or if they would storm past him into the house and keep him company by force. They looked at each other, and I could smell their anxiety; I wished that Denny would understand the depth of their concern for him.

"You'll be all right?" Mike asked. "We don't have to worry about the gas oven being left on and you lighting a cigarette or something?"

"It's electric," Denny said. "And I don't smoke."

"He'll be all right," Tony said to Mike.

"You want us to keep Enzo or anything?" Mike asked.

"No."

"Bring you some groceries?"

Denny shook his head.

"He'll be all right," Tony said again, and tugged at Mike's arm.

"My phone's always on," Mike said. "Twenty-four-hour crisis hotline. Need to talk, need anything, call me."

They retreated down the walk.

"We fed Enzo!" Mike called from the alley.

They left, and Denny and I went inside. He took his hands from his pockets and held them up to look at them shaking.

"Rapists don't get custody of their little girls," he said. "See how that works?"

I followed him into the kitchen, for a moment concerned that he had lied to Mike and Tony and that perhaps we did have a gas oven after all. But he didn't go to the oven, he went to the cupboard and took out a glass. Then he reached into where he kept the liquor and took out a bottle. He poured a drink.

It was absurd. Depressed, stressed, hands shaking, and now he was going to get himself drunk? I couldn't stand for it. I barked sharply at him.

He looked down at me, drink in hand, and I up at him. If I'd had hands, I would have opened one of them and slapped him with it.

"What's the matter, Enzo, too much of a cliché for you?"

I barked again. Too much of a *pathetic* cliché for me.

"Don't judge me," he said. "That's not your job. Your job is to support me, not judge me."

He drank the drink and then glared at me, and I did judge him. He was acting just as they wanted him to act. They were rattling him, and he was about to quit and then it would be over and I'd have to spend the rest of my life with a drunkard who had nothing to do but stare lifelessly out from his dead eyes at pictures flashing by on the TV screen. This wasn't my Denny. This was a pathetic character from a hackneyed television drama. And I didn't like him at all.

I left the room thinking I would go to bed, but I didn't want to sleep in the same room as this Denny impostor. This Denny facsimile. I went into Zoë's bedroom, curled up on the floor next to her bed, and tried to sleep. Zoë was the only one I had left.

Later—though I don't know how much—he stood in the doorway.

"The first time I took you for a drive in my car when you were a puppy, you puked all over the seat," he said to me. "But I didn't give up on you."

I lifted my head from the ground, not understanding his point.

"I put the booze away," he said. "I'm better than that."

He turned and walked away. I heard him shuffle around in the living room and then turn on the TV.

So he didn't fall hopelessly into the bottle, the refuge of the weak and the maudlin. He got my point. Gestures are all that I have.

I found him on the couch watching a video of Eve, Zoë, and me, from years ago when we went to Long Beach, on the Washington coast. Zoë was a toddler. I remembered that weekend well; we were all so young, it seemed, chasing kites on the wide beach that went on for miles. I sat next to the couch and watched, too. We were so naive; we had no knowledge of where the road would take us, no idea that we would ever be separated. The beach, the ocean, the sky. It was there for us and only for us. A world without end.

"No race has ever been won in the first corner," he said. "But plenty of races have been lost there."

I looked at him. He reached out, settled his hand on the crown of my head, and scratched my ear like he has always done.

"That's right," he said to me. "If we're going to be a cliché, let's be a positive cliché."

Yes: the race is long—to finish first, first you must finish.

36

I love very few things more than a nice long walk in the drizzle of Seattle. I don't care for the heaviness of real rain; I like the misting, the feeling of the tiny droplets on my muzzle and eyelashes. The freshness of the air, which has been suddenly infused with ozone and negative ions. While rain is heavy and can suppress the scents, a light shower actually amplifies smells; it releases the molecules, brings odor to life, and then carries it through the air to my nose. Which is why I love Seattle more than any other place, even Thunderhill Raceway Park. Because, while the summers are very dry, once the damp season begins, nary a day goes by without a helping of my much-loved drizzle.

Denny took me for a walk in the drizzle, and I relished it. Eve had only been dead for a few days, but since her death,

I had felt so bottled up and congested, sitting with Denny in the house for much of the time, breathing the same stale air over and over. Denny seemed to crave the change, too; instead of jeans, a sweatshirt, and his yellow slicker, he put on a pair of dark slacks, and he wore his black trench coat over a high-necked cashmere sweater.

We walked north out of Madison Valley and into the Arboretum. Once past the dangerous part, where there is no walkway and the cars drive well over the safe speed limit, we turned off on the smaller road, and Denny released me from my leash.

This is what I love to do: I love to run through a field of wet grass that has not been mowed recently, I love to run, keeping my snout low to the ground so the grass and the sparkles of water cover my face. I imagine myself as a vacuum cleaner, sucking in all the smells, all the life, a spear of summer grass. It reminds me of my childhood, back on the farm in Spangle, where there was no rain, but there was grass, there were fields, and I ran.

I ran and I ran that day. And Denny walked on, trudging steadily. At the point where we usually turned around, we kept going. We crossed the pedestrian bridge and curled up into Montlake. Denny reattached my leash and we crossed a larger road and we were in a new park! I loved this one, too. But it was different.

"Interlaken," Denny said to me as he unleashed me.

Interlaken. This park was not fields and flatland. It was

a gnarled and twisty ravine painted with vines and bushes and groundcover, tented by the tallest of trees and a canopy of leaves. It was wonderful. As Denny followed the path, I bounded up and down the hillside, hiding in the low brush and pretending I was a secret agent, or running as fast as I could through the obstacles and pretending I was a predator like in the movies, hunting something down, tracking my prey.

For a long time we walked and ran in this park, me running five paces for every one of Denny's, until I was exhausted and thirsty. We emerged from the park and walked in a neighborhood that was foreign to me. Denny stopped in a café to purchase a cup of coffee for himself. He brought some water for me, which was in a paper cup and difficult to drink, but sated me nonetheless.

And we continued walking.

I have always loved activity and walking, especially with Denny, my favorite walking partner, and especially in the drizzle, but I have to admit, at that time I was getting quite tired. We had been out for more than two hours, and after a long walk like that, I like to go home for a playful toweling off, and then settle down for a nice long nap. But there was no nap; we kept walking.

I recognized Fifteenth Avenue when we reached it, and I knew Volunteer Park quite well. But I was surprised when we went into the Lake View Cemetery. Of course, I knew the importance of Lake View Cemetery, though I had never been there. I had seen a documentary on Bruce Lee; Lake View is where he is buried, alongside his son, Brandon, who was a wonderful actor until his untimely death. I feel very badly for Brandon Lee, because he fell victim to the family curse, but also because the last film he made was *The Crow*, an unfortunate title for an unfortunate film based on a comic book written by someone who clearly had no idea of the real nature of crows. But that's a discussion for another time. We entered the cemetery, and we did not seek out the graves of Bruce and Brandon Lee, two very fine actors. We sought something else. Following the paved road to the north we looped around the central hill and came upon a temporary tent structure, under which many people were assembled.

They were all dressed nicely and those who weren't protected from the drizzle by the tent were holding umbrellas. Immediately, I saw Zoë.

Ah. The light switch—it's either on or it's off. Denny had dressed for the event.

We approached the people, who were slightly disorganized, milling about, their collective attention fragmented. The proceedings had not yet begun.

We got very close to them, and then, suddenly, someone broke off from the group. A man. And then another man, and another. The three of them walked toward us.

One of them was Maxwell. The others were Eve's brothers, whose names I never knew because they showed themselves so infrequently.

"You're not welcome here," Maxwell said sternly.

"She's my wife," Denny said calmly. "The mother of my child."

She was there, the child. Zoë saw her father. She waved at him, and he waved back.

"You're not welcome here," Maxwell said again. "Leave, or I'll call the police."

The two brothers raised themselves. Pre-battle posturing.

"You already called them, didn't you?" Denny asked.

Maxwell sneered at Denny.

"You were warned," he said.

"Why are you doing this?"

Maxwell pushed up into Denny's personal space.

"You've never been good to Eve," Maxwell said. "And with what you did to Annika, I will not trust you with Zoë."

"Nothing happened that night—"

But Maxwell had already turned. "Please escort Mr. Swift away from here," he said to his two sons, and he abruptly walked away.

In the distance, I saw Zoë, unable to contain herself any longer; she jumped out of her seat and ran toward us.

"Beat it," one of the men said.

"It's my wife's funeral," Denny said. "I'm staying."

"Get the hell out of here," the other man said, jabbing Denny in the ribs.

"Punch me if you want," Denny said. "I won't fight back."

"Child molester!" the first man hissed, flinging his

hands into Denny's chest. Denny didn't budge. A man who drives a two-thousand-pound car at one hundred seventy miles per hour does not get flustered by the honking of the geese.

Zoë reached us and leapt at Denny. He hoisted her into the air and propped her on his hip and kissed her cheek.

"How's my baby?" he asked.

"How's my daddy?" she replied.

"I'm getting by," he said. He turned to the brother who had just pushed him. "Sorry, I didn't catch what you just said. Maybe you'd like to repeat it in front of my daughter."

The man took a step back, and then Trish rushed up to us. She inserted herself between Denny and the brothers. She told them to leave, and she turned to Denny.

"Please," she said. "I understand why you're here, but it can't be done like this. I really don't think you should stay." She hesitated for a moment, and then she said: "I'm sorry. You must be so alone."

Denny didn't respond. I looked up at him, and his eyes were full of tears. Zoë noticed, too, and started crying with him.

"It's okay to cry," she said. "Grandma says crying helps because it washes away the hurting."

He looked at Zoë for a long moment and she at him. Then he sighed sadly.

"You help Grandma and Grandpa be strong, okay?" he said. "I have some important business to take care of. About

Mommy. There are things that have to be done."

"I know," she said.

"You'll stay with Grandma and Grandpa for a little bit longer, until I get everything worked out, okay?"

"They told me I might stay with them for a while."

"Well," he said regretfully, "Grandma and Grandpa are very good at thinking ahead."

"We can all compromise," Trish said. "I know you're not a bad person—"

"There is no compromise," Denny said.

"Given time, you'll see. It's what's best for Zoë."

"Enzo!" Zoë called out suddenly, locating me beneath her. She squirmed loose of Denny and grabbed me around the neck. "Enzo!"

I was surprised and pleased by her hearty greeting, so I licked her face.

Trish leaned in to Denny.

"You must have been missing Eve terribly," she whispered to him. "But to take advantage of a fifteen-year-old girl—"

Denny abruptly straightened and pulled away from her.

"Zoë," he said. "Enzo and I are going to watch from a special spot. Come on, Enzo."

He bent down and kissed her forehead, and we walked away.

Zoë and Trish watched us go. We continued on the circular path and walked up the bump of a hill to the top, where we stood underneath the trees, and, protected from the lightly falling rain, watched the whole thing. The people coming to attention. The man reading from a book. The people laying roses on the coffin. And everyone leaving in their cars.

We stayed. We waited for the workers who came and dismantled the tents. The workers who came and used a strange winch device to lower the coffin into the ground.

We stayed. We watched the men with their little Caterpillar as they shoveled all the dirt over her. We waited.

When they were all gone, we walked down the hill and we stood before the mound of dirt and we cried. We kneeled and we cried and we grabbed at handfuls of the dirt, the mound, and we felt the last bit of her, the last part of her that we could feel, and we cried.

And finally, when we could do no more, we stood. And we began the long walk home.

37

The morning after Eve's funeral, I could barely move. My body was so stiff, I couldn't even stand, and Denny had to look for me because I usually got up immediately and helped him with breakfast. I was eight years old, two years older than Zoë, though I felt much more like her uncle than her brother. While I was still too young to suffer an arthritic condition in my hips, that's exactly what I suffered from. Degenerative arthritis caused by hip dysplasia. It was an unpleasant condition, yes; but in a sense it was a relief that I could concentrate on my own difficulties rather than dwell on other things that preoccupied my thoughts: specifically, Zoë being stranded with the Twins.

I was quite young when I understood that my hips were

abnormal. I had spent most of my first months of life running and playing with Denny, just the two of us, and so I had little opportunity to compare myself with other dogs. When I was old enough to frequent dog parks, I realized that keeping my hind legs together in my gait—though much more comfortable for me—was an obvious sign that my hips were defective. The last thing I wanted was to be seen as a misfit, and so I trained myself to walk and run in certain ways to disguise my defect.

As I matured and the protective cartilage at the ends of my bones wore away, as cartilage tends to do, the pain became more acute. And yet, instead of complaining, I tried to hide my problem. Perhaps I have always been more like Eve than I've ever admitted, for I distrusted the medical world immensely, and I found ways to compensate for my disability so I could avoid a diagnosis that would undoubtedly hasten my demise.

As I mentioned, I do not know the source of Eve's distrust of medicine; the origins of my distrust, however, are all too clear. When I was just a pup, not more than a week or two old, the alpha man on the farm in Spangle introduced me to a friend of his. The man held me in his lap and petted me, feeling my forelegs at length.

"They should come off," he said to the alpha man.

"I'll hold him," the alpha man said.

"He needs anesthetic, Will. You should have called me last week."

"I'm not wasting my money on a dog, Doc," the alpha man said. "Cut."

I had no idea what they were talking about, but then the alpha man gripped me tightly around my midsection. The other man, "Doc," took hold of my right paw and, with shiny scissors that glinted in the sunlight, snipped off my right dew claw. My right thumb. The pain blazed through my body, a wracking, shattering pain. It was bloody and horrible and I cried out. I struggled mightily to free myself, but the alpha man squeezed me so tightly I could barely breathe. Then Doc took hold of my left paw and, without hesitating for a moment, cut off my left thumb. *Click*. I remember that perhaps more than the pain. The sound. *Click*. So loud. And then the blood was everywhere. The pain was so intense it left me shivering and weak. Later, Doc applied salve to my wounds and wrapped my forelegs tightly and whispered to me, "It's a mean bastard who won't pay for a little local anesthetic for his pups."

Do you see? This is why I distrust them. It's a mean bastard who will do the cutting without anesthetic because he wants to get paid.

The day after Eve's funeral, Denny took me to the vet, a thin man who smelled of hay, and who had a bottomless pocket full of treats. He felt my hips and I tried not to wince, but I couldn't help myself when he squeezed certain places. He diagnosed me, prescribed anti-inflammatory medication, and said there was nothing else he could do except, some day in the future, perform expensive surgery to replace my defective parts.

Denny thanked the man and drove me home.

"You have hip dysplasia," he said to me.

If I'd had fingers, I'd have shoved them into my ears until I burst my own eardrums. Anything to avoid hearing.

"Hip dysplasia," he repeated, shaking his head in amazement.

I shook my head, too. With my diagnosis, I knew, would come my end. Slowly, perhaps. Painfully, without a doubt; marked by the signposts laid out by the veterinarian. The visible becomes inevitable. The car goes where the eyes go. Whatever the trauma that led to Eve's distrust of medicine, I was able to see only the effects: she had been unable to look away from where the others had told her to look. It is a rare person who can hear the blunt authority of a terminal diagnosis, refuse to accept it, and choose a different path. I thought of Eve and how quickly she embraced her death once the people around her agreed to it; I considered the foretelling of my own end, which was to be full of suffering and pain, as death is believed to be by most of the world, and I tried to look away.

38

Because of the criminal charges against Denny, the Twins had been granted a temporary restraining order that meant, pending challenge in court, Denny didn't get to see Zoë at all for several months. Minutes after he was arrested, Maxwell and Trish filed a motion to terminate Denny's right to custody of any kind, since he was clearly an unfit parent. A pedophile. A sex offender.

Well. We all play by the same rules; it's just that some people spend more time reading those rules and figuring out how to make them work in their behalf.

I have seen movies that involve abducted children and the grief and terror that suffocate the parents when their children are taken by strangers. Denny felt every bit of that grief, and, in my own way, I did, too. And we knew where

Zoë was. We knew who had taken her. And, still, we could do nothing.

Mark Fein suggested it would be inflammatory to tell Zoë about the legal proceedings, and he suggested that Denny invent a story about driving race cars in Europe to explain his prolonged absence. Mark Fein also negotiated a letter exchange: notes and drawings made by Zoë would be delivered to Denny, and Denny could write letters to his child, as long as he agreed to allow those letters to be censored by the Twins' counsel. I will tell you, every vertical surface in our house was decorated with Zoë's delightful artwork, and many long nights were spent by Denny and me crafting the letters we sent to Zoë, telling of Denny's exploits on the European race circuit.

As much as I wanted Denny to act, to lash out against the establishment in a bold and passionate way, I respected his restraint. Denny has long admired the legendary driver Emerson Fittipaldi. "Emmo," as he was called by his peers, was a champion of great stature and consistency, and was known for his pragmatism on the track. Taking chances is not a good idea if choosing wrong may send you into the wall at Indy, twist your car into a fiery metal sculpture that emergency workers struggle to untangle while your flesh is melted from your bones by the invisible flames of burning ethanol. Not only did Emmo never panic, Emmo never put himself in a position where he might have to; like Emmo, Denny never took unnecessary risks.

While I, too, admire and try to emulate Emmo, I still think that I would like to drive like Ayrton Senna, full of emotion and daring. I would like to have packed our necessities in the BMW, driven by Zoë's school one day to pick her up unannounced, and then headed directly for Canada. From Vancouver, we could have driven east to Montreal— where they have many fabulous road courses and where they host a Formula One Grand Prix every summer—to live by ourselves in peace for the rest of our lives.

But it was not my choice. I was not behind the wheel. No one cared a whit about me. Which is why they were all in such a state of panic when Zoë asked her grandparents if she could see me. You see, no one had accounted for my whereabouts. The Twins, not knowing where their elaborate fiction had placed me, immediately called Mark Fein, who immediately called Denny to outline the nature of our predicament.

"She believes it all," I could hear Mark shout over the phone, even though the phone was pressed to Denny's ear. "So where did you leave the fucking dog? You could have taken him with you, but there are quarantine rules! Does she know about quarantine?"

"Tell her of course she can see Enzo," Denny said calmly. "Enzo is staying with Mike and Tony while I'm in Europe; Zoë likes them, and she'll believe it. I'll have Mike bring Enzo over on Saturday."

And that's what happened. In the early afternoon Mike

picked me up and drove me over to Mercer Island, and I spent the afternoon playing with Zoë on the great lawn. Before dinnertime, Mike returned me to Denny.

"How did she look?" Denny asked Mike.

"She looked terrific," Mike said. "She has her mother's smile."

"They had a good time together?"

"A fantastic time. They played all day."

"Fetch?" Denny asked, thirsty for details. "Did she use the Chuckit? Or did they play chase? Eve never liked it when they played chase."

"No, mostly fetch," Mike said kindly.

"I never minded when they played chase because I know Enzo, but Eve was always . . ."

"You know," Mike said, "sometimes they just flopped down on the grass and cuddled together. It was really sweet."

Denny wiped his nose quickly.

"Thanks, Mike," he said. "Really. Thanks a lot."

"Anytime," Mike said.

I appreciated Mike's effort to appease Denny, even though he was avoiding the truth. Or maybe Mike didn't see what I saw. Maybe he couldn't hear what I heard. Zoë's profound sadness. Her loneliness. Her whispered plans that she and I would somehow smuggle ourselves off to Europe and find her father.

That summer without Zoë was very painful for Denny.

In addition to feeling isolated from his daughter, his career was derailed: though he was offered the opportunity to drive again for the racing team he was with the previous year, he was forced to decline, as the pending criminal case demanded that he remain in the state of Washington at all times or he would forfeit his bond. Further, he was not allowed to accept any of the lucrative teaching jobs and commercial work offers that came his way—after his spectacular experience at Thunderhill, he was highly recommended in the commercial industry and received offers over the phone fairly frequently. These jobs almost always took place in California, or sometimes in Nevada or Texas, and occasionally in Connecticut, and therefore were forbidden to him. He was a prisoner of the state.

And yet.

We are all afforded our physical existence so we can learn about ourselves. So I understand why Denny, on a deeper level, allowed this situation to befall him. I won't say he created the situation, but he *allowed* it. Because he needed to test his mettle. He wanted to know how long he could keep his foot on the accelerator before lifting. He chose this life, and therefore he chose this battle.

And I realized, as the summer matured and I frequently visited Zoë without Denny, that I was a part of this, too. I was integral to the drama. Because on those late Saturday afternoons in July, after Mike reviewed the events of the day with Denny and then returned to his own world, Denny would sit with me on the back porch and quiz me. "Did you play fetch? Did you tug? Did you chase?" He would ask, "Did you cuddle?" He would ask, "How did she look? Is she eating enough fruit? Are they buying organic?"

I tried. I tried as hard as I could to form words for him, but they wouldn't come. I tried to beam my thoughts into his head via telepathy. I tried to send him the pictures I saw in my mind. I twitched my ears. I cocked my head. I nodded. I pawed.

Until he smiled at me and stood.

"Thanks, Enzo," he would say on those days. "You're not too tired, are you?"

I would stand and wag. I'm never too tired.

"Let's go, then."

He would grab the Chuckit and the tennis ball and walk me down to the Blue Dog Park, and we would play fetch until the light grew thin and the mosquitoes came out of hiding, thirsty for their dinner.

39

There was an occasion that summer when Denny found a teaching engagement in Spokane and, via Mike, our faux-Intercontinental liaison, asked if the Twins could take me for the weekend; they agreed, as they had grown accustomed to my presence in their home, and I always handled myself with the utmost dignity when I was around them, never soiling their expensive rugs or carpets, never begging for food, and never drooling when I slept.

I would much rather have gone to racing school with Denny, but I understood that he depended on me to take care of Zoë, and also to act as some kind of a witness on his behalf. Though I could not relate to him the details of our visits, my presence, I think, reassured him in some way.

On a Friday afternoon, I was delivered by Mike into

Zoë's waiting embrace. She immediately ushered me into her room, and we played a game of dress-up together; to say that I was taking one for the team would be an understatement, considering the crazy outfits I was forced to wear. But that's my ego speaking; I knew my role as jester in Zoë's court, and I was happy to play the part.

That evening Maxwell took me outside earlier than usual, urging me to "get busy." When I came back inside, I was led to Zoë's room, which already had my bed in it. Apparently, she had requested I sleep with her rather than by the back door or, God forbid, in the garage. I curled into a ball and quickly dozed off.

A bit later, I woke. The lights were dim. Zoë was awake and active, encircling my bed with piles of her stuffed animals.

"They'll keep you company," she whispered to me as she surrounded me.

Seemingly hundreds of them. All shapes and sizes. I was being surrounded by teddy bears and giraffes, sharks and dogs, cats and birds and snakes. She worked steadily and I watched, until I was nothing more than a small atoll on the Pacific, and the animals were my coral reef. I found it somewhat amusing and touching that Zoë cared to share me with her animals in that way, and I drifted off to sleep feeling protected and safe.

I awoke later in the night and saw that the wall of animals around me was quite high. Still, I was able to shift my weight and change position to make myself more comfortable. But when I did, I was shocked by a frightening sight. One of the animals. The one on top. Staring straight at me. It was the zebra.

The replacement zebra. The one she had chosen to fill in for the demon that had dismantled itself before me so long ago. The horrifying zebra of my past.

The demon had returned. And, though it was dark in the room, I know I saw a glint of light in its eyes.

As you can imagine, my sleep that night was sparse. The last thing I wanted was to awaken amid animal carnage because the demon had returned. I forced myself to stay awake; yet I couldn't help but drift off. Each time I opened my eyes, I found the zebra staring at me. Like a gargoyle, it stood on a cathedral of animals above me, watching. The other animals had no life; they were toys. The zebra alone knew.

I felt sluggish all day, but I did my best to keep up, and I tried to catch up on my sleep by napping quietly. To any observer, I'm sure I gave off the impression of being quite contented; however, I was anxious about nightfall, concerned that, once again, the zebra would torture me with its mocking eyes.

That afternoon, as the Twins took their alcohol on the deck as they tended to do and Zoë watched television in the TV room, I dozed outside in the sun. And I heard them.

"I know it's for the best," Trish said. "But still, I feel badly for him."

"It's for the best," Maxwell said.

"I know. But still . . ."

"He forced himself on a teenage girl," Maxwell said sternly. "What kind of a father preys on innocent young girls?"

I lifted my head from the warm wood of the deck and saw Trish cluck and shake her head.

"What?" Maxwell demanded.

"From what I hear, she's not that innocent."

"What you *hear*!" Maxwell blurted. "He forced himself on a young girl! That's *rape*!"

"I know, I know. It's just that the timing of her coming forward is . . . a big coincidence."

"Are you suggesting that she made it up?"

"No," Trish said. "But why did Pete wait to tell us about it until after you complained to him so bitterly that you were certain we wouldn't get custody of Zoë?"

"I don't care about any of that," Maxwell said, waving her off. "He wasn't good enough for Eve, and he's not good enough for Zoë. And if he's stupid enough to get caught with his pants down and his pecker in his fist, you're going to be damn sure I'm going to seize the moment. Zoë will have a better childhood with us. She will have a better moral raising, a better financial raising, a better family life, and you know it, Trish. You know it!"

"I know, I know," she said, and sipped her amber drink with the bright red cherry drowned at the bottom of the glass. "But he's not a bad person."

He poured his drink down his gullet and slapped the glass down on the teak table.

"It's time to start dinner," he said, and he went inside.

I was stunned. I, too, had noted the coincidence of events, and I had been suspicious since the beginning. But to hear the words, the coldness in Maxwell's tone.

Imagine this. Imagine having your wife die suddenly of a brain cancer. Then imagine having her parents attack you mercilessly in order to gain custody of your daughter. Imagine that they exploit allegations of sexual molestation against you; they hire very expensive and clever lawyers because they have much more money than you have. Imagine that they prevent you from having any contact with your six-year-old daughter for months on end. And imagine they restrict your ability to earn money to support yourself and, of course, as you hope, your daughter. How long would you last before your will was broken?

They had no idea who they were dealing with. Denny would not kneel before them. He would never quit; he would never break.

With disgust, I followed them into the house. Trish began her preparations and Maxwell took his jar of peppers from the refrigerator; inside me, a darkness brewed. Contrivers. Manipulators. They were no longer people to me. They were now the Evil Twins. Evil, horrible, dastardly people who stuffed themselves with burning hot peppers in order to fuel the bile in their stomachs. When they laughed, flames shot out of their noses. They were not worthy of life, these people. They were disgusting creatures, nitrogen-based life forms that lived in the very darkest corners of the very deepest lakes where there is no light and the pressure crushes everything to sand; deep, dark places where oxygen would never dare venture.

My anger with the Evil Twins fed my thirst for revenge. And I was not above using the tools of my dogness to exact justice.

I presented myself to Maxwell as he stuffed another pepper into his mouth and pulverized it with the ceramic teeth he removed at night. I sat before him. I lifted a paw.

"Want a treat?" he asked me, clearly surprised by my gesture.

I barked.

"Here you go, boy."

He extracted a pepper from the bottle and held it before my nose. It was a very large one, long and artificially green and smelling of sulfites and nitrates. The devil's candy.

"I don't think those are good for dogs," Trish said.

"He likes them," Maxwell countered.

My first thought was to take the pepperoncini and a couple of Maxwell's fingers with it. But that would have caused real problems, and I likely would have been euthanized before Mike could return to save me, so I didn't take his fingers. I did, however, take the pepper. I knew it was bad for me, that I would suffer immediate discomfort. But I knew my discomfort would pass, and I anticipated the unpleasant rebound effect, which is what I wanted. After all, I am just a stupid dog, unworthy of human scorn, without the brains to be responsible for my own bodily functions. A dumb dog.

I observed their dinner carefully because I wanted to see for myself. The Twins served Zoë some kind of chicken covered in a creamy sauce. They didn't know that while Zoë loved chicken cutlets, she never ate them with sauce, and certainly never with cream; she disliked the consistency. When she didn't eat the string beans they served, Trish asked if she would like a banana instead. Zoë replied affirmatively and Trish made some banana slices, which Zoë barely picked at because they were crudely sliced and speckled with brown spots, which she always avoided. (When Denny prepared her bananas for her, he took great care in slicing them in uniform thickness after removing any and all brown spots he could find.)

And these agents of evil—these supposed grandparents!— thought Zoë would be better off with them! Bah! They didn't spend a moment thinking about her welfare; after dinner, they didn't even ask why she hadn't eaten the bananas. They allowed her to leave the table having eaten almost nothing. Denny never would have allowed that. He would have prepared for her something she liked and he would have required that she eat a sufficient dinner to continue to grow in a healthy way.

All the while I watched, I seethed. And in my stomach, a foul concoction steeped.

When it was time to take me out that night, Maxwell opened the French door to the back deck and began his idiotic chanting: "Get busy, boy. Get busy."

I didn't go outside. I looked up at him and I thought about what he was doing, how he was rending our family, pulling apart the fabric of our lives for his own smug, self-congratulatory purposes; I thought about how he and Trish were grossly inferior guardians for my Zoë. I crouched in my stance right there, inside the house, and I shat a massive, soupy, pungent pile of diarrhea on his beautiful, expensive, linen-colored Berber carpet.

"What the hell?" he shouted at me. "Bad dog!"

I turned and trotted cheerfully to Zoë's room.

"Get busy, motherfucker," I said as I left. But, of course, he couldn't hear me.

As I settled into my lagoon of stuffed animals, I heard Maxwell exclaim loudly and call for Trish to clean up my mess. I looked at the zebra, still perched on his throne of lifeless animal carcasses, and I growled at it very softly but very ominously. And the demon knew. The demon knew not to mess with me that night.

Not that night, or ever again.

40

Oh, a breath of September!

The vacations were done. The lawyers were back at work. The courts were at full staff. The postponements were finished. The truth would be had!

He left that morning wearing the only suit he owned, a crumpled khaki two-piece from Banana Republic, and a dark tie. He looked very good.

"Mike will come by at lunch and take you for a walk," he said to me. "I don't know how long this will go."

Mike came and walked me briefly through the neighborhood so I wouldn't be lonely, and then he left again. Later that afternoon, Denny returned. He smiled down at me.

"Do I need to reintroduce you two?" he asked.

And behind him was Zoë!

I leapt in the air. I bounded. I *knew* it! I *knew* Denny would vanquish the Evil Twins! I felt like doing flips. Zoë had returned!

It was an amazing afternoon. We played in the yard. We ran and laughed. We hugged and cuddled. We made dinner together and sat at our table and ate. It felt so good to be together again! After dinner, they ate ice cream in the kitchen.

"Are you going back to Europe soon?" Zoë asked out of the blue.

Denny froze in place. The story had worked so well, Zoë still believed it. He sat down across from her.

"No, I'm not going back to Europe," he said.

Her face lit up.

"Yay!" she cheered. "I can have my room back!"

"Actually," Denny said, "I'm afraid not yet."

Her forehead crinkled and her lips pursed as she attempted to puzzle out his statement. I was puzzled, too.

"Why not?" she asked, finally, frustration in her voice. "I want to come home."

"I know, honey, but the lawyers and judges have to make the decision on where you'll live. It's part of what happens when someone's mommy dies."

"Just *tell* them," she demanded. "Just *tell* them that I'm coming home. I don't want to live there anymore. I want to live with you and Enzo."

"It's a little more complicated than that," Denny hemmed.

"Just *tell* them," she repeated angrily. "Just *tell* them!"

"Zoë, someone has accused me of doing something very bad—"

"Just *tell* them."

"Someone said I did something very bad. And even though I know I didn't do it, now I have to go to court and prove to everyone that I didn't do it."

Zoë thought about it for a moment.

"Was it Grandma and Grandpa?" she asked.

I was very impressed with the laserlike accuracy of her inquiry.

"Not—" Denny started. "No. No, it wasn't them. But . . . they *know* about it."

"I made them love me too much," Zoë said softly, looking into her bowl of melted ice cream. "I should have been bad. I should have made them not want to keep me."

"No, honey, no," Denny said, dismayed. "Don't say that. You should shine with all of your light all the time. I'll work this out. I promise I will."

Zoë shook her head without meeting his eyes. Understanding that the conversation was over, Denny cleared her bowl and began to clean the dishes. I felt badly for them both, but more so for Zoë, who continued to face situations that were loaded with subtleties beyond her experience and fraught with the conflicting desires of those around her, fighting for supremacy like vines entangled on a trellis. Sadly, she went into her bedroom to play with the animals she had left behind.

Later in the evening, the doorbell rang. Denny answered it. Mark Fein was there.

"It's time," he said.

Denny nodded and called for Zoë.

"This was a major victory for us, Dennis," Mark said. "It means a lot. You understand that, right?"

Denny nodded, but he was sad. Like Zoë.

"Every other weekend, Friday after school until Sunday after dinner, she's yours," Mark said. "And every Wednesday, you pick her up after school and deliver her before eight o'clock, right?"

"Right," Denny said.

Mark Fein looked at Denny for a long time without speaking.

"I'm fucking proud of you," he said, finally. "I don't know what goes on in that head of yours, but you're a fucking competitor."

Denny breathed in deeply.

"That's what I am," he agreed.

And Mark Fein took Zoë away. She had just returned and she was going away again. It took me some time to fully grasp the situation, but I understood, ultimately, that the court case earlier in the day was not Denny's criminal trial, but a custody hearing, a hearing that had been delayed over and over, put off for months because the lawyers were going to their houses on Lopez Island with their own families and the judge was going to Cle Elum to his ranch. I felt betrayed;

I knew that those people, those officials of the court, had no clue as to the feelings I had witnessed that night at the dinner table. If they had, they would have stopped everything, canceled all of their other obligations, and ensured a swift resolution to our situation.

As it was, we had taken only our first step. The restraining order had been quashed. Denny had won visitation rights. But Zoë was still in the custody of the Evil Twins. Denny was still on trial for a felony charge he didn't deserve. Nothing had been solved.

And yet. I had seen them together. I had seen them look at each other and giggle with relief. Which reaffirmed my faith in the balance of the universe. And while I understood that we had merely successfully navigated the first turn of a very long race, I felt that things boded well for us; Denny was not one to make mistakes, and with fresh tires and a full load of fuel, he would prove a formidable foe to anyone challenging him.

41

The flash and fury of a sprint race are grand. The strategies and skill of a race of five hundred miles are spectacular. But the race for the true racer is the enduro. Eight hours, twelve hours. Twenty-four. Even twenty-five. I introduce you to one of the forgotten names in automotive racing history: Luigi Chinetti.

Chinetti was a tireless driver who participated in every motorsports race at Le Mans from 1932 through 1953. He is known mostly for winning the first ever Ferrari victory at the 24 Hours of Le Mans, in 1949. Chinetti drove more than twenty-three-and-one-half of those twenty-four hours. For twenty minutes, he relinquished control of the car to his co-driver, Peter Mitchell-Thompson, the car's owner, a baron from Scotland. That is all. Chinetti drove all but twenty minutes of the twenty-four hours. And he won.

A brilliant driver, mechanic, and businessman, Luigi Chinetti later convinced Ferrari to sell their cars in the United States, and he convinced them to grant him the first—and for many years, the only—Ferrari dealership in this country. He sold expensive red automobiles to very rich people, and they paid very rich prices for their toys. Chinetti always kept his client list confidential, shunning the garish light of conspicuous consumption.

A great man, Luigi Chinetti. Clever and smart and resourceful. He died in 1994 at the age of ninety-three years. I often wonder who he is now, who possesses his soul. Does a child know his own spiritual background, his own pedigree? I doubt it. But somewhere, a child surprises himself with his endurance, his quick mind, his dexterous hands. Somewhere a child accomplishes with ease that which usually takes great effort. And this child, who has been blind to his past but whose heart still beats for the thrill of the race, this child's soul awakens.

And a new champion walks among us.

42

How quickly.

How quickly a year passes, like a mouthful of food snatched from the maw of eternity.

How quickly.

With little drama, comparatively speaking, to mark the months, they slipped by, one by one, until another fall lay before us. And still, almost nothing had changed. Back and forth, round and round, the lawyers danced and played their game, which was merely a game to them. But not to us.

Denny took Zoë on schedule, every other weekend, every Wednesday afternoon. He took her to places of cultural enrichment. Art museums. Science exhibits. The zoo and the aquarium. He taught her things. And sometimes, on secret missions, he took us to the go-karts.

Ah. The electric karts. She was just big enough to fit when he took her. And she was good. She knew the karts immediately, as if she had been born to them. She was quick.

How quickly.

With little instruction she climbed behind the wheel, tucked her golden hair into a helmet, buckled her harness, and was off. No fear. No hesitation. No waiting.

"You take her to Spanaway?" the worker boy asked Denny after her very first session.

Spanaway was a place south of us where children often practiced go-karting on an outdoor course.

"Nope," Denny replied.

" 'Cause she could kick your ass," the kid said.

"I doubt it." Denny laughed.

The worker kid glanced nervously at the clock. He looked through the glass barrier to the cash register people. It was mid-afternoon, after the lunch rush and before anyone showed up for the evening activities. The place was empty except for us; they only let me in because I had been there before and I had never created a problem.

"So take a session," the kid said. "She wins, you pay. You win, you don't pay."

"You're on," Denny said, grabbing a helmet from the rack of helmets that people can borrow—he hadn't bothered to bring his own.

They started their race, a flying start, with Denny giving Zoë a bit of an edge, taking it easy on her. For several laps he dogged her, stayed on her back tires, let her know he was there. Then he tried to pass her.

And she slammed the door on him.

He tried again to pass. She slammed the door.

Again. Same result. It was like she knew where he was at every moment. In a kart with no mirrors. Wearing a helmet that allowed no peripheral vision. She *felt* him. She *knew*.

When he made his moves, she shut him down. Every single time.

Consider that she had a tremendous advantage, being only sixty pounds to his one hundred fifty. That's a huge weight differential in karting. Still. Consider that he was a thirty-year-old semiprofessional race car driver and she was a seven-year-old neophyte. Consider the possibilities.

She took the checker, God bless her little soul. She took the checker and beat her old man. And I was so happy. I was so happy that I didn't mind it when I had to wait in the car while they went into Andy's Diner for French fries and milk shakes.

How did Denny sustain himself for the duration of this ordeal? Here's how: He had a secret. His daughter was better and quicker and smarter than he was. And while the Evil Twins may have restricted his ability to see her, when he *was* allowed to see her, he received all the energy he needed to maintain his focus.

43

"This is not a conversation I like to have," Mark Fein said, leaning back on the iron chair until it groaned with fatigue. "It's one I have too often."

Spring, again. Victrola. Dark chocolate eyes.

I slept at my master's feet on the sidewalk of Fifteenth Avenue, which had been warmed by the sun like a cooking stone. Slept and sprawled, barely lifting my head to acknowledge the occasional petting I received from the passersby, all of whom, on some level, wanted to be more like me: able to enjoy a nap in the sun without guilt, without worry. Little did they know that, in fact, I was quite apprehensive, as I always was at our meetings with Mark.

"I'm ready," Denny said.

"Money."

Denny nodded to himself and sighed. "I've missed some invoices."

"You owe me a shitload, Dennis," Mark clarified. "I've been giving you slack, but I have to cut you off."

"Give me another thirty days of slack," Denny said.

"Can't do it, friend."

"Yes, you can," Denny said firmly. "Yes. You can."

Mark sucked on his latte.

"I have investigators. Lie detector specialists. Paralegals. Support staff. I have to pay these people."

"Mark," Denny said. "I'm asking you for a favor. Give me thirty days."

"You'll be paid in full?" Mark asked.

"Thirty days."

Mark finished his coffee drink and stood.

"Okay. Thirty days. Our next meeting is at Café Vita."

"Why Café Vita?" Denny asked.

"My dark chocolate eyes. They left for a richer roast. She's at Café Vita, so that's where our next meeting will be. As long as you pay your bill. Thirty days."

"I'll pay," Denny said. "You keep working."

44

The solution had been put to Denny by Mark Fein: if Denny were to quit his claim to Zoë, the criminal charges would vanish. That's what Mark Fein said. As simple as that.

Of course, that was speculation on his part. The Evil Twins didn't tell him that outright, but, drawing on his experience, Mark Fein knew. Because the mother of the girl was Trish's cousin, was part of it. And also because their lawyer had made it clear in the initial hearings that they did not wish for Denny to spend any time in jail for his offense. They simply wanted him to be registered as a sex offender. Sex offenders don't get custody of their little girls.

"They're very devious," Mark noted. "And they're very good."

"As good as you?" Denny wondered.

"No one is as good as me. But they're very good."

At one point Mark even counseled Denny that perhaps the best thing for Zoë would be to stay with her grandparents, as they were better able to provide for the comforts of her childhood, as well as pay for her college education, when that became necessary. Further, Mark suggested, were Denny not to be the principal caregiver for Zoë, he would be much more able to accept instructing and driving jobs out of state, as well as participate in racing series worldwide, if he so chose. He noted that a child needs a stable home environment, which, he said, could be best provided in a single housing location and with consistent schooling, preferably in the suburbs, or at a private school in an urban neighborhood. Mark assured Denny he would settle for nothing short of a liberal visitation schedule. He spent quite a long time convincing Denny of these truths.

I wasn't convinced. Of course, I understood that a race car driver must be selfish. Success at any endeavor on an elite level demands selfishness. But for Mark Fein to say Denny should put his own needs above the needs of his family because concurrent success in both fields was impossible was simply wrong. Many of us have convinced ourselves that compromise is necessary to achieve our goals, that all of our goals are not attainable so we should eliminate the extraneous, prioritize our desires, and accept less than the moon. But Denny refused to yield to that idea. He wanted his daughter and he wanted his racing career and he refused to give up one for the other.

Things change quickly on a racecourse. I remember watching one of Denny's races, when I had accompanied him to the track and was looked after by his crew. We watched near the start/finish line as, with one lap remaining, Denny was in third place, behind two other cars. They drove past us, and when they came back around for the checkered flag, Denny was by himself; he won the race. When asked how he had overtaken two cars on the final lap, he simply smiled and said that when he saw the starter wag one finger, meaning it was the last lap, he got a flash, and he said to himself, "I will win this race." One of the racers ahead of him spun off the track, the other locked up his wheels and gave Denny an easy opening to pass.

"It's never too late," Denny said to Mark. "Things change."

Very true. Things change quickly. And, as if to prove it, Denny sold our house.

We had no money left. They had sucked him dry. Mark had threatened to cease working for Denny's defense. There was little else Denny could do.

He rented a truck from U-Haul and called on his friends, and one weekend that summer, we moved all of our belongings from our house in the Central District to a one-bedroom apartment on Capitol Hill.

I loved our house. It was small, I know. Two bedrooms and one bathroom. And the yard was too small for a good running. And sometimes at night the buses on the street were too loud. But I had grown attached to my spot in the living room on the hardwood floor, which was very warm in the winter when the sun streamed in through the window. And I loved using my dog door, which Denny had installed for me so I could venture into the backyard at will. I would often go out on the back porch on a cold and rainy day when Denny was at work and sit and breathe and watch the movement of the tree branches and smell the rain.

But that was no more. That was gone. From that point forward, my days were spent in an apartment with carpeting that smelled of chemicals, insulated windows that didn't breathe properly, and a refrigerator that hummed too loudly and seemed to work too hard to keep the food cold. And no cable TV.

Still, I tried to make the best of it. If I squeezed myself into the corner between the arm of the sofa and the sliding glass door that opened onto a balcony that was too small to be considered a balcony at all, if I wedged myself just so, I could see past the building across the street and, through a narrow gap, I could see the Space Needle with its little bronze elevators that tirelessly whisked visitors from the ground to the sky and back again.

45

Denny paid his account with Mark Fein. Shortly afterward, Mark Fein was appointed to be a circuit judge, something about which I know little, except that it is a lifetime appointment, it is quite prestigious, and it is not refusable. Denny found a new lawyer who didn't meet at Café Vita or Victrola Coffee because he didn't care for young girls with eyebrow piercings and chocolate eyes. Whereas Mark Fein was a letter B, this new one was a letter L. Mr. Lawrence. Laconic, laid-back, lugubrious . . . Mark had spark and fire. This one had very large ears.

This one asked for a continuance, which is what you can do in the legal world if you need time to read all the paperwork. And while I understood it was necessary, I was still concerned. Mark Fein had carried himself with the energy of someone who had already won the game and was politely waiting for you to count the chips to discover your loss. Mr. Lawrence might have been very capable, but he carried himself more like a hound without a hunt: a let-me-know-when-you're-ready look on his sad face. And so while it had seemed like we were getting close to the reckoning, suddenly the horizon shot away from us and, again, we were waiting for the legal wheels to turn, which they did, but exceedingly slowly.

Shortly after Denny began working with our new representation, we received more bad news. The Evil Twins were suing Denny for child support.

Dastardly, is how Mark Fein had described them. So now, in addition to taking his child from him, they demanded he pay for the food they fed her?

Mr. Lawrence defended their action as a legitimate tactic, ruthless as it might be. He posed to Denny a question: "Does the end always justify the means?" And then, he answered it: "Apparently, for them, it does."

I have an imaginary friend. I call him King Karma. I know that karma is a force in this universe, and that people like the Evil Twins will receive karmic justice for their actions. I know that this justice will come when the universe deems it appropriate, and it may not be in this lifetime but in the next, or the one after that. The current consciousness of the Evil Twins may never feel the brunt of the karma they have incurred, though their souls absolutely will. I understand this concept.

But I don't like it. And so my imaginary friend does things for me. If you are mean to someone, King Karma will swoop out of the sky and call you names. If you kick someone, King Karma will bound from an alley and kick you back. If you are cruel and vicious, King Karma will administer a fitting punishment.

At night, before I sleep, I talk to my imaginary friend and I send him to the Evil Twins, and he exacts his justice. It may not be much, but it's what I can do. Every night, King Karma gives them very bad dreams in which they are chased mercilessly by a pack of wild dogs until they awaken with a start, unable to fall asleep again.

46

It was an especially difficult winter for me. Perhaps it was the stairs in our apartment building. Or maybe it was my genetic deficiency catching up to me. Or maybe I was just tired of being a dog.

I so longed to shed this body, to be free of it. I spent my lonely, joyless days watching the people who walked by on the street below, all going somewhere, all with important destinations. And me. Unable to unlock the door and go to greet them. And, even if I had been able to greet them, I had a dog's tongue and therefore would have been unable to speak to them. Unable to shake their hands. How I wanted to talk to these people! How I wanted to engage them in life! I wanted to participate, not just to observe; I wanted to judge the world around me, not merely be a supportive friend.

And, looking back, I can tell you it was my state of mind, it was my outlook on life, that attracted me to that car and attracted that car to me. That which we manifest is before us.

We walked back from Volunteer Park late in the night, extending our usual quick jaunt because of the special weather conditions. It was not too cold and not too warm, a gentle breeze blew, and snow fell from the sky. I was unsettled by the snow, I remember. Seattle is rain. Warm rain or cold rain, Seattle is rain. Seattle is not snow. There are far too many hills for Seattle to be able to tolerate snow. And yet there was snow.

Denny often allowed me to walk home from the park without my leash, and that night I strayed too far from him. I was watching the flakes fall and gather in a thin layer on the sidewalk and on the street, ahead on Tenth Avenue, which was devoid of both cars and people.

"Yo, Zo!" he called. He whistled for me, his sharp whistle.

I looked up. He was on the other side of Aloha. He must have crossed without my noticing.

"Come here, boy!"

He slapped his thigh and, feeling detached from him, feeling somehow like there was a world between us, not merely a two-lane road, I bounded toward him into the street.

He suddenly cried out, "No! Wait!"

The tires did not scream, as tires do. The ground was covered with a thin layer of snow. The tires hushed. They shushed. And then the car hit me.

So stupid, I thought. I am so stupid. I am the stupidest dog on the planet, and I have the audacity to dream of becoming a man? I am stupid.

"Settle down, boy."

His hands were on me. Warm.

"I didn't see—"

"I know."

"He shot out—"

"I totally understand. I saw the whole thing."

Denny lifted me. Denny held me.

"What can I do?"

"I'm several blocks from home. He's too heavy to carry. Will you drive me?"

"Sure, but—"

"You tried to stop. The street is snowy."

"I've never hit a dog before."

"You just clipped him."

"I'm totally freaking—"

"He's more scared than he is anything else."

"I've never hit—"

"What just happened isn't important," Denny said. "Let's think about what's going to happen next. Get in your car."

"Yeah," the boy said. He was just a boy. A teenager. "Where I should go?"

"Everything's fine," Denny said, sliding into the backseat with me on his lap. "Take a deep breath and let's drive."

47

Ayrton Senna did not have to die.

This came to me in a flash as I lay, whimpering in pain, in the backseat of Denny's car on the way to the animal hospital that night. It came to me: on the Grand Prix circuit in the town of Imola. In the Tamburello corner. Senna did not have to die. He could have walked away.

Saturday, the day before the race, Senna's friend and protégé Rubens Barrichello was seriously injured in an accident. Another driver, Roland Ratzenberger, was killed during a practice session. Senna was very upset about the safety conditions of the track. He spent Sunday, race morning, assembling the other drivers to form a new driver's safety group; Senna was elected the head of the group.

People say that he was so ambivalent about that race, the

San Marino Grand Prix, that he thought seriously of retiring as a driver on Sunday morning. He almost quit. He almost walked away.

But he did not walk away. He raced, that fateful first day of May in 1994. And when his car failed to turn in at the fabled Tamburello corner, a corner known for its excessive danger and speed, his car left the track at nearly one hundred ninety miles per hour and struck a concrete barrier; he was killed instantly by a piece of suspension that penetrated his helmet.

Or he died in the helicopter on the way to the hospital.

Or he died on the track, after they had pulled him out of the wreckage.

Enigmatic is Ayrton Senna, in death as well as in life.

To this day, there is still great controversy over his death. On-board camera footage mysteriously disappeared. Accounts of his death differed. The politics of the Fédération Internationale de l'Automobile came into play. It is true that, in Italy, if a driver dies while on the track, the death is investigated immediately and the race is stopped. It is true that, if a race were to be stopped in such a way, millions of dollars would be lost by the FIA, its sponsors, the track, television revenue, and so forth. Commerce would be affected. Whereas if that same driver were to die in a helicopter, for instance, en route to the hospital, the race could continue.

It is also true that the first man to reach Senna after that moment, Sidney Watkins, said: "We lifted him from the cockpit and laid him on the ground. As we did, he sighed and, although I am totally agnostic, I felt his soul departed at that moment."

What is the real truth regarding the death of Ayrton Senna, who was only thirty-four years old?

I know the truth, and I will tell you now:

He was admired, loved, cheered, honored, respected. In life as well as in death. A great man, he is. A great man, he was. A great man, he will be.

He died that day because his body had served its purpose. His soul had done what it came to do, learned what it came to learn, and then was free to leave. And I knew, as Denny sped me toward the doctor who would fix me, that if I had already accomplished what I set out to accomplish here on earth, if I had already learned what I was meant to learn, I would have left the curb one second later than I had, and I would have been killed instantly by that car.

But I was not killed. Because I was not finished. I still had work to do.

48

Separate entrances for cats and dogs. That's what I remember most. And still another entrance for infectious animals, which did not discriminate by genus. Apparently, dogs and cats are equal when they are infectious.

I remember the doctor painfully manipulating my hips. Then he gave me a shot and I was very much asleep.

When I awoke, I was still groggy, but no longer in pain. I heard snippets of conversation. Terms like "dysplasia," and "chronic arthritis," and "nondisplaced fracture of the pelvic bone." Others like "replacement surgery," and "salvage operation," "knitting," and "pain threshold," "calcification," and "fusing." And my favorite, "old."

Denny carried me to the lobby and laid me down on the brown carpeting, which was somehow comforting in the dim room. The assistant spoke to him and said more things that were confusing to me due to my drugged state. "X-ray." "Sedative." "Examination and diagnosis." "Cortisone injection." "Pain medications." "Nighttime emergency fee." And, of course, "Eight hundred twelve dollars."

Denny handed the assistant a credit card. He kneeled down and stroked my head.

"You'll be all right, Zo," he said. "You cracked your pelvis, but it will heal. You'll just take it easy for a while, and then you'll be good as new."

"Mr. Swift?"

Denny stood and returned to the counter.

"Your card has been declined."

Denny stiffened.

"That's not possible."

"Do you have another card?"

"Here."

They both watched the blue machine that took the cards, and a few moments later, the assistant shook his head.

"You've exceeded your limit."

Denny frowned and took out another card.

"Here's my ATM card. It will work."

They waited again. Same result.

"That's not right," Denny said. I could hear his breath quicken, his heart beat faster. "I just deposited my paycheck. Maybe it hasn't cleared yet."

The doctor appeared from the back.

"A problem?" he asked.

"Look, I have three hundred dollars from when I deposited my check, I took some of it out in cash. Here."

Denny fanned bills in front of the doctor.

"They must be holding the rest of the check or something, waiting for it to clear," Denny said, his voice sounding panicky. "I know I have money in that account. Or I can transfer some into it tomorrow morning from my savings."

"Relax, Denny," the doctor said. "I'm sure it's just a misunderstanding."

He said to the assistant, "Write Mr. Swift a receipt for the three hundred, and leave a note for Susan to run the card in the morning for the balance."

The assistant reached out and took Denny's cash. Denny watched closely as the young man wrote up the receipt.

"Could I keep twenty of it?" Denny asked hesitantly. I could see his lip quivering. He was exhausted and shaken and embarrassed. "I need to put some gas in my car."

The assistant looked to the doctor, who lowered his eyes and nodded silently and turned away, calling good night over his shoulder. The assistant handed Denny a twenty-dollar bill and a receipt, and Denny carried me to the car.

When we got home and Denny placed me on my bed, he sat in the dark room, lit only by the streetlamps outside, and he held his head in his hands for a long time.

"I can't," he said. "I can't keep going."

I looked up, and he was talking to me. He was looking at me.

"They won," he said. "You see?"

How could I respond? What could I say?

"I can't even afford to take care of you," he said to me. "I can't even afford gas for my car. I've got nothing left, Enzo. There's nothing left."

Oh, how I wished I could speak. How I wished for thumbs. I could have grabbed his shirt collar. I could have pulled him close to me, so close he could feel my breath on his skin, and I could have said to him, "This is just a crisis. A flash! A single match struck against the implacable darkness of time! You are the one who taught me to never give up. You taught me that new possibilities emerge for those who are prepared, for those who are ready. You have to believe!"

But I couldn't say that. I could only look at him.

"I tried," he said.

He said that because he couldn't hear me. Because he had not heard a word I'd just said. Because I am a dog.

"You are my witness," he said. "I tried."

If I could have stood on my hind legs. If I could have raised my hands and held him. If I could have spoken to him.

"I have not *witnessed*," I would have said. "I *am witnessing*!"

And he would have understood what I meant. And he would have realized.

But he could not hear me. Because I am what I am.

And so he returned his head to his hands and he sat.

I provided nothing.

He was alone.

49

Days later. A week. Two. I don't know. After Denny's deflation, time meant little to me; he looked sickly, he had no energy, no life force, and so neither did I. At a point when my hips still bothered me—not so long as to have healed, not so soon that the pain was acute—we went to visit Mike and Tony.

They didn't live far from us. Their house was small but reflected a different level of income; Tony had stood in the right place at the right time, Denny once told me, and would never have to worry about money again. Such is life. Such is manifesting. Your car goes where your eyes go.

We sat in their kitchen, Denny with a cup of tea and a manila folder before him. Tony wasn't present. Mike paced nervously.

"It's the right decision, Den," Mike said. "I totally support you."

Denny didn't move, didn't speak, just stared dully at the folder.

"This is your youth," Mike said. "This is your time. Principle is important, but so is your life. So is your reputation."

Denny nodded.

"Lawrence got what you wanted him to get, right?"

Denny nodded.

"Same visitation schedule but with two weeks in the summer and one week over Christmas break, and the February school break?" Mike asked.

Denny nodded.

"And you don't have to pay support anymore. They'll put her in a private school on Mercer Island. And they'll pay for her college education."

Denny nodded.

"And they'll settle for misdemeanor harassment and probation; no sex offense on your record."

Denny nodded.

"Denny," Mike said seriously, "you're a smart guy. One of the smartest guys I've ever met. Let me tell you, this is a smart decision. You know that, right?"

Denny looked confused for a moment, scanned the tabletop, checked his own hands.

"I need a pen," he said.

Mike reached behind him to the telephone table and picked up a pen. He handed it to Denny.

Denny hesitated, his hand poised over the documents in the folder. He looked up at Mike.

"I feel like they've sliced open my guts, Mike. Like they've sliced me open and cut out my intestines and I'll have to carry around a plastic shit-bag for the rest of my life. For the rest of my life, I'll have this plastic bag of shit tied to my waist and a hose, and whenever I empty my shit-bag into the toilet, I'll have to think about how they cut me open and gutted me and I just lay there with a dead smile on my face and said, 'Well, at least I'm not broke.'"

Mike seemed at a loss. "It's rough," he said.

"Yeah," Denny agreed. "It's rough. Nice pen."

Denny held up the pen. It was one of those souvenir pens with the sliding thing in the plastic top with the liquid.

"Woodland Park Zoo," Mike said.

I looked closer. The top of the pen. A little plastic savannah. The sliding thing? A zebra. When Denny tipped the pen, the zebra slid across the plastic savannah. The zebra is everywhere.

I suddenly realized. The zebra. It is not something outside of us. The zebra is something *inside* of us. Our fears. Our own self-destructive nature. The zebra is the worst part of us when we are face-to-face with our worst times. The demon is us!

Denny brought the tip of the pen to the paper and I could see the zebra sliding forward, inching toward the signature line, and I knew it wasn't Denny who was signing. It was the zebra! Denny would never give up his daughter for a few weeks of summer vacation and an exemption from child support payments!

I was an old dog. Recently hit by a car. And yet I mustered what I could, and the pain medication Denny had given me earlier helped with the rest. I pushed up onto his lap with my paws. I reached out with my teeth. And the next thing I knew, I was standing at the kitchen door with the papers in my mouth and both Mike and Denny staring at me, completely stunned.

"Enzo!" Denny commanded. "Drop it!"

I refused.

"Enzo! Drop!" he yelled.

I shook my head.

"Come here, boy!" Mike said.

I looked over at him; he was holding a banana. Playing good cop to Denny's bad cop. Which was totally unfair. He knew how much I loved bananas. But still, I refused.

"Enzo, get the hell over here!" Denny shouted, and he lunged at me.

I slipped away.

It was a low-speed chase, to be sure, my mobility being restricted as it was. But it was a chase nonetheless. One in which I feinted and dodged and slid and evaded the hands that grasped for my collar. I held them off.

I still had the papers, even when they cornered me in the living room. Even when they were about to catch me and wrest the papers from my jaws, I had a chance. I was trapped, I know. But Denny taught me that the race isn't over until the checker flies. I looked around and noticed that one of the windows was open. It wasn't open much, and there was a screen on it, but it was open, and that was enough.

Despite all of my pain, I lunged. With all of my might, I dove. I cleared the opening; I crashed into that screen and through it. And suddenly I was on the porch. I scurried into the backyard.

Mike and Denny flew out the back door, panting, and yet not pursuing. Instead, they seemed somewhat impressed by my feat.

"He dove," Mike said, breathless.

"Out the window," Denny finished for him.

Yes, I did. I dove.

"If we had a videotape of that, we could win ten thousand dollars on *America's Funniest Home Videos*," Mike said.

"Give me the papers, Enzo," Denny said.

I shook them vigorously in my mouth. Mike laughed at my refusal.

"It's not funny," Denny admonished.

"It's kind of funny," Mike replied in his defense.

"Give me the papers," Denny repeated.

I dropped the papers before me and pawed at them. I dug at them. I tried to bury them.

Again, Mike laughed.

Denny, however, was very angry; he glared at me.

"Enzo," he said. "I'm warning you."

What could I do? Had I not made myself clear? Had I not communicated my message? What else was there for me to do?

One thing only. I lifted my hind leg and I urinated on the papers.

Gestures are all that I have.

When they saw what I had done, they couldn't help themselves; they laughed. Denny and Mike. They laughed so hard. Denny laughed harder than I'd seen him laugh in years. Their faces turned red. They could barely breathe. They fell to their knees and laughed until they could laugh no more.

"Okay, Enzo," Denny said. "It's okay."

I went to him then, leaving the urine-soaked papers on the grass.

"Call Lawrence," Mike said to Denny. "He'll print them again and you can sign them."

Denny stood.

"No," he said, "I'm with Enzo. I piss on their settlement, too. I don't care how smart it is for me to sign it. I didn't do anything wrong, and I'm not giving up. I'm never giving up."

"They're going to be mad," Mike said with a sigh.

"Screw them," Denny said. "I'm going to win this thing or I'm going to run out of fuel on the last lap. But I'm not going to quit. I promised Zoë. I'm not going to quit."

When we got home, Denny gave me a bath and toweled me off. Afterward, he turned on the TV in the living room.

"What's your favorite?" he asked, looking at the shelf of videotapes he kept, all the races we loved to watch together. "Ah, here's one you like."

He started the tape. Ayrton Senna driving the Grand Prix of Monaco in 1984, slicing through the rain in pursuit of the race leader, Alain Prost. Senna would have won that race, had they not stopped it because of the conditions; when it rained, it never rained on Senna.

We watched the race together without pause, side by side, Denny and me.

50

The summer of my tenth birthday came along and there was a sense of balance to our lives, though none of completeness. We still spent alternate weekends with Zoë, who had grown so tall recently, and who never let a moment pass without questioning an assumption or challenging a theory or offering an insight that made Denny smile with pride.

My hips had healed poorly from my accident, but I was determined not to cost Denny any more money, as I had at the animal hospital that night. I pushed through the pain, which at times prevented me from sleeping through the nights. I tried my best to keep up with the pace of life; my mobility was severely limited and I couldn't gallop or canter, but I could still trot fairly well. I felt that I pulled off my end of it, as I sometimes heard people who knew my background comment on how frisky I looked or how dogs in general heal quickly, and easily adapt to their disabilities.

Money was still a constant struggle for us, since Denny had to give the Evil Twins a portion of his paycheck, and Mr. Lawrence, the levelheaded lawyer, always demanded that Denny's account be kept up to date. Fortunately, Denny's bosses were generous in allowing him to change his schedule frequently so he could attend his various meetings, and also so he could teach driving on certain days at Pacific Raceways, which was an easy way for Denny to make more money to pay for his defense.

Sometimes, on his driving school days, Denny would take me with him to the track, and while I was never allowed to ride with him, I did enjoy sitting in the stands and watching him teach. I became known as a bit of a track dog, and I especially liked trotting through the paddock, looking at the latest fashion in cars purchased by the rich young men and women whose bank accounts were fed with heaping piles of technology monies. From the nimble Lotus Exige to the classic Porsche to the more flamboyant Lamborghini, there was always something good to see.

On a hot day at the end of July, we were teaching, I remember, and while they were all out on the course, I watched as a beautiful red Ferrari F430 drove through the paddock and up to the school headquarters. A small, older man climbed out and the owner of the school, Don Kitch, came to meet him. They embraced and spoke for several minutes.

The man strolled to the bleachers to get a view of the track, and Don radioed to his corner workers to checker the session and bring in the students for lunch break.

As the drivers climbed out of their vehicles and the instructors gave them helpful comments and pointers, Don called for Denny, who approached, as did I, curious about what was going on.

"I need a favor," Don said to Denny.

And suddenly the small man with the Ferrari was with us.

"You remember Luca Pantoni, don't you?" Don asked. "We came to dinner at your place a couple of years ago."

"Of course," Denny said, shaking Luca's hand.

"Your wife cooked a delightful dinner," Luca said. "I remember it still. Please accept my sincere and heartfelt condolences."

When I heard him speak with his Italian accent, I recognized him immediately. The man from Ferrari.

"Thank you," Denny said quietly.

"Luca would like you to show him our track," Don said. "You can grab a sandwich between sessions, right? You don't need lunch."

"No problem," Denny said, pulling on his helmet and walking to the passenger side of the exquisite automobile.

"Mr. Swift," Luca called out. "Perhaps you would do me the favor of allowing me to be the passenger so that I may see more."

Surprised, Denny looked at Don.

"You want me to drive *this* car?" he asked. After all, the F430 is priced at nearly a quarter of a million dollars.

"I accept full liability," Luca said.

Don nodded.

"I'd be pleased to," Denny said, and he climbed into the cockpit.

It was an extremely beautiful car, and it was outfitted not for street use, but for the track, with ceramic brake rotors, one-piece FIA homologated racing seats and harnesses, a full roll cage, and, as I had suspected, F1-style paddle shifters. The two men strapped in and Denny pressed the electronic start button and the car fired to life.

Ah, what a sound. The whine of the fantastic engine layered over the throaty rumble of the massive exhaust. Denny flicked the paddle shifter and they cruised slowly through the paddock toward the track entrance.

I followed Don into the school classroom, where the students were clutching thick hunks of a giant sandwich, chewing and eating and laughing, their intense morning of track time having injected a week's worth of joy into their lives.

"If you drivers want to see something special," Don said, "grab your sandwiches and come out to the bleachers. There's a lunch session going on."

The Ferrari was the only car on the track, as the track was usually closed during the lunch hour. But this was a special occasion.

"What's going on?" one of the other instructors asked Don.

"Denny's got an audition," Don replied cryptically.

We all went out to the bleachers in time to see Denny come around turn 9 and streak down the straight.

"I figure it will take him three laps to learn the sequential shifter," Don said.

Sure enough, Denny started slowly, like he had driven with me back at Thunderhill. Oh, how I wished I could have traded places with Luca, that lucky dog! To be copilot to Denny in an F430 must be an amazing experience.

He was driving easy, but as he came around for the third time, there was a noticeable change to the car. It was no longer a car, it was a red blur. It no longer whined, it screamed as it shot down the straightaway so fast that the students laughed at each other as if someone had just told a dirty joke. Denny was laying down a hot lap.

A minute later, so fast one wondered if he had taken a shortcut, the Ferrari popped out of the cluster of trees at the exit of turn 7, cresting the rise until its suspension was totally extended, and then with a *pock-pock-pock* sound we heard the electronic clutch quickly downshift from sixth to third and we saw the ceramic brake rotors glow red between the spokes of the magnesium wheels, and then we heard the throttle open full and watched the car slam through the sweeping turn 8 as if it were a rocket sled, as if it were on rails, its hot rubber racing-compound tires grabbing the greasy pavement like Velcro, and then—*pock!*—shifting up and—*pock!*—blasting past us at turn 9 no more than two inches from the concrete barrier. The Doppler effect of the passing car converted its snarl into an angry growl, and off it rocketed—*pock!*—shifting again at the Kink and it was gone.

"Holy shit!" a student said.

I looked back at them, and their mouths were agape. We all were silent, and we could hear that sound—*pock, pock*—as Denny set himself up for turn 5A on the backside of the track, which we couldn't see but which we could imagine, given such wonderful sound effects, and again Denny careened past us at a million miles an hour.

"How close to the edge is he?" someone asked aloud.

Don smiled and shook his head.

"He's way past the edge," he said. "I'm sure Luca told him to show him what he could do, and that's what he's doing." Then he turned to the group and shouted: "DON'T YOU EVER DRIVE LIKE THAT! DENNY IS A PROFESSIONAL RACE CAR DRIVER AND THAT'S NOT HIS CAR! HE DOESN'T HAVE TO PAY FOR IT IF HE BREAKS IT!"

Lap after lap, around they went until we were dizzy and exhausted from watching them. And then the car slowed considerably—a cool-down lap—and pulled off into the paddock.

The entire class gathered around as Denny and Luca emerged from the burning hot vehicle. The students were abuzz; they touched the scalding glass window that shielded the magnificent power plant and exclaimed at the spectacular drive.

"Everyone into the classroom!" Don barked. "We'll go over corner notes from your morning sessions."

As they headed off, Don clasped Denny's shoulder firmly. "What was it like?"

"It was incredible," Denny said.

"Good for you. You deserve it."

Don went off to teach his class; Luca approached and extended his hand. In it was a business card.

"I would like you to work for me," Luca said with his thick accent.

I sat next to Denny, who reached down and scratched my ear out of habit.

"I appreciate that," Denny said. "But I don't think I'd make a very good car salesman."

"Neither do I," Luca said.

"But you're with Ferrari."

"Yes. I work in Maranello, at Ferrari headquarters. We have a wonderful track there."

"I see," Denny said. "So you'd like me to work . . . where?"

"At the track. There is some need, as often our clients would like track instruction in their new cars."

"Instructing?"

"There is some need. But mostly, you would be testing the vehicles."

Denny's eyes got extremely large and he sucked in a huge breath of air, as did I. Was this guy saying what we thought he was saying?

"In Italy," Denny said.

"Yes. You would be provided with an apartment for you and your daughter. And of course, a company car—a Fiat—as part of your compensation package."

"To live in Italy," Denny said. "And test-drive Ferraris."

"*Si.*"

Denny rolled his head around. He turned around in a circle, looked down at me, laughed.

"Why me?" Denny asked. "There are a thousand guys who can drive this car."

"Don Kitch tells me you are an exceptional driver in the wet weather."

"I am. But that can't be the reason."

"No," Luca said. "You are correct." He stared at Denny, his clear blue eyes smiling. "But I would prefer to tell you more about those reasons when you join me in Maranello, and I can invite you to my house for dinner."

Denny nodded and chewed his lip. He tapped Luca's business card against his thumbnail.

"I appreciate your generous offer," he said. "But I'm afraid certain things prevent me from leaving this country—or even this state—at the moment. So I have to decline."

"I know about your troubles," Luca said. "That is why I am here."

Denny looked up, surprised.

"I will keep the position available for you until your situation is resolved and you can make your decision free from the burden of circumstance. My telephone is on my card."

Luca smiled and shook Denny's hand again. He slipped into the Ferrari.

"I wish you would tell me why," Denny said.

Luca held up his finger.

"Dinner, at my home. You will understand."

He drove away.

Denny shook his head in bewilderment as the high-performance driving school students emerged from the classroom and headed for their cars. Don appeared.

"Well?" he asked.

"I don't understand," Denny said.

"He's taken an interest in your career since he first met you," Don said. "Whenever we talk, he asks how you're doing."

"Why does he care so much?" Denny asked.

"He wants to tell you himself. All I can say is that he respects how you're fighting for your daughter."

Denny thought for a moment.

"But what if I don't win?" he asked.

"There is no dishonor in losing the race," Don said. "There is only dishonor in not racing because you are afraid to lose." He paused. "Now get to your student, Grasshopper, and get the hell out on the track! That's where you belong!"

51

"You need to go out? Let's go out."

He was holding my leash. He wore his jeans and a light jacket for the fall chill. He lifted me to my unsteady feet and clipped on the leash. We went out into the darkness; I had fallen asleep early, but it was time for me to urinate.

I had been experiencing a decline in my health. I don't know if my accident the previous winter had knocked something loose in my plumbing, or if it was somehow associated with the medication that Denny gave me, but I had developed an inconvenient case of urinary incontinence. After even mild activity, I often slept deeply and awoke having soiled my bedding. It was usually only a few dribbles, though on occasion it was more extensive, and it was always horribly embarrassing.

I also was having great difficulty with my hips. Once I was up and moving, once I had warmed up my joints and ligaments, I felt fine and was able to move well. However, whenever I slept or lay in one spot for any amount of time, my hind joints locked in place, and I found it difficult to get them moving again, or even to rise to a standing position.

The net result of my health issues was that Denny could no longer leave me alone for an entire workday. He began visiting at lunchtime so he could take me out to relieve myself. He was very kind, and explained to me that he was doing it for himself: he was feeling stagnant, he said, and frustrated. The lawyers continued at their glacial pace, and there was nothing Denny could do to speed them along, so he looked at the short walk from his work to the apartment and back as a tonic; it allowed him a certain amount of cardiovascular exercise, yes, but it also gave him a purpose; a mission; something to do other than wait.

That evening—it was around ten, I knew, because *The Amazing Race* had just finished—Denny took me out. The night was bracing, and I enjoyed the feeling of wakefulness as I breathed in through my nostrils. The energy.

We crossed Pine Street and I saw people smoking outside the Cha Cha Lounge. I forced myself to ignore the urge to sniff the gutter. I refused to shove my nose into the butt of another dog making the rounds. And yet I urinated on the street like an animal because that was the only alternative I was afforded. To be a dog.

We walked down Pine toward the city, and then she was there.

Both of us stopped. We held our breaths. Two young women at an outdoor table at Bauhaus Books and Coffee, and one of them was Annika.

Temptress! Seducer! Vixen!

How awful for us to have to see this horrid girl. I wanted to leap at her and take her nose in my teeth and twist! How I hated this young girl who attacked my Denny with her unrestrained sexuality and then blamed him for the attack. How I despised she who would rend this family because of her own agenda. A woman scorned, indeed! Kate Hepburn would smash her with a single blow and laugh while doing it. How my anger burned.

At Bauhaus, she sat at an outdoor table with another girl. At this hip and cool coffee shop in *our* neighborhood, she sat drinking coffee and smoking cigarettes! She was at least seventeen by now, possibly eighteen, and was legally allowed to function in society on her own. Technically, she could sit at any coffee shop in any city and stew in her wretchedness. I couldn't stop her. But I didn't have to deal with her—immature finger pointer, inflicter of wounds!

I thought we would cross the street to avoid a confrontation, but instead, we headed straight for her. I didn't understand. Perhaps Denny hadn't seen her. Perhaps he didn't know?

But I knew, and so I resisted. I set my weight, I ducked my head.

"Come on, boy," Denny ordered me. He tugged at my leash.

I refused.

"With me!" he snapped.

No! I would not go with him!

And then he leaned down. He kneeled and held my muzzle and looked me in the eyes.

"I see her, too," he said. "Let's handle this with dignity."

He released my muzzle.

"This can work *for* us, Zo. I want you to go up to her and love her more than you've ever loved anyone before."

I didn't understand his strategy, but I acquiesced. After all, he had the leash.

As we drew abreast of her table, Denny stopped and looked surprised.

"Oh, hey!" he said brightly.

Annika looked up, feigning shock, clearly having seen us, but hoping there would be no interaction.

"Denny. Good to see you!"

I played my part. I greeted her enthusiastically, I nuzzled her, I pushed my nose into her leg, I sat and looked at her with great anticipation, which is something people find very appealing. But inside, I was churning. Her facial makeup. Her hair. Her tight sweater and heaving bosom. Yuck.

"Enzo!" she said.

"Hey," Denny said, "can we talk for a minute?"

Annika's friend started to get up.

"I'll go get more coffee," she said.

"No," Denny stopped her with a wave of his hand. "Please stay."

She hesitated.

"It's important that you witness that there is no impropriety taken here," Denny explained. "If you leave, I'll have to leave."

The girl looked to Annika, who nodded her agreement.

"Annika," Denny said.

"Denny."

He pulled up a chair from the next table, which was empty. He sat down next to her.

"I totally understand what's going on," he said.

Which was strange, because I certainly didn't. I didn't understand it at all. She had attacked him. She then accused him of attacking her and because of that we only got to see Zoë on certain days of the week. Why we were speaking with her rather than roasting her on a spit was unfathomable to me.

"I may have given you signals," he said. "That's totally my fault. But just because the light is green doesn't mean you shouldn't look both ways before stepping into the street."

Annika screwed up her face in puzzlement and looked to her friend.

"A metaphor," her friend said.

Ha! A metaphor, she said! Fantastic! This one knows how to decode the English language! We will save her for roasting tomorrow!

"I should have handled the situation entirely differently," Denny said. "I haven't had the chance to say this to you because we've been kept apart, but I made all the mistakes.

It's all my fault; you did nothing wrong. You're an attractive woman, and I understand my noting that attractiveness— even to myself—may have signaled to you that I was available. But, you know, I wasn't available. I was married to Eve. And you were far too young."

Annika dipped her head at the mention of Eve.

"Maybe I even thought of you as Eve for a minute," Denny said. "And maybe I looked at you like I used to look at Eve. But, Annika, while I understand how angry you must be, I wonder if you understand what's going on, what the fallout is. They won't let me have my daughter. Do you realize that?"

Annika looked up at him and shrugged.

"They want me to be registered as a sex offender, and that will mean that I will always have to register with the police, wherever I live. And I will never be able to see my daughter again without supervision. Did they tell you about that?"

"They said . . ." she said softly, but didn't finish.

"Annika, when I saw Eve for the first time, I couldn't breathe. I couldn't walk. I felt if she were out of my sight for a moment, I might wake up from a dream and find her gone. My entire world revolved around her."

He paused, and none of us said anything for a moment. A crowd of people emerged from a restaurant across the street and said their good-byes loudly and with much laughter, kissing and hugging before they went their separate ways.

"It never could have worked between you and me. There are a million reasons. My daughter, my age, your age, Eve. In a different time, in a different place? Maybe. But not now. Not three years ago. You're a wonderful woman, and I know that you will find the right partner and you will be very happy for the rest of your life."

She looked up at him, and her eyes were so big.

"I'm very sorry that it won't be me, Annika," he said. "But one day you will find someone who stops the world for you as Eve stopped the world for me. I promise you."

She looked deeply into her latte.

"Zoë's my daughter," he said. "I love her like your father loves you. Please, Annika, don't take her away from me."

Annika didn't look up from her coffee, but I glanced at her friend. Tears hung on her lower lids.

We paused a moment, and then we turned and walked away briskly, and Denny's gait seemed lighter than it had been for years.

"I think she heard me," he said.

I thought so, too, but how could I respond? I barked twice.

He looked at me and laughed.

"Faster?" he asked.

I barked twice again.

"Faster, then," he said. "Let's go!" And we trotted the rest of the way home.

52

The couple who stood in the doorway were entirely foreign to me. They were old and frail. They wore threadbare clothing. They toted old fabric suitcases that bulged awkwardly. They smelled of mothballs and coffee.

Denny embraced the woman and kissed her cheek. He picked up her bag with one hand and shook the man's hand with the other. They shuffled into the apartment and Denny took their coats.

"Your room is in here," he said to them, carrying their bags into the bedroom. "I'll sleep on the sofa."

Neither of them said a word. He was bald except for a crescent of stringy black hair. His skull was long and narrow. His eyes were sunken like his cheeks; his face was covered with a gray bristle that looked painful. The woman had white hair that was quite thin and left most of her scalp visible. She wore sunglasses, even in the apartment, and she often stood completely still and waited until the man was next to her before she moved.

She whispered into the man's ear.

"Your mother would like to use the washroom," the man said.

"I'll show her," Denny said. He stood next to the woman and held out his arm.

"*I'll* show her," the man said.

The woman took the man's arm, and he led her toward the hall where the bathroom was.

"The light switch is hidden behind the hand towel," Denny said.

"She doesn't need a light switch," the man said.

As they went into the bathroom, Denny turned away and rubbed his face with the palms of his hands.

"Good to see you," he said into his hands. "It's been so long."

53

Had I known I was meeting Denny's parents, I might have acted more receptive to these strangers. I had been given no advance notice, no warning, and so my surprise was completely justified. Still, I would have preferred to greet them like family.

They stayed with us for three days, and they hardly left the apartment. For the afternoon on one of those days, Denny retrieved Zoë, who was so pretty with her hair in ribbons and a nice dress, and who had obviously been coached by Denny, as she willingly sat for quite a long time on the couch and allowed Denny's mother to explore the terrain of her face with her hands. Tears ran down Denny's mother's cheeks during the entire encounter, raindrops spotting Zoë's flower-print dress.

Our meals were prepared by Denny, and were simple in nature: broiled steaks, steamed string beans, boiled potatoes. They were eaten in silence. The fact that three people could occupy such a small apartment and speak so few words was quite strange to me.

Denny's father lost some of his gruff edge while he was with us, and he even smiled at Denny a few times. Once, in the silence of the apartment, while I sat in my corner watching the Space Needle elevators, he came and stood behind me.

"What do you see, boy?" he asked quietly, and he touched the crown of my head and his fingers scratched at my ears just the way Denny does. How the touch of a son is so like the touch of his father.

I looked back at him.

"You take good care of him," he said.

And I couldn't tell if he was talking to me or to Denny. And if he was talking to me, did he mean it as a command or as an acknowledgment? The human language, as precise as it is with its thousands of words, can still be so wonderfully vague.

On the last night of their visit, Denny's father handed Denny an envelope.

"Open it," he said.

Denny did as instructed, and looked at the contents.

"Where the hell did this come from?" he asked.

"It came from us," his father replied.

"You don't have any money."

"We have a house. We have a farm."

"You can't sell your house!" Denny exclaimed.

"We didn't," his father said. "They call it a reverse mortgage. The bank will get our house when we die, but we thought you needed the money now more than you would later, so."

Denny looked up at his father, who was quite tall and very thin; his clothes draped on him like clothes on a scarecrow.

"Dad—" Denny started, but his eyes filled with tears and he could only shake his head. His father reached for him and embraced him, held him close and stroked his hair with long fingers and fingernails that had large, pale half-moons near the quick.

"We never did right by you," his father said. "We never did right. This makes it right."

They left the next morning. Like the last strong autumn wind that rattles the trees until the remaining leaves fall, brief but powerful was their visit, signaling that the season had changed, and soon, life would begin again.

54

A driver must have faith. In his talent, his judgment, the judgment of those around him, physics. A driver must have faith in his crew, his car, his tires, his brakes, himself.

The apex sets up wrong. He is forced off his usual line. He carries too much speed. His tires have lost grip. The track has gotten greasy. And he suddenly finds himself at turn exit with no more track and too much speed.

As the gravel trap rushes at him, the driver must make decisions that will impact his race, his future. To tuck in would be devastating: wrenching the front wheels against their nature will only spin the car. To lift is equally bad, taking grip away from the rear of the car. What is to be done?

The driver must accept his fate. He must accept the fact that mistakes have been made. Misjudgments. Poor decisions. A confluence of circumstance has landed him in this position. A driver must accept it all and be willing to pay the price for it. He must go off-track.

To dump two wheels. Even four. It's an awful feeling, both as a driver and as a competitor. The gravel that kicks up against the undercarriage. The feeling of swimming in muck. While his wheels are off the track, other drivers are passing him. They are taking his spot, continuing at speed. Only he is slowing down.

At this moment, a driver feels a tremendous crisis. He *must* get back on the gas. He *must* get back on the track.

Oh! The folly!

Consider the drivers who have been taken out of races by snapping their steering wheels, by overcorrecting to extremes and spinning their cars in front of their competitors. A terrible position to find oneself in—

A winner, a champion, will accept his fate. He will continue with his wheels in the dirt. He will do his best to maintain his line and gradually get himself back on the track when it is safe to do so. Yes, he loses a few places in the race. Yes, he is at a disadvantage. But he is still racing. He is still alive.

The race is long. It is better to drive within oneself and finish the race behind the others than it is to drive too hard and crash.

55

So much information came out in the following days, thanks to Mike, who plagued Denny with questions until he answered. About his mother's blindness, which came on when Denny was a boy; he cared for her until he left home after high school. About how his father told Denny that if he didn't stay to help with the farm and his mother, he shouldn't bother keeping in touch at all. About how Denny called every Christmas for years until his mother finally answered the phone and listened without speaking. For years, until she finally asked how he was doing and if he was happy.

I learned that his parents had not paid for the testing program in France, as Denny had claimed; he paid for that with a home equity loan. I learned that his parents had not contributed to the sponsorship of the touring car season, as

Denny had said; he paid for that with a second mortgage, which Eve had encouraged.

Always pushing the extremes. Finding himself broke. And finding himself on the telephone with his blind mother, asking her for some kind of help, any kind of help, so that he could keep his daughter; and her response that she would give him everything if only she could meet her grandchild. Her hands on Zoë's hopeful face; her tears on Zoë's dress.

"Such a sad story," Mike said, pouring himself another shot of tequila.

"Actually," Denny said, examining his can of Diet Coke, "I believe it has a happy ending."

56

"All rise," the bailiff called out, such old-fashioned formality in such a contemporary setting. The new Seattle courthouse: glass walls and metal beams jutting out at all angles, concrete floors and stairs with rubber treads, and all of it lit by a strange, bluish light.

"The Honorable Judge Van Tighem."

An elderly man, clad in a black robe, strode into the room. He was short and wide, and he had a wave of gray hair swept to one side of his head. His dark, bushy eyebrows hung over his small eyes like hairy caterpillars; he spoke with an Irish lilt.

"Sit," he commanded. "Let us begin."

* * *

Thus, the trial commenced. At least in my mind. I won't give you all the details because I don't know them. I wasn't there because I am a dog, and dogs are not allowed in court. The only impressions I have of the trial are the fantastic images and scenes I invented in my dreams. The only facts I know are the ones I gathered from Denny's retelling of events; my only idea of a courtroom, as I have said before, is what I learned from watching my favorite movies and television shows. I pieced together those days as one conjures a partially completed jigsaw puzzle—the frame is finished, the corners filled in, but handfuls of the heart and belly are missing.

The first day of the trial was devoted to pretrial motions, the second to jury selection. Denny and Mike didn't talk much about those events, so I assume everything went as expected. Both days, Tony and Mike arrived at our apartment early in the morning; Mike escorted Denny to court while Tony stayed behind to look after me.

Tony and I didn't do much with our time together. We sat and read the paper, or went for short walks, or ventured to Bauhaus so he could check his e-mail on their free wi-fi network. I liked Tony, despite the fact that he had washed my dog years earlier. Or maybe because he had. That dog, poor thing, finally went the way of all flesh and fell to threads and was tossed into the trash bin without ceremony, without eulogy. "My dog," was all I could think to say. My dog. And I watched Denny drop it into the bin and close the drawer, and that was that.

On the third morning, there was a definite change in the air when Tony and Mike arrived. There was much more tension, fewer banal pleasantries, no one-liners. It was the day the case was to begin in earnest, and we were all filled with trepidation. Denny's future was at stake, and it was no laughing matter.

Apparently, I later learned, Mr. Lawrence delivered an impassioned opening statement. He agreed with the prosecution's assertion that sexual molestation is about power, but he pointed out that baseless allegation is an equally destructive weapon, and is just as much about power. And he pledged to prove Denny innocent of the charges against him.

The prosecution led off their case with a parade of witnesses, all of whom had stayed with us that week in Winthrop, each of them testifying to Denny's inappropriate flirtatious manner and his predator-like stalking of Annika. Yes, they agreed, she was playing the game with him, but she was a child! ("As was Lolita!" Spencer Tracy might have shouted.) Denny was an intelligent, strong, good-looking man, the witnesses said, and should have known better. One by one, they depicted a world in which Denny maneuvered sneakily in order to be with Annika, to brush against her, to hold her hand illicitly. Each convincing witness was followed by another even more convincing, and another after that. Until, finally, the alleged victim herself was called to take the stand.

Wearing a subdued skirt and high-collared blouse, her

hair pinned back and eyes downcast, Annika proceeded to catalog every look, glance, and breath, every incidental touch and near miss. She admitted that she was a willing—even eager—accomplice, but insisted that, as a child, she had no idea what she was getting herself into. Visibly upset, she spoke about how the entire episode had tormented her ever since.

Tormented her in what way, I would have asked, by her innocence, or by her guilt? But I wasn't there to pose the question. By the time Annika's direct examination was finished, not a person in the courtroom, save Denny himself, was absolutely certain that he had not taken liberties with her that week. And even Denny's confidence in himself was shaken.

Early that afternoon—it was Wednesday—the weather was oppressive. The clouds were heavy, but the sky refused to rain. Tony and I walked down to Bauhaus so he could get his coffee. We sat outside and stared at the traffic on Pine Street until my mind shut down and I lost track of time.

"Enzo—"

I raised my head. Tony pocketed his cell phone.

"That was Mike. The prosecutor asked for a special recess. Something's going on."

He paused, waiting for my response. I said nothing.

"What should we do?" he asked.

I barked twice. We should go.

Tony closed up his computer and got his bag together. We hurried down Pine and across the freeway overpass. He was moving very quickly, and I had a hard time keeping up. When he felt the leash go taut, he looked back at me and slowed. "We have to hurry if we want to catch them," he said. I wanted to catch them, too. But my hips ached so. We hustled past the Paramount Theater to Fifth Avenue. We rushed south, zigzagging from Walk to Don't Walk signals until we reached the plaza before the courthouse on Third Avenue.

Mike and Denny were not there. Only a small cluster of people in one corner of the plaza, speaking urgently, gesturing with agitation. We started toward them. Perhaps they knew what was going on. But at that moment, the rain began to fall. The group immediately disbanded, and I saw Annika among them. Her face was drawn and pale; she was crying. When she saw me, she winced, turned away quickly, and vanished into the building.

Why was she so upset? I didn't know, but it made me very nervous. What could be going on inside that building, in the dark chambers of justice? What might she have said to further incriminate Denny and destroy his life? How I prayed for some kind of intervention, for the spirit of Gregory Peck or Jimmy Stewart or Raul Julia to descend on the plaza and lead us to the truth. For Paul Newman or Denzel Washington to step out of a passing bus and deliver a rousing speech that would set everything right.

Tony and I took refuge underneath an awning; we stood tensely. Something was going on, and I didn't know what it was. I wished that I could have injected myself into the process, snuck into the courtroom, leapt on a table, and made my voice heard. But my participation was not part of the plan.

"It's done now," Tony said. "We can't change what's already been decided."

Can't we? I wondered. Even just a little? Can we not will ourselves to achieve the impossible? Can we not use the power of our life force to change something: one small thing, one insignificant moment, one breath, one gesture? Is there nothing we can do to change what is around us?

My legs were so heavy I could no longer stand; I lay on the wet concrete, and I fell into an unsteady sleep filled with very strange dreams.

"Ladies and gentlemen of the jury," Mr. Lawrence said, *standing before the jury box. "It is important to note that the case put forth by the prosecution is entirely circumstantial. There is no evidence whatsoever of violation. The truth of what really happened that night is known by two people alone. Two people, and a dog."*

"A dog?" the judge asked incredulously.

"Yes, Judge Van Tighem," Mr. Lawrence said, stepping forth boldly. "The entire event was witnessed by the defendant's dog. I call to the stand Enzo!"

"I object!" the prosecutor barked.

"Sustained," the judge said. "For the time being."

He produced a large volume from beneath his desk and paged through it at length, reading many passages.

"Does this dog speak?" the judge asked Mr. Lawrence, his head still buried in the book.

"With the help of a voice synthesizer," Mr. Lawrence said, "yes, the dog speaks."

"I object!" the prosecutor piped in.

"Not yet," the judge said. "Tell me about this device, Mr. Lawrence."

"We've borrowed a special voice synthesizer that was developed for Stephen Hawking," Mr. Lawrence continued. "By reading the electrical pulses of the inner brain—"

"Enough! You had me at 'Stephen Hawking'!"

"With this device, the dog can speak," Mr. Lawrence said.

The judge clapped shut his massive tome.

"Objection overruled. Let's have him, then, this dog! Let's have him!"

The room was filled with hundreds of people, and I was sitting on the witness stand, strapped to Stephen Hawking's voice simulator; the judge swore me in.

"Do you swear to tell the truth, the whole truth, and nothing but the truth, so help you God?"

"I do," I said in my scratchy, metallic voice, which was not at all as I had imagined. I had always hoped I would sound more commanding and present, like James Earl Jones.

"Mr. Lawrence," the judge said, astonished. "Your witness."

"Enzo," Mr. Lawrence said, "you were present for the alleged molestation?"

"I was," I said.

Suddenly there was silence in the gallery. Suddenly no one dared to speak, to titter, or even to breathe. I was talking, and they were listening.

"Tell us in your own words what you witnessed in Mr. Swift's bedroom that night."

"I will tell you," I said. "But first, with permission, I would like to address the court."

"You may," the judge said.

"Inside each of us resides the truth," I began, "the absolute truth. But sometimes the truth is hidden in a hall of mirrors. Sometimes we believe we are viewing the real thing, when in fact we are viewing a facsimile, a distortion. As I listen to this trial, I am reminded of the climactic scene of a James Bond film, The Man with the Golden Gun. James Bond escaped his hall of mirrors by breaking the glass, shattering the illusions, until only the true villain stood before him. We, too, must shatter the mirrors. We must look into ourselves and root out the distortions until that thing which we know in our hearts is perfect and true, stands before us. Only then will justice be served."

I looked over the faces in the room and saw each of them considering my words, nodding appreciatively.

"Nothing happened between them," I said, finally. "Nothing at all."

"But we've heard so much of these accusations," Mr. Lawrence said.

"Your Honor"—I raised my voice—"Ladies and gentlemen of the jury, I assure you that my master, Dennis Swift, in no way acted inappropriately around this young lady, Annika. It was clear to me that she loved him more than anything in the world, and she offered herself to him. He declined her offer. After driving us over a harrowing mountain pass, after exhausting himself, draining himself of all physical energy in order to deliver us safely home, Denny is guilty only of falling asleep. Annika, this girl, this woman, as unaware of the ramifications of her actions as she might have been, assaulted my Denny."

A murmur rose from the gallery.

"Miss Annika, is this true?" the judge demanded.

"It is true," Annika replied.

"Do you disavow these accusations?" Van Tighem asked.

"I do," she cried. "I'm so sorry for the pain I've put you all through. I disavow!"

"This is a stunning revelation!" Van Tighem announced. "Enzo the dog has spoken! The truth is known. This case is dismissed. Mr. Swift is free to go, and he is awarded custody of his daughter."

I leapt from the witness stand and embraced Denny and Zoë. At last, we were a family, together again.

* * *

"It's over."

My master's voice.

I opened my eyes. Denny was flanked by Mike and Mr. Lawrence, who held a very large umbrella. How much time had passed, I didn't know. But Tony and I were both very wet from the rain.

"That recess was the longest forty-five minutes of my life," Denny said.

I waited for his answer.

"She recanted," he said. "They dropped the charges."

He fought it, I know, but it was hard for him to breathe.

"They dropped the charges, and I'm free."

Denny might have been able to hold it off if we had been alone, but Mike wrapped him in a hug, and Denny unleashed the years of tears that had been dammed behind mud and determination and the ability to always find another finger to stick in the leaking dike. He cried so hard.

"Thank you, Mr. Lawrence," Tony said, shaking Mr. Lawrence's hand. "You did a fantastic job."

Mr. Lawrence smiled, perhaps for the first time in his life.

"They had no physical evidence," he said. "All they had was Annika's testimony. I could tell, on direct, she was wavering—there was something more she wanted to say—so I went after her on cross, and she broke down. She said that up until now she'd been telling people what she had *hoped* might have happened. Today, she admitted that nothing happened at all. Without her testimony, it would have been foolish for the prosecutor to move forward with the case."

Is that what she testified? I wondered where she was, what she was thinking. I glanced around the plaza and spotted her leaving the courthouse with her family. She seemed somehow fragile.

She looked over and saw us. She was not a bad person, I knew then. One can never be angry at another driver for a track incident. One can only be upset at himself for being caught in the wrong place at the wrong time.

She gave a quick wave meant for Denny, but I was the only one who saw because I was the only one looking. So I barked to let her know.

"You've got a good master, there," Tony said to me, his attention still on our immediate circle.

He was right. I have the best master.

I watched Denny as he held on to Mike and swayed back and forth, feeling the relief, the release, knowing that another path might have been easier for him to travel, but that it couldn't possibly have offered a more satisfying conclusion.

57

The very next day, Mr. Lawrence informed Denny that the Evil Twins had dropped their custody suit. Zoë was his. The Twins had requested forty-eight hours to assemble her belongings and spend a little more time with her before delivering her to Denny, but he was under no obligation to agree.

Denny could have been mean. He could have been spiteful. They took years of his life, they took all of his money, they robbed him of work, they tried to destroy him. But Denny is a gentleman. Denny has compassion for his fellow man. He granted them their request.

He was baking cookies last night in anticipation of Zoë's return, making the batter from scratch like he used to do, when the phone rang. Since his hands were covered with sticky oatmeal goop, he tapped the speaker button on the kitchen phone.

"You're on the air!" he said brightly. "Thanks for calling. What's on your mind?"

There was a long pause filled with static.

"I'm calling for Dennis Swift."

"This is Denny," Denny called from his cookie bowl. "How can I help you?"

"This is Luca Pantoni, returning your call. From Maranello. Am I catching you at a bad time?"

Denny's eyebrows shot up, he smiled at me.

"Luca! *Grazie*, for returning my call. I'm making cookies so I have you on the speakerphone. I hope you don't mind."

"No problem."

"Luca, the reason I called . . . The issues that were keeping me in the States have been resolved."

"I can tell by the tone of your voice they were resolved to your satisfaction," Luca observed.

"Very much so," Denny said. "Yes, indeed. I was wondering if the position you offered me earlier was still available?"

"Of course."

"My daughter and I—and my dog, Enzo—would very much like to join you for dinner in Maranello, then."

"Your dog is named Enzo? How propitious!"

"He is a race car driver at heart," Denny said, and he

smiled at me. I love Denny so much. I know everything about him, and yet he always surprises me. He called Luca!

"I look forward to meeting your daughter and to seeing Enzo again," Luca said. "I will have my assistant make the arrangements. It will be necessary to retain your services under contract. I hope you understand. The nature of our business, as well as the expense of developing a test driver—"

"I understand," Denny replied, plopping oatmeal and raisins onto the cookie sheet.

"You do not object to a three-year commitment?" Luca asked. "Your daughter will not mind living here? There is an American school, if she would prefer it to our Italian schools."

"She told me she wants to try the Italian school," Denny said. "We'll have to see how it goes. Either way, she knows it will be a great adventure, and she's very excited. She's been studying a children's book I gave her that teaches some simple Italian phrases. She says she feels confident ordering pizza in Maranello, and she loves pizza."

"*Bene!* I love pizza, too! I like the way your daughter thinks, Denny. I am so pleased I can be a part of your fresh start."

Denny plopped more cookies, almost as if he had forgotten about the telephone call.

"My assistant will be in touch with you, Denny. We will expect to see you in a few weeks."

"Yes, Luca, thank you." *Plop, plop.* "Luca."

"*Si?*"

"Now will you tell me why?" Denny asked.

Another long pause.

"I would prefer to tell you—"

"Yes, I know, Luca. I know. But it would help me so much if you could see your way to telling me now. For my own peace of mind."

"I understand your need," Luca said. "I will tell you. Many years ago, when my wife passed away, I almost died from grief."

"I'm sorry," Denny said, no longer working the cookie batter, simply listening.

"Thank you," Luca said. "It took me a long time to know how to respond to people offering their condolences. Such a simple thing, yet filled with much pain. I'm sure you understand."

"I do," Denny said.

"I *would* have died from grief, Denny, if I had not received help, if I had not found a mentor who offered me his hand. Do you understand? My predecessor at this company offered me a job driving cars for him. He saved my life, not merely for me, but for my children as well. This man passed away recently—he was very old—but still, sometimes I see his face, I hear his voice, and I remember him. What he offered me is not for me to keep, but for me to give to another. That is why I feel very fortunate that I am able to offer my hand to you."

Denny stared at the phone as if he could see Luca in it.

"Thank you, Luca, for your hand, and for telling me why you have offered it."

"My friend," Luca said, "the pleasure is entirely mine. Welcome to Ferrari. I assure you, you will not want to leave."

They said their good-byes, and Denny pressed the button with his pinkie. He crouched down and held out his sticky hands for me, and I obligingly licked them clean.

"Sometimes I believe," he said to me as I indulged in the sweetness of his hands, of his fingers, of his opposable thumbs. "Sometimes I really do believe."

58

The dawn breaks gently on the horizon and spills its light over the land. My life seems like it has been so long and so short at the same time. People speak of a will to live. They rarely speak of a will to die. Because people are afraid of death. Death is dark and unknown and frightening. But not for me. It is not the end.

I can hear Denny in the kitchen. I can smell what he's doing; he's cooking breakfast, something he used to do all the time when we were a family, when Eve was with us and Zoë. For a long time they have been gone, and Denny has eaten cereal.

With every bit of strength I have in my body, I wrench myself to a standing position. Though my hips are frozen and my legs burn with pain, I hobble to the door of the bedroom.

Growing old is a pathetic thing. It is full of limitations and reduction. It happens to us all, I know; but I think that it might not have to. I think it happens to those of us who request it. And in our current mind-set, our collective ennui, it is what we have chosen to do. But one day a mutant child will be born who refuses to age, who refuses to acknowledge the limitations of these bodies of ours, who lives in health until he is done with life, not until his body no longer supports him. He will live for hundreds of years, like Noah. Like Moses. This child's genes will be passed to his offspring, and more like him will follow. And their genetic makeup will supplant the genes of those of us who need to grow old and decay before we die. I believe that one day it will come to pass; however, such a world is beyond my purview.

"Yo, Zo!" he calls to me when he sees me. "How are you feeling?"

"Like shit," I reply. But, of course, he doesn't hear me.

"I made you pancakes," he says, cheerfully.

I force myself to wag my tail, and I really shouldn't have, because the wagging jostles my bladder and I feel warm droplets of urine splash my feet.

"It's okay, boy," he says. "I've got it."

He cleans up my mess and tears me a piece of pancake. I take it in my mouth, but I can't chew it, I can't taste it. It sits on my tongue limply until it finally falls out of my mouth and onto the floor. I think Denny notices, but he doesn't say anything; he keeps flipping the pancakes, setting them on the rack to cool.

I don't want Denny to worry about me. I don't want to force him to take me on a one-way visit to the vet. He loves me so much. The worst thing I could possibly do to Denny is make him hurt me. The concept of euthanasia has some merit, yes, but it is too fraught with emotion. I much prefer the idea of assisted suicide, which was developed by the inspired physician Dr. Kevorkian. It's a machine that allows an ailing elder to push a button and take responsibility for his own death. There is nothing passive about the suicide machine. A big red button. Press it or don't. It is a button of absolution.

My will to die. Perhaps, when I am a man, I will invent a suicide machine for dogs.

When I return to this world, I will be a man. I will walk among you. I will lick my lips with my small, dexterous tongue. I will shake hands with other men, grasping firmly with my opposable thumbs. And I will teach people all that I know. And when I see a man or a woman or a child in trouble, I will extend my hand, both metaphorically and physically. I will offer my hand. To him. To her. To you. To the world. I will be a good citizen, a good partner in the endeavor of life that we all share.

I go to Denny, and I push my muzzle into his thigh.

"There's my Enzo," he says.

And he reaches down out of instinct; we've been together

so long, he touches the crown of my head, and his fingers scratch at the crease of my ears. The touch of a man.

My legs buckle and I fall.

"Zo?"

He is alarmed. He crouches over me.

"Are you okay?"

I am fine. I am wonderful. I am. I am.

"Zo?"

He turns off the fire under the frying pan. He places his hand over my heart. The beating that he feels, if he feels anything at all, is not strong.

In the past few days, everything has changed. He is going to be reunited with Zoë. I would like to see that moment. They are going to Italy together. To Maranello. They will live in an apartment in the small town, and they will drive a Fiat. Denny will be a wonderful driver for Ferrari. I can see him, already an expert on the track because he is so quick, so smart. They will see his talent and they will pluck him from the ranks of test drivers and give him a tryout for the Formula One team. Scuderia Ferrari. They will choose him to replace the irreplaceable Schumi.

"Try me," he will say, and they will try him.

They will see his talent and make him a driver, and soon, he will be a Formula One champion just like Ayrton Senna. Like Juan Manuel Fangio. Jim Clark. Like Jackie Stewart, Nelson Piquet, Alain Prost, Niki Lauda, Nigel Mansell. Like Michael Schumacher. My Denny!

I would like to see that. All of it, beginning this afternoon when Zoë arrives and is once again together with her father. But I don't believe I will get the chance to see that moment. And, anyway, it is not for me to decide. My soul has learned what it came to learn, and all the other things are just things. We can't have everything we want. Sometimes, we simply have to believe.

"You're okay," he says. He cradles my head in his lap. I see him.

I know this much about racing in the rain. I know it is about balance. It is about anticipation and patience. I know all of the driving skills that are necessary for one to be successful in the rain. But racing in the rain is also about the *mind*! It is about owning one's own body. About believing that one's car is merely an extension of one's body. About believing that the track is an extension of the car, and the rain is an extension of the track, and the sky is an extension of the rain. It is about believing that you are not you; you are everything. And everything is you.

Racers are often called selfish and egotistical. I myself have called race car drivers selfish; I was wrong. To be a champion, you must have no ego at all. You must not exist as a separate entity. You must give yourself over to the race. You are nothing if not for your team, your car, your shoes, your tires. Do not mistake confidence and self-awareness for egotism.

I saw a documentary once. It was about dogs in Mongolia.

It said that the next incarnation for a dog—a dog who is ready to leave his dogness behind—is as a man.

I am ready.

And yet . . .

Denny is so very sad; he will miss me so much. I would rather stay with him and Zoë here in the apartment and watch the people on the street below as they talk to each other and shake each other's hands.

"You've always been with me," Denny says to me. "You've always been my Enzo."

Yes. I have. He's correct.

"It's okay," he says to me. "If you need to go now, you can go."

I turn my head, and there, before me, is my life. My childhood. My world.

My world is all around me. All around the fields of Spangle, where I was born. The rolling hills covered with the golden grasses that sway in the wind and tickle my stomach when I move over them. The sky so perfectly blue and the sun so round.

This is what I would like. To play in those fields for a little longer. To spend a little more time being me before I become someone else. This is what I would like.

And I wonder: Have I squandered my dogness? Have I forsaken my nature for my desires? Have I made a mistake by anticipating my future and shunning my present?

Perhaps I have. An embarrassing deathbed regret. Silly stuff.

"The first time I saw you," he says, "I knew we belonged together."

Yes! Me, too!

"It's okay."

I saw a film once. A documentary. On the television, which I watch a lot. Denny once told me not to watch so much. I saw a documentary about dogs in Mongolia. It said that after dogs die, they return as men. But there was something else—

I feel his warm breath on my neck, his hands. He leans down to me, though I can no longer see him, he leans down to my ear.

The fields are so large I could run forever in one direction and then run forever back. There is no end to these fields.

"It's okay, boy," he says softly, gently, into my ear.

—I remember! This documentary said that after a dog dies, his soul is released into the world around us. His soul is released to run in the world, run through the fields, enjoy the earth, the wind, the rivers, the rain, the sun, the—

When a dog dies, his soul is released to run until he is ready to be reborn. I remember.

"It's okay."

When I am reborn as a man, I will find Denny. I will find Zoë. I will walk up to them and shake their hands and tell them that Enzo says hello. They will see.

"You can go."

Before me I see my world: the fields around Spangle.

There are no fences. No buildings. No people. There is only me and the grass and the sky and the earth. Only me.

"I love you, boy."

I take a few steps into the field, and it feels so good, so nice to be in the cool air, to smell the smells all around me. To feel the sun on my coat. I feel like I am here.

"You can go."

I gather my strength and I start off and it feels good, like I have no age at all, like I am timeless. I pick up speed. I run.

"It's okay, Enzo."

I don't look back, but I know he's there. I bark twice because I want him to hear, I want him to know. I feel his eyes on me but I don't turn back. Off into the field, into the vastness of the universe ahead, I run.

"You can go," he calls to me.

Faster, the wind presses against my face as I run, faster, I feel my heart beating wildly and I bark twice to tell him, to tell everyone in the world, to say *faster*! I bark twice so he knows, so he remembers. What I want now is what I've always wanted.

One more lap, Denny! One more lap! *Faster!*

IMOLA, ITALY

After it is all over, after the last race has been won, after the season's champion has been crowned, he sits alone in the infield of the Tamburello corner, on the grass that is soggy from many days of rain. A bright figure in his Ferrari-red Nomex racing suit, which is covered with patches of the many sponsors who want him as their figurehead, their image, as the one whom they can hold before the world as their symbol, the champion sits alone. All around Japan, Brazil, around Italy, Europe, the world, people celebrate his victory. In the trailers and the back rooms, the other drivers, some of whom are half his age, shake their heads in amazement. To have accomplished what he has accomplished. To have endured what he has endured. To have become a Formula One champion out of nowhere. At his age. It is nothing less than a fairy tale.

An electric golf cart stops on the tarmac near him, driven by a young woman with long, golden hair. With her in the cart are two other figures, one large and one small.

The young woman climbs out and walks toward the champion.

"Dad?" she calls.

He looks to her, though he had hoped to be alone just a little longer.

"They're big fans," she says.

He smiles and rolls his eyes. The idea that he has fans at all—big or small—is very silly to him and something he has to get used to.

"No, no," she says, because she knows his thoughts almost before he can think them. "I think you'd really like to meet them."

He nods at her because she is always right. She beckons the two people in the cart. A man steps out, hunched beneath a rain poncho. Then a child. They walk toward the champion.

"Dení!" the man calls.

He does not recognize them. He does not know them.

"Dení! Speravamo di trovarla qui!"

"Eccomi," the champion replies.

"Dení, we are your biggest fans. Your daughter brought us to find you. She said you would not mind."

"She knows me," the champion says warmly.

"My son," says the man. "He worships you. He talks about you always."

The champion looks at the boy, who is small with sharp features and icy blue eyes and light curly hair.

"*Quanti anni hai?*" he asks.

"*Cinque,*" the boy replies.

"Do you race?"

"He races the karts," the father says. "He is very good. The first time he sat in a kart, he knew how to drive it. It's very expensive for me, but he is so good, such a talent, that we do it."

"*Bene, che bello,*" the champion says.

"Will you sign our program?" the father asks. "We watched the race from the field over there. The grandstand is very expensive. We drove from Napoli."

"*Certo,*" the champion says to the father. He takes the program and the pen. "*Come ti chiami?*" he asks the boy.

"*Enzo,*" the boy says.

The champion looks up, startled. For a moment, he doesn't move. He doesn't write. He doesn't speak.

"Enzo?" he asks, finally.

"*Si,*" the boy says. "*Mi chiamo Enzo. Anch'io voglio diventare un campione.*"

Stunned, the champion stares at the boy.

"He says he wants to be a champion," the father translates, misinterpreting the pause. "Like you."

"Ottima idea," the champion says, but he continues staring at the boy until he realizes he's been staring too long and shakes his head to stop himself. *"Mi scusi,"* he says. "Your son reminds me of a good friend of mine."

He catches his daughter's eye, then he signs the boy's program and hands it to the father, who reads it.

"Che cos'é?" the father asks.

"My telephone number in Maranello," the champion says. "When you think your son is ready, call me. I'll make sure he gets proper instruction and the opportunity to drive."

"Grazie! Grazie mille!" the man says. "He talks about you always. He says you are the best champion ever. He says you are better, even, than Senna!"

The champion rises, his racing suit still wet from the rain. He pats the boy's head and ruffles his hair. The boy looks up at him.

"He is a race car driver at heart," the champion says.

"Grazie," the father says. "He studies all of your races on videotapes."

"La macchina va dove vanno gli occhi," the boy says.

The champion laughs, then looks to the sky.

"Sì," he says. "The car goes where the eyes go. It is true, my young friend. It is very, very true."

acknowledgments

Thanks to the wonderful people at Harper, especially Jennifer Barth, Tina Andreadis, Christine Boyd, Jonathan Burnham, Kevin Callahan, Michael Morrison, Kathy Schneider, Brad Wetherell, Leslie Cohen; my fantastic team at Folio Literary Management, most notably Jeff Kleinman, Ami Greko, Adam Latham, Anna Stein; my resident experts and facilitators, including but not limited to Scott Driscoll, Jasen Emmons, Joe Fugere, Bob Harrison, Soyon Im, Doug Katz, David Katzenberg, Don Kitch Jr., Michael Lord, Layne Mayheu, Kevin O'Brien, Nick O'Connell, Luigi Orsenigo, Sandy and Steve Perlbinder, Jenn Risko, Bob Rogers, Paula Schaap, Jennie Shortridge, Marvin and Landa Stein, Dawn Stuart, Terry Tirrell, Brian Towey, Cassidy Turner, Andrea Vitalich, Kevin York, Lawrence Zola . . .

Caleb, Eamon, and Dashiell . . .

and the one who makes my world possible,

Drella.

ALSO BY
GARTH STEIN

RAVEN STOLE THE MOON
A NOVEL
Available in Paperback and eBook

"Deeply moving, superbly crafted and highly unconventional."
—*Washington Times*

A profoundly poignant and unforgettable story of a grieving mother's return to a remote Alaskan town to make peace with the loss of her young son, *Raven Stole the Moon* combines intense emotion with Native American mysticism and a timeless and terrifying mystery, and earned raves for a young writer and his uniquely captivating imagination.

RACING IN THE RAIN
MY LIFE AS A DOG
Available in Paperback, eBook, and Digital Audio

In this young readers' edition of the *New York Times* bestselling adult novel *The Art of Racing in the Rain*, meet one funny mutt—Enzo, the lovable dog who tells this story.

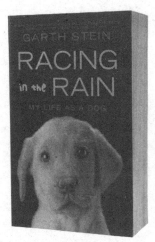